Peter Willi...
Grammar sc...
years in the Royal Air Force and later
a career as a sports journalist, writing
for British national newspapers. Married,
has a son and daughter and now semi-
retired, he finds the slower paced life on
Spain's Costa Blanca ideal for pursuing
his enthusiasm for writing.

"No Flowers for Frankie" is his debut
novel and a second book is now under
way.

To, Mel and Dave —
with very best wishes,

Peter Williams

2nd DEC
2006

No Flowers
for Frankie

by

Peter Williams

Moyhill Publishing

First Published in 2006 by Moyhill Publishing

A CIP catalogue record for this book is available
from the British Library.

ISBN 1-905597-05-3
ISBN 978-1-905597-05-5

This is a work of fiction. Any resemblance to characters living
or dead is purely coincidental.

Designed & typeset by *Moyhill* Publishing

Cover Photography credits:
"Smoke" background by Maria Kaloudi

Printed in UK

Book Sales in Ireland and UK
Moyhill Publishing,
12 Eaton Brae, Shankill, Co. Dublin, Ireland.

Book Sales in continental Europe
Moyhill Publishing,
Avenida Sicilia 54, 28420 Galapagar, Madrid, Spain.

Order online at *http://www.moyhill.com*
or **e-mail** *orders@moyhill.com*

This book is dedicated to my wife Sheila
for her support and encouragement
that resulted in a better novel.

MAIN CHARACTERS

CARDIFF

Nell Gallagher	Head of Gallagher Family
Charles Gallagher	Nell's Scots-born husband, book-keeper
Frankie Gallagher	Nell's middle son – leader of the pack
	Nell's other sons. *Danny, Joe, Bobby, Gerry, Jack, Nick, Eddie and Chaz Junior.*
Lydia	Nell's eldest daughter
Alec Edwards	Lydia's husband, ex-Welsh Guards
Katie	One of Nell's eight daughters
Peggy Steele	Frankie G's teenage girlfriend
Dave Parker	Police Officer, and former classmate of Frankie G and Peggy Steele
George Davies	Dave Parker's boss
Jim Cooper	Dave Parker's assistant.
Ian James	Local Bank manager
Jeff Brown	Ian James' assistant manager
Jessie Jenkins	District midwife, delivered all Nell's children

LONDON

Sabra	Frankie G's number one girlfriend
Eva	Sabra's identical twin sister
Hetty	Frankie G's former London girlfriend
Mal	Owns small night club – drug dealer
Leroy	Mal's business partner and enforcer
Maurice Green	Owner of expensive call girls night club
Lisa Jones	Photo/Journalist for leading UK magazine

SPAIN, Costa Blanca

Juan Luis Garcia	Guardia Civil officer (Lt.), Costa Blanca
Karl	German, Boat owner, water-sports enthusiast, wheeler-dealer
Maxie	German, Water-sports teacher, wheeler-dealer – former Hamburg brothel manager
Gail	Neighbour, friend of Sabra
John Smith	English-born arms dealer, based in Portugal

Prologue

Nellie Gallagher's love for her children – all twenty of them, is spontaneous, even compelling in its intensity. True, she has a soft spot for several of the youngest children but her love for all is deep enough for none to feel denied. Seventeen of her offspring survive the rigours of their early childhood. The other three succumb to the illnesses endemic to their harsh environment before any reach their third birthday. Now neatly though cruelly divided by fate into nine boys and eight girls, Nell and her family face a future burdened by poverty and an alcoholic father.

To many, the responsibility of bringing up seventeen children in such squalid surroundings and surviving a world war would be deemed a crushing burden from which there are few prospects of escape. Not to Nell. She labours painstakingly, channelling her family's fierce loyalty and passion for life until they gain recognition, notorious though it may be, in a society which until then, they are a passing shadow on the city's seamier side of life.

One son in particular stands out from the rest. Frankie Gallagher, age twenty and junior to several of his siblings, displays a zest for life and a recklessness for pursuing it that singles him out as a natural leader. Standing just under six feet tall, Frankie's rugged good looks are slightly marred by a one-time broken nose that simply refuses to respond to medical re-adjustment. Women who cast an appraising eye over this athletically-built young man, can't fail to notice his clear blue eyes, white even teeth and dark brown curly hair.

1

When he smiles, it is enough to make them forget everything they were ever taught about good behaviour.

His intense feelings of love during his school-days and for several years after are directed at only one woman. Former classmate Peggy Steele, even at fifteen years of age had the body of a well-developed woman. She was well aware of her effect on grown men, never mind her classmates.

Her presence is the nectar that attracts attention from all quarters. But it is the attention that Peggy draws from their former mutual classmate Dave Parker that causes Frankie plenty of grief. Parker, the son of a vicar and born into a more settled household, is blessed with fine features and dark matinee-idol looks reminiscent of a Spanish bullfighter. Fractionally taller than Frankie and matching his athletic build, he too has to fend off numerous females during his pursuit of Peggy. Unintentionally, she becomes the spark that triggers off a lifetime of bitterness between the two rivals for her affections.

Parker's feelings of hostility towards Frankie explode into sheer hatred when Peggy reveals she is pregnant with Frankie's child. When, later in life, the two rivals find themselves on opposite sides of the law, it is inevitable that tragedy will follow.

Chapter 1

Jessie Jenkins perspired freely as she propelled her plump body and the heavy, black-framed bicycle with its cavernous square dark leather bag mounted over the rear wheel, along the dusty city back-streets. It was a journey she'd made numerous times in her life's mission as a district midwife and it wasn't getting easier as her fiftieth birthday approached.

Few women, or men for that matter ventured out alone at dusk in Cardiff's Riverside area. Even the police patrolled their beat in pairs in nearby Butetown for safety's sake. Riverside was one of a number of rundown districts in the Welsh capital where petty crime and violence thrived alongside daily life as its inhabitants struggled to scrape a living of sorts amid the misery created by the depression of the mid 1930s.

But it wasn't the neighbourhood and its dismal streets that occupied Jessie's thoughts as she pedalled vigorously. She was visualising the task ahead – to deliver not one, but possibly two children in the same household. It didn't surprise Jessie that Nellie Gallagher was expecting yet another kid – her twentieth in just thirty years of marriage. After all, she'd had a lot of practise and there were plenty of families in Cardiff with upwards of a dozen or so kids. But this time, Nell's eldest daughter Lydia was also about to give birth, albeit only her second and probably her last, she had confided in Jessie.

The midwife was surprised Lydia had stayed on to live with her family after marrying her childhood sweetheart Alec. Especially as

3

her mother had burdened her with the majority of daily domestic chores as a kind of unpaid skivvy despite Lydia's newly-married status. This provided Nell with plenty of time to indulge her favourite pastimes of cinema-going and boozing. It was a situation Lydia bitterly resented, but felt compelled to put up with out of a sense of duty until she and Alec could get some money together and rent a place of their own. Nellie Gallagher was the kind of person to take advantage where she could. She felt she had suffered plenty bringing her kids into the world. Now it was their turn to make her life easier – and she made sure they did. But for now, Nell had other matters to occupy her mind – yet another baby.

Jessie hauled the heavy bike onto the stone forecourt of the neglected four storey, red brick house trapped between its equally grimy neighbours. What, she wondered, lay in store for the two little unborn mites that would soon be part of the Gallagher family, bless their souls.

It was most likely a difficult future that Nell's baby would face in which Jessie was about to play the role she done so many times before in the family – that of delivering yet another Gallagher offspring fathered by her sexually-slothful husband Charlie.

Charles James Gallagher, Edinburgh-born and betraying evidence of a well-educated earlier life, had finally dropped anchor in Cardiff by way of Glasgow and Liverpool docks. There had always been a hint that Charlie had stolen money from a family member and had been kicked out of the household in disgrace.

Ellen Kate Reynolds, born in Cardiff, was the only child of a passionate Welsh–Gypsy union. Ellen had despaired of her lonely childhood, impatiently awaiting adulthood. She had dreamt only of meeting and marrying the right man in her life. The reality was somewhat different.

Despite his short, stocky figure and rolling gait, Charlie's ten year age advantage, air of wisdom and cosmopolitan outlook captured the heart of fifteen-year-old Ellen long enough to make her pregnant. They married shortly after her sixteenth birthday, her parents grateful for the semblance of respectability it bestowed on the ill-matched pair. The young lovers consummated their betrothal with a lusty disregard for the disciplines of family planning. It was a practise given scant attention by working class couples in Britain during the years between the two world wars.

Married life and the hard, physical demands of a constantly-growing family had taken its toll on Ellen's appearance. Once a soft, plump pretty young woman, she now possessed the bones and muscles of a man, only too ready to give vent to a fearsome temper when upset. It was a state fortified by the vitriolic coarseness of her tongue.

Not surprisingly, she had few real friends, to whom she is known as Nell. Those less favourably disposed refer to her by her baptismal name out of a fearful respect. Her style of discipline and the heavy-handed manner in which she dispensed it soon became the tool by which she controlled but never tamed the youthful feelings of defiance and aggression among her brood.

Jessie knocked on the battered front door whose coat of brown varnish had long since given up the unequal struggle to protect its host from the elements. She didn't have long to wait. The curly headed teenage girl who answered her knock was clearly relieved. "We saw you coming Mrs Jenkins. Thank God you're here. We think our sister's baby is due any time now and Mam's in a right temper 'cos it looks like she's ready to drop hers earlier than expected. Can you please hurry," she added, her face reflecting her concern. The youngster scuttled back down the hallway and continued upstairs as Jessie freed her heavy case from its leather straps, her mind focusing on the job ahead. "Tell your sister not to worry love. I'll be up in a minute," she called to the disappearing figure on the staircase.

She paused at the door of the middle ground floor room before knocking. The loud, rasping voice, coarsened by years of smoking cheap cigarettes cut through the shadow of the gloomy hallway like a woodcutter's saw through a sapling. "Has that bloody midwife turned up yet? If she doesn't show up soon, I'll get that idle bastard of a husband of mine to help me out with what he put in there. Where the hell are you anyway Charlie? Charlie!"

Jessie eased the door open with some small difficulty. She knew it was going to jam against the floor. It had been doing just that for some years now. The aggrieved tone of the obese, middle-aged woman on the bed subsided throatily as Nellie Gallagher shifted her position on the soft yielding mattress. Her movement was made all the more difficult by her fifteen stone bulk. Being pregnant didn't help either. Short of stature and stout of girth, Nell's once-dark luxurious, wavy hair now showed many traces of grey. The faint facial lines of her soft skin had deepened to fleshy furrows as the excesses of her lifestyle took their toll.

Nell glowered as the midwife struggled into the room, hauling her heavy bag on her hip. Jessie's eyes took in the scene with the experience born of many years in her profession. Charlie lay there slumped almost out of sight on a low-slung armchair in the corner. Nell lay there looking plain evil. She was breathing wheezily, legs spread wide.

Jessie approached the large, ornate brass bedstead, the overstuffed mattress striving to retain its shape under Nell's bulk. "How are you feeling Nell," she enquired gently, her genuine concern evident in her quiet tone.

"It's nice of you to ask Jessie," growled her patient sarcastically, "but I'm feeling fucking rotten right now. I think this little sod is going to give me more gip than any of the others."

The midwife sat on the side of the bed, taking Nell's fleshy hand in hers. "It's time you took my advice Nell and give this business a rest. You're getting too old for this game. That's why you lost your last two. I'm not getting any younger myself," thought Jessie ruefully.

Nell smiled, squeezing the midwife's hand. "Perhaps you're right Jess. But it's that bastard Charlie who's to blame. It's all he's ever got on his mind. Christ knows how he manages seeing he's pissed out of his mind most of the time." Jessie rose. "You'll be alright for a while yet Nell, so I'll pop upstairs and see Lydia. Your girls think she's due pretty soon now. I'll be back down to see you later. Stop worrying. You've got some gin there haven't you? Take a little nip. It'll help you relax."

The midwife retreated from the room leaving Nell puffing with exertion as she struggled to retrieve the gin bottle from underneath her pile of pillows. Jessie climbed the first flight of stairs, arriving at the doorway of the dingy bedroom, now occupied by the youngster and her year-older sister, both of whom had kept a six-hour vigil over the slightly-built figure on the bed. Lydia opened her eyes, a wan smile touching her lips.

"It's good to have you here Jessie," she murmured. The midwife smoothed Lydia's moist, clammy brow. "Just relax my love, it won't take long now."

Little more than an hour later, the first cries of the infant, now released from its warm protective cocoon, pierced the silence. "It's a girl," exclaimed Jessie, "and she's so beautiful." Her remarks were directed to the sweat-soaked, exhausted figure on the bed but were received with sighs of delight by her two sisters, their vigil finally rewarded.

Both eagerly craned forward as the midwife expertly severed the umbilical cord before bathing and finally swathing the infant in a clean, white cotton towel. Handing the infant to her mother she asked, "have you decided on a name yet, Lydia?" Her patient's slight body seemed more fragile than ever following the tension and stress of giving birth, as she eased herself onto her elbows, cradling her newly-born daughter. "Jessica Mary – that's the names me and Alec want to call her. We decided on Jessica after you – and Mary after his mam. It's not easy choosing names with so many kids already in the family," added Lydia.

Two sharp knocks on the bedroom door were followed by a muffled "can I come in?" The young sister's elder brother Frankie stood hesitantly in the doorway, his role as a young man in these circumstances somewhat uncertain. "Mrs Jenkins, I think you'd better get downstairs. Mam is asking for you. It looks as though she's about to start." Frankie's announcement was calmly received by the midwife. "Tell her I'll be with her in a minute, Frankie. You can also tell her she's a grandmother again."

Frankie remained in the doorway still not assured by the midwife's message. "Make it quick will you Mrs Jenkins. I don't want anything to go wrong with Mam." He crossed to the large bed upon which his eldest sister lay, clasping her newly-arrived daughter. "How are you doing Sis? You okay?" Frankie stroked the baby's damp, downy head with a surprising softness of touch. "We're both doing fine thanks Frankie," murmured Lydia, her body wanting to drift off to sleep, her energy drained. "How's Mam?" Her question was answered as if on cue by a bellow from the floor below as Nell gave her verdict on the timing of the impending arrival of her own latest offspring "Jessie, if you don't bloody well get down here quick, I'm going to drop this next bugger on the lino."

The midwife gathered the contents of her bag, said a brief farewell to the new mother, Frankie and his other sisters and returned to Nell's room. As she entered, she noted that Charlie had barely moved from his slumped position on the armchair in the corner of the room. He was breathing noisily, the smell of alcohol now quite noticeable. "Do you mind if I open a window Nell," she asked, moving to do so without waiting for an answer. "The old bastard stinks. He's not going to be much help, is he," growled Nell, gesturing towards her prostrate husband. "We can manage quite nicely on our own," replied Jessie. "We've done this plenty of times before haven't we Nell, so just relax." Jessie tied her fair hair back into a bunch before continuing her preparations. She glanced over her shoulder at Charlie.

She had often wondered where the old bastard got the energy to father so many children. He certainly wasn't her idea of a husband or a lover, God forbid, despite his sexual appetite. Indeed, she thought him utterly repulsive. Charlie slumbered on, snoring noisily, totally unaware he was the subject of such sexual conjecture. His bald, shiny pate reflected the pale evening sunlight that shafted through the gap in the grimy curtains, creating an unexpected soft highlight in the shadowy room. His fringe of grey hair, now turning a dirty white, gave him the appearance of a monk. Such an unlikely comparison was rarely evident to others due to his insistence on wearing a well-thumbed greasy cap that now lay across his ample paunch.

"Any chance of a drink Nell, water – or perhaps something a bit stronger before we have a look?," enquired Jessie, more in hope than expectation. Nell motioned to her husband. "Hey Charlie! Charlie! For Christ's sake! Wake up! Get Jessie a cup of tea!" Several seconds elapsed before he stirred sleepily, slowly reacting to his wife's bellowing. Although she didn't know it, she had disturbed one of his better dreams – the one where he owned a brewery and was its best customer.

"You'll find the teapot under the cushions on the sofa, Jess. It keeps it warm you see love," Nell added by way of explanation to her guest. Charlie grunted once or twice as he struggled to collect his senses. He rose unsteadily to his feet from the armchair in which he had collapsed since returning from his daily lunchtime drinking session. "Two spoonfuls of sugar please Charlie," murmured Jessie helpfully as the old soak retrieved a cup that had already been used at least once, probably twice that morning. He made no move to wash it out.

Nell duly gave birth to the twentieth child of her union with Charlie. Once again, it was just like shelling peas. She thanked Jessie for her contribution and, as is the way among working class people, thrust a pound note into the midwife's hand despite her half-hearted protests. Jessie carefully tucked the money away. Her final task was to check on Lydia and her new arrival before leaving to attend yet another miracle of birth elsewhere on her patch.

As she pedalled off into the darkening gloom, her bicycle lights now switched on, Jessie's thoughts reached back into the gloomy, though passionately intense house she had just visited. "God knows, those Gallagher's are a real handful. Let's hope the latest couple of kids have a chance at leading a normal life. If they do, they'll be the first."

Chapter 2

The smell hung heavily in the grey, damp early morning air. It was even strong enough to permeate the clothes worn by the small, disjointed bunches of children as they trudged reluctantly from the tightly-packed rows of squalid terraced houses to their school, located some two miles distant in the central area of the city. As for the ever-present smell, none of them were aware of anything different from all the other days of their young lives.

The scruffy gaggle of youngsters was joined at intervals by others, equally scruffy and equally reluctant to complete their journey that would see them passing eventually through the portals of St John's School. From their thin under-fed faces it was clear they were resigned to their fate. Resigned to spending yet another tortuous day at the mercy of the monsters masquerading as teachers-but more recognisable in the kids' eyes as dispensers of swift discipline achieved with long, whippy canes and strong arms. The teachers on the other hand, viewed their daily duties with evangelistic-like enthusiasm and the supreme satisfaction of nurturing and broadening a host of receptive young minds, openly thirsting for more knowledge.

The overpowering reek of hops and malt discharging from the tall chimneys of the large, local brewery they passed along the way, continued to impoverish the air in the city's central area as the children discovered reasons to make even slower progress schoolwards. The chimneys, ignoring everyone's presence except their own, belched out their existence as they had done for more than a hundred years. They contributed as much as any other social factor in the city's central area, casting the neighbouring streets indelibly into their 'working-class' role.

The ever-present smell also explained why such a brewery and its accompanying activity was never constructed in one of Cardiff's more affluent areas.

The tolling of the school bell, subdued at first, gradually grew louder as the straggle of children, now numbering about sixty, neared the end of their journey. It was a scene being repeated from other directions as pupils converged on their place of daily persecution. The school bell clanged its challenge with renewed vigour as the reluctant army turned the final corner to be confronted by the tall, green painted wrought iron double gates still glistening damply from the early morning rain.

Standing just inside the gates, hands clasped behind his back, deputy headmaster Trevor Jenkins stood, rocking back and forth on his heels, his recently bathed bald head shining a welcome. He smiled and nodded in recognition as his charges for the day stepped through the gates. Few pupils made eye contact, preferring instead to slouch by, heads lowered. Those that did were either attempting to ingratiate themselves with Mr Jenkins, or new to the school – or both.

As the pupils split into their tribal groups and headed for the classrooms, it looked like being just another day for the Gallaghers, with very little gained in terms of educational achievement. Danny Gallagher stood, wiping his nose on one of the sleeves of his rough, grey woollen jersey as a prelude to exploring the damp cavities of both nostrils with a grubby index finger. He carefully inspected the results of his examination before flicking the offending bogey onto the floor. He waited for Frankie to approach then said, "One of the Murphy sisters just told me she saw Peggy with Dave Parker on Sunday night. She told me not to tell you," added Danny without the slightest trace of betrayal.

Frankie stopped abruptly in mid-stride, turning and grabbing his brother by the shoulders. "Are you sure about that? Which of the Murphy sisters was it? Where did she say she saw them? Peggy said she was going to stay in Sunday night." Danny shook himself free and shrugged his shoulders. "It was Mary Murphy – and you'd better ask Peggy about that – or Dave Parker. They're both in school today." Frankie glared at his brother, his inner anger rising by the second. "Yeah – you're right. I'll sort Parker out in the break."

With that he turned on his heel and bounded up the wrought-iron circular staircase that led to the senior pupils' classrooms. As he entered, Frankie noted that Dave Parker was already seated in his usual place two rows away. If Frankie's glare at his rival was intended to convey any message of threat, Dave Parker was seemingly unaware, concerning himself with fishing out his books from the sturdy oak desk. Its heavy lid was disfigured by the numerous carvings of former pupils, who had spent at least some productive time in class, even if it was only carving forgotten names and unimportant dates.

It didn't take long for the word to flash around the grapevine that a fight was on in the break involving Frankie and Parker behind the outside toilets. Within minutes of the break bell clanging out its message, many of the pupils, their faces reflecting their hopes of a real scrap, had already formed a circle before Frankie and Dave showed up.

As they moved to the centre of the space provided, Peggy pushed her way through the throng, her blue eyes brimming with barely-supressed tears, to confront the pair. "I know why the two of you are going to fight but if you think it should be over me you're both very much mistaken." Her eyes pleaded more eloquently than her words as she stood between the pair. "If you'll only listen Frankie, I can explain why I didn't see you on Sunday night, so for God's sake, don't behave like a pair of idiots and stop this at once!"

Dave Parker took her gently by her slim shoulders. "Please Peggy just stay out of this. He's been itching for a real scrap for ages and this time, he's going to get one." With that he led her into the hands of one of her classmates before turning to again confront Frankie. Unable to watch what followed, Peggy took one last despairing look at the pair before leaving for the school building along with two of her classmates.

It took very few angry words of exchange before the two were squaring up and throwing punches at each other. Frankie's advantage of being a keen amateur boxer didn't prevent his rival from giving as good as he got as they lashed into each other with a flurry of punches, before grappling and then rolling on the ground, urged on by their respective supporters.

The teachers were well aware of the commotion in the playground but hesitated to break it up. Not so the music teacher, a slightly-built, middle-aged female, who though fearful, threw caution to the wind, stepped in and somehow successfully separated the two. They parted reluctantly, chests heaving from their exertions, the evidence of battle showing on their bruised faces. The teacher, still terrified by her own unexpected bravery, was joined by the headmaster, belatedly exerting his authority. Their fight was over- at least for the time being.

Ordering the rest of the pupils to return to their classes, he instructed the two perspiring combatants to accompany him to his study. They were to receive six of the best from his trusty cane followed by being sent home in disgrace. The pair took their punishment without any complaint. For Frankie, leaving school early for the day was a real bonus. But Dave Parker would have some explaining to do to his more demanding parents.

From Frankie's point of view, it meant another day nearer the time that he could turn his back on the school for keeps. He hated the bloody place. It was a place for losers. Just two more weeks and he would be away for good seeking his own way in the world of adults. It was something he had longed for, craved for, convinced there was a fortune to be made by a smart kid who knew his way around.

There were plenty in the school who would be glad to see the back of Frankie. He had gained a grudging respect borne out of fear even from older pupils, mainly by his forceful personality and hard-earned reputation as a playground battler. Having so many brothers in the same school only helped to seal his reputation. Take on one Gallagher and you usually had to take on the lot.

But there was always Dave Parker. It was hard to believe he was a vicar's son. Parker possessed a really hard edge and had never shirked a showdown with any of the Gallaghers if the need demanded. Parker and Frankie had long been crossing swords and had plenty of punch-ups in and out of school, but lately it had really come to the crunch. They had developed a natural dislike of each other which had worsened in recent months over their mutual passion for the same girl. Peggy Steele was something special – even at fifteen years of age. Full-breasted, a head of thick blonde wavy hair and the possessor of the shapely, firm body of a mature woman, Peggy was fully aware of the impact she had on men, never mind teenage boys.

A number of the male teachers, including Mr Jenkins, often fantasised over her statuesque looks and innocent sensuality. Her naturally blonde hair and nubile body made her stand out in a crowd – any crowd, but particularly in school where her classmates seemed little more than dowdy schoolgirls by comparison. It was little wonder that Dave Parker and Frankie were smitten. Their only consolation was they had the field clear to themselves. Few if any rivals for her affections would make known their feelings for her with Frankie Gallagher and Dave Parker to contend with.

Frankie let himself in at the family home. He was one of the few of Nell's kids trusted with a front door key. Nell lay slouched on an overstuffed sofa that had seen better days. A half bottle of gin stood on a small table, within easy reach of Nell's plump hands. "Who gave you that bunger Frankie?," she enquired hoarsely, referring to his black eye, as he busied himself cutting two chunks of bread and a thick slice of cheese, which he put on a plate. He fished out a jar from the nearby cupboard and then proceeded to smother the thick sandwich with a mustard and onion sauce.

He sat down at the large wooden table before replying. "Nobody gave it to me – I had to fight for it. That bastard Dave Parker really upsets me and I'll be glad to finish in that poxy school. With luck, he'll have a bleeding accident and then I'll be rid of him." Nell poured herself another generous measure of gin, savouring its fragrance before taking a long slow sip. "Parker's too smart to have accidents – they only happen to other people," she growled. "Anyway, just forget about Parker, He'll probably become a priest just like his old man and then he'll be out of your life for good." But the issue over Peggy and Parker still gnawed at Frankie's guts. Hadn't Danny said they were seen together the night she was supposed to staying home? That final thought made his mind up. He would go around to her house that night and talk things through. He was convinced Peggy had very strong feelings for him, but Christ, it was really hard work being a teenager in love!

Later, as made his way home from Peggy's, he replayed parts of their earlier moments together in his mind. Lovers, he had now decided, were very special people. But were Peggy and he special as a couple, particularly as they hadn't yet made love? Could they really be called lovers-true lovers? Frankie smiled to himself as he pondered the question. "Yeah, they were special and they would prove that before long."

As he lay resting on his bed later that night, trying to ignore the contrasting snores of his two brothers on the single beds squeezed into the attic, Frankie took comfort from his flashbacks of their meeting that night. "I'll prove my love for Peggy before long and that should see that bastard Parker out of my hair for good." They were his final thoughts before he slipped into an untroubled sleep – his bruises long since forgotten. Little did he know then that his problems with Dave Parker were just beginning.

Chapter 3

The young man closed the front door of the family home behind him, turned and stood quietly taking in the Monday morning sights sounds and smells of a brand new beginning – and it smelt good, bloody good.

Frankie Gallagher's school days were at last behind him and despite Nell's firm reminders that he'd have to contribute much more to the household kitty, he wanted to spend the next few days enjoying his freedom from the shackles of St John's school. Then there was Peggy, Yeah, Peggy. Now there's some girl!

His daydreaming was shattered as the front door burst open behind him. Several of his younger brothers and sisters pushed past him noisily, their cold toast sandwiches coated either with pork or beef dripping wrapped in small newspaper packets clasped in their sticky hands. For them it was breakfast on the run as they headed for school. Then with a final chorus that sounded like "see you Frankie," they were on their way jostling and joking. Was it their defence against the later disciplines the day held in store?

Frankie closed the wrought iron gate and crossed the busy Tudor Street to the tram stop opposite. Cardiff's numerous electric trams criss-crossed the city in all directions, providing a cheap and reliable form of transport whose convenience was rarely appreciated by its passengers. The trams were there, so everyone expected them to be on time.

Normally he would have walked into town centre but today was different. He was different. He was an adult now and he was going to travel like one. The double-decker tram, shiny and resplendent in its amber and maroon livery, lurched jerkily around the bend some eighty or so yards distance down Tudor Street, its twin steel arms somehow maintaining contact with the overhead electric wires. Sometimes they didn't, causing a shower of blue sparks to cascade over the roof of the tram.

It skidded to a stop, its wheels squealing in protest on the twin metal rails embedded in the road surface as the manual handbrake was applied by the driver. The several passengers in front of Frankie clambered aboard, the conductor adroitly checking that the correct fare was dropped into the glass-fronted 'fare box'. Only then did he push a small metal catch on the bottom of the glass box, sending the coins hurtling down a large tube fitted to a padlocked black metal box. It seemed a lot of fuss over tuppence, thought Frankie, having found a spare space on one of the varnished wooden-slatted seats. The conductor pulled the cord, the bell clanged and they were on their swaying, jolting journey as the driver at the controls up front responded.

The adverts pasted to the panels fixed above the passengers' heads briefly caught Frankie's attention. They didn't seem to have changed much since the last time he had enjoyed the luxury of a tram journey. The tram overtook his brothers and sisters who had been joined by several others on their trek to school. Frankie's eyes followed them until they were out of sight. He had four more stops before he eventually reached his destination – the central shopping and street market area located in The Hayes.

There was an encouraging bustle of movement and noise as the city's workers went about their early morning business. He headed for the large cluster of fruit and vegetable stalls erected next to the popular Hayes Island Cafe, a well known local landmark and meeting place.

Having bought a steaming hot mug of strong tea, he chose to stand under the protection offered by the cafe's awning. That way, he avoided the droppings of the hundreds of pigeons that inhabited the tree-lined square in which the cafe was located. Others, visitors usually, more romantically minded and less well-versed in the bloody-mindedness of Cardiff's resident pigeons, chose to sit in the open on green-painted, metal slatted seats, seemingly oblivious to the pigeon shit that had been added to their sandwiches or cakes – at no extra charge. Why, thought Frankie idly, are most of the seats in Cardiff's public places or services, slatted? They last a long time, he guessed, but by Christ, they were hard!

"Hey Frankie! Frankie, over here," called his brother Chaz pausing briefly, a box of lettuces in hand, unloaded moments before from the van parked alongside. Chaz beckoned him over. Frankie put his near-empty tea mug on the counter and strolled over. "Hiya Chaz," he called out. "Still screwing that Chinese bint from the cafe down the Docks?" Chaz paused, crate still in hand. "Yeah, now and again. Well, maybe four or five times a week. She says she likes me, but I'm sure she's getting it elsewhere as well." Frankie shrugged. "That's some problem you've got there – only four or fives times a week."

Chaz dropped the box on the floor. "Some of the market boys tell me that bastard George Davies was sniffing around again last Friday asking lots of questions about Mam and the family. He said Mam has been selling a lot of stolen goods to the brasses (prostitutes) in Westgate Street. That's the stuff that Joe and Doug got when they did that warehouse in Collingdon Road the week before last – you remember, all that women's underwear stuff."

Frankie stared at his brother for several moments before replying. "Davies is putting the pressure on hoping somebody is going to grass us up. He's always trying to pin something on the family. He's got a one track mind." That was certainly true. Chief Superintendent George Davies of the city's Crime Squad, had long been a thorn in the side of the Gallagher family and had conducted his pursuit of them on a personal level for a number of years.

He likened the Gallagher boys to a football team. No sooner had the elder brothers qualified as professionals in the bigger league, along came another two or three of them, relinquished their amateur shoplifting status and signed on as 'pros' in their own right. Still, he felt he was gradually winning the game.

Three of Frankie's elder brothers had already sampled the hospitality of Cardiff Jail on various burglary charges, courtesy of Mr Davies. He had also conducted a running battle with Nell over the years for the production line of potential criminals she and her husband Charlie had unfailingly produced.

Chaz continued to unload his stock from the battered van. He called to Frankie. "Give us a hand our kid, will you, otherwise I'll be away to a late start." Frankie nodded his assent and stacked the remainder of the loaded boxes onto the pavement, from where Chaz selected his stock to display on his portable stall.

Frankie glanced up at the large square clock bolted above the facia on the outside wall of David Morgan's department store. "Hey Chaz, I'm just off for a leak and then I'm on my way," he said heading for the steps of the underground public toilet, when a shadow fell across his path.

"Hello Frankie. Giving your brother a hand? Shouldn't you be in school, or have they expelled you yet, you little shit." The question was directed at him by one of two men, whom he instantly recognised as plain-clothes policemen. A crack that passed for a smile creased the face of the one that had spoken to him. The other just remained silent, taking in the activity around him.

Swallowing his apprehension of the pair that confronted him, Frankie took one pace back and composed himself before answering. "Just for the record – your records – I've finished with school. I'm a big boy now," he added, his blue eyes staring steadily at his questioner's face. The detective returned Frankie's gaze, studying the young man in front of him. "This young pup seemed brighter and more self-assured than most of his elder brothers," he mused. "We're definitely going to have trouble with this cocky sod."

He turned to address Chaz. "Give my regards to Nell, will you Chaz? Oh and ask her to save a few pairs of knickers for my missus – she's running short." With that, he motioned to his companion who had remained silent throughout the exchanges. They picked their way through the clutter of scattered boxes and cartons with measured steps, acknowledging calls of recognition from several of the other stall holders with nods of the head.

Chaz walked over to Frankie, still poised on the top step of the urinal. "You bet I'll ask Mam to save some gear for that arsehole's missus. After all, Mam is flogging the stuff to the brasses on the street corners," he laughed, amused at his own witticism. Frankie

19

hesitated, then spoke. "That lot haven't got anything on us right now. He was only fishing and waiting to see if he got a bite." Frankie turned and descended the steps. "Anyway Chaz," he called, "I'm busting for a slash and if I don't get down there soon and have one, you'll have to re-label your honeydews as water melons!"

Just a mile away from the market where Frankie had been exchanging pleasantries with the local guardians of peace and justice, Dave Parker climbed the marble staircase leading off from the main foyer in the City Hall to the first floor. He studied the polished wood panels with their gold painted lettering adorning the walls of the long corridor. "Room twelve, that's the one I want."

His appointment for the job interview was only ten minutes later as he slipped into the nearest gents toilet to give himself a final checkover in the large, bevelled glass mirror. Smartly dressed in a dark grey suit, crisp white shirt, striped tie and highly polished shoes, his dark brown hair neatly combed, he felt ready and confident.

An hour later as he sat alone, waiting in an oak-panelled room, he cast his mind back over the questions delivered by his two stern-faced, clipped moustached interviewers, their starch-winged collars seeming to move up and down in time with their Adam's apple when they spoke. Everything considered, he felt he had acquitted himself well, with high hopes of being offered the job of a lowly-paid counter clerk and general dogsbody in the city's Accounts Department. At least, it was a foot on the ladder however low, but he had made his mind up not to follow his father into the Church – a decision that hadn't gone down too well with his parents.

The heavy oak door opposite opened slowly and number one moustache beckoned him to enter with a single flick of his nico-tined-stained forefinger. Dave rose, followed him in and sat on the chair pointed at by the same finger. The man then joined his companion on the other side of the table.

The second moustache spoke, his top lip not moving. Dave could hardly contain his excitement as he was informed his application had been successful. There followed a sermon not unlike one of his father's lesser efforts on the need for punctuality, honesty, cleanliness, diligence, respect and enthusiasm. Oh, and he was expected to report any illness well in advance of absenting himself from work!

Dave Parker thanked both moustaches for their kindness, left their office in the company of a buxom secretary, signed two official-looking pieces of paper and was welcomed to his job, commencing the following Monday. As he left, he was totally unaware of the glances of female staff, inwardly marvelling at the prospect of a handsome young man with gorgeous eyes and friendly smile working in their midst in just seven days time. How, they wondered, could they possibly wait that long?

It was only eighteen months since Frankie had left school but things were really looking up for him. He was earning good money from a variety of activities, some of which wouldn't stand too close an examination, particularly his job as 'back-up' man to a collector employed by local money lender Leo Reubens. He had spent just one day in Leo's office gaining a rudimentary knowledge of the money lending business, but it was on the streets with ex-boxing professional Jack Miller that he learnt the finer points of the game. Like beating the shit out of borrowers when they failed to come up with their payments.

Miller's 'hard man' collector's reputation had become part of local folklore after he had nailed a defaulter's hands to the floorboards of his living room with the unfortunate fellow's wife looking on. Needless to say, she found the money from somewhere!

From then on, the expression, *'don't fuck around with Miller or he'll crucify you'* was said with real feeling among those down on their luck. The incident was never reported to the police and the victim recovered after hospital treatment from 'his accident at work.'

Frankie's mentor demonstrated another of his skills in making friends and influencing people while both were handing in a day's takings in Reubens' office. A borrower facing the money-lender across the desk, was bemoaning the high level of interest charged on loans. Reubens looked over the top of his spectacles at

21

the man opposite. "Mr Harris, one day when I'm dead and gone, you'll realise what a good friend I've been to you."

Harris looked at him contemptuously before replying. "So why don't you drop dead right now so that we can test your theory?" he queried. His cynicism earned him a powerful right hand smash to the side of his chest from the on-looking Miller, resulting in three broken ribs.

Frankie's sharp mind and an instinct for taking full advantage of the opportunities that came his way, meant that even now, in his later teens, his ability to earn plenty of ready cash amid the poverty that surrounded him didn't go unnoticed. As a result, a steady stream of attractive young women were usually drawn to him and his brothers on their nights out on the town.

Their activities centred around the numerous social clubs scattered throughout the city. The political clubs, dockers, railwaymen and steelworkers clubs were immensely popular for being open seven days a week, when on Sundays, every pub in Wales was closed by law. Talented amateur singers, musicians and dancing provided most of the entertainment. The out-of-club night-time activities of the younger members rubbing their bodies together provided the rest.

For many, the next day and the Monday morning blues that went with it meant a return to the daily grind of earning a living. For the Gallagher family, it meant seizing whatever opportunity, rarely honest, presented itself to make some money. For the local police force, it meant trying to stop them and the other villains that walked the streets they had sworn to protect. Life in the city was about to go on as usual.

Chapter 4

Saturday morning and the prospects of a whole weekend away from work lay ahead. Peggy stared up at the glossy photographs lining one entire wall of the Central Cinema in The Hayes, each capturing the smiling features of a Hollywood film star, their teeth gleaming unnaturally. Among them were several of her favourites who stared back at her. Clark Gable, who didn't give a damn, dapper George Raft, Humphrey Bogart's hooded eyes and dependable Spencer Tracy had all caused her young heart to flutter. But it was left to the even more glamourous females to steal their hearts, usually by the last reel. Jean Harlow, Greta Garbo, Hedy Lamarr and Lana Turner always appeared flawless and their photographs on this wall of fame reflected that.

As Peggy glanced over to the other wall, mostly displaying posters, she couldn't suppress a giggle as her eyes alighted on the one featuring the 'King Kong' film. The heroine, Fay Wray, lay trapped in the grasp of the giant gorilla's huge hand – but his face! He really looked funny!

She made her way back to the entrance. Frankie was late. He had promised this was going to be a weekend they'd never forget. His promise of sharing a pleasure previously unknown to either of them had kept her awake most of the previous night. She glanced at the cinema clock. Five more minutes and they would miss the start of the midday matinee. To her relief, she spotted him weaving his way through the general flow of pedestrians, his athletic figure and confident walk singling him out from the crowd.

"Hello beautiful," he smiled, the evenness of his teeth matching those of the paper heroes behind her. Seeing her concern for the time, he felt an explanation was due. "You know that I've always wanted a car and I've seen one that is just what I want, but the bloke selling it wants too much." Peggy pulled him close, kissing him briefly. "You're here now. That's all that matters."

The ticket cashier, her nose buried in a picture magazine, wasn't aware of their presence until Frankie thrust one shilling and a sixpenny piece under the plate glass window. "Two ninepennies, please." She pulled the coins towards her, pressed a button twice causing two tickets to appear through a narrow slot. Frankie collected them and spoke again to the cashier. "Is there any part of the cinema which is non-smoking?" he enquired. He was rewarded by a beaming smile from the cashier. "No luv. You can smoke anywhere you like." He looked at Peggy, both bursting out with laughter at the unintended humour, leaving a somewhat puzzled cashier ruminating on the strangeness of some people!

The darting light of the usherette's torch signalled her presence to the couple. "Is there any room in the back row?" enquired Peggy, an instant before Frankie could ask the same question. They settled in their seats, their eyes gradually adjusting to the semidarkness and noting that there were plenty of empty seats on either side of them. "Whatever happened to courting couples" thought Frankie as he slipped an arm around Peggy's shoulder.

They emerged from the cinema blinking in the bright sunlight. Having spent most of their time in the cinema exploring each other as much as their surroundings permitted, they were well prepared for the next stage of their adventure. This was, after all, a very special day.

The bus trip from Cardiff city centre to the famous Merthyr Mawr sand dunes some twenty-five miles down the coast, towards Porthcawl, took the best part of an hour. Even when they alighted they still had a mile or so to walk through a country lane that wound its way past cud-chewing cows and sheep-dip troughs before they arrived at the famous dunes that towered above them. At around one hundred feet high, they were indeed impressive. Its visitors were keen to test their physical prowess, intent on ploughing their way slowly up the shifting sands – two steps forward, one step backward.

It was a hard slog as Frankie could testify, having previously tackled the slopes in company with some of his brothers. But for those who persisted, they were rewarded with magnificent views of the sweeping, sun-bathed coastline and its wave-swept sandy beaches stretching four or five miles in both directions.

The couple stood marvelling at the space that surrounded them, the happy sounds filtering down from the hot, sandy dunes. They kissed, a long slow kiss full of the passion previously stifled by the presence of school, family or friends. As they broke off, Frankie guided her towards a cluster of thick bushes growing on the last vestiges of short grass flourishing on the edge of the mini-desert.

He pulled several branches of the bush aside allowing Peggy room enough to squeeze through into the small, clear space beyond, large enough for them both to lie down. The thicket provided perfect cover despite the proximity of others in the area. They again embraced, the tempo of their passion increasing as they fumbled inexpertly with awkward buttons. They finally shed their clothes and lay there stroking and caressing each other, while looking searchingly into each others eyes and finding only mutual consent. Neither were strangers to the pleasures of self-masturbation. It was a common-enough occurrence among their former school friends. But intercourse – that was a barrier neither had ever breached.

Peggy's ample young breasts responded to the encouragement of Frankie's eager fingers, her large pink nipples now firm and erect. As he explored the secret place between her thighs, she responded, gently stimulating the foreskin around the bulbous head of his penis until it swelled to its full, hard erection. From the ease with which Frankie's fingers now slid moistly in and out of her vagina, she knew she was ready to accept him.

It was the moment that both had ached for. She guided him inside until she could feel his swollen member pulsing, pushing forward insistently until she was breached. The initial stab of pain was replaced by waves of erotic sensation that took over her entire body, forcing involuntary groans of pleasure from her lips. Frankie, desperate to prolong the sensuousness he had also surrendered to, eased the strength behind his thrusts.

Gradually, the peak of their climax subsided. Frankie eased himself away from Peggy's thighs, conscious of how sore he felt. She lay there, her eyes searching his for signs of fulfilment or perhaps even disillusionment. They had until now, been strangers to the innermost secrets of each others bodies. Their uncertainties were dispelled instantly by the feelings of love that now flowed between them.

They dressed slowly, then sat facing each other. "How do you feel, Peggy?" asked Frankie gently, his hands caressing her smooth young face. She closed her eyes, savouring once again the fresh feelings and new sensations. "Magic, Frankie. That was sheer magic," she breathed. "It was better than I ever thought it would be." Frankie pulled her closer. "It certainly was for me too," he replied, his strength slowly renewing itself. "But the next time – and I just can't wait for the next time, I want it to be in bed – or somewhere like that," he added. "You see, Peg, I got a lot of sand under my foreskin somehow. It's gritty as hell and bloody uncomfortable," at which point, they burst into barely restrained laughter, finally betraying their presence to passers-by. But they emerged from their hiding place as lovers, true lovers now. Nothing else in the world mattered.

"Are you certain you know you're pregnant Peg? I mean, when did you find out? When?" Frankie's face was a picture of astonishment mingled with happiness as he drew Peggy close to him, still stunned by her wondrous news that he was to become a father – not just a father, but a father to Peggy's child! She looked at him, still uncertain of his reaction. "I'm sure, Frankie. I've known for about two weeks now, but I wanted to be certain before I told you."

He could smell the fragrance of her soft hair as they held each other tightly – her fragrance a memory that vividly recalled many of their earlier meetings when their feelings gave way to unbridled expressions of passion. With surprising tenderness, he smoothed away the beginnings of the tears that were brimming over into her astonishingly beautiful eyes. "Why are you crying Peg? Is it because you're frightened we're having a baby," he murmured, gently kissing her forehead.

She raised her face to his, fleetingly brushing his lips with hers. "No Frankie, no. It could never be that," she whispered. "It's just that I thought you might be very upset and not want me to have our baby." She hesitated before continuing. "I know my parents won't be at all happy." He again drew her closer and looked deeply into her eyes. "There's nothing in this world Peg, nothing at all I want more than sharing our baby together – nothing!" he emphasised.

He whirled her around at arms length two or three times before realising she might now be so fragile it could only hurt her and the baby. "Jesus Peg, I'm sorry," he mumbled in embarrassment. "I forgot for a moment that from now on, you'll have to be handled with kid gloves."

Her infectious peal of laughter in response calmed his apprehension. "Frankie Gallagher, while I have you to look after me and our baby, I don't think there's anything in this world for us to worry about."

Chapter 5

The strains of music drifting across the from the distant band-stand and the sunshine playing on her face were perfect partners as Peggy dozed on the grass, eyes barely closed, her mind drifting gently, enjoying the calmness of the balmy summer evening.

Her thoughts wondered lazily, but Frankie, her Frankie was at the centre of most of them. Well, he always seemed so, didn't he?

As the seriousness of their relationship deepened, so too had the significance of their obvious attraction for one another imposed itself upon the minds of her parents. If matters between the young couple continued to develop at the same pace, Peggy's parents were going to be faced with the totally unwholesome prospects of their daughter marrying into the Gallagher family. Good God! Could anything imaginable be worse?

Well yes, it certainly could. Her parents weren't aware, for example, that their beloved only daughter was pregnant – by Frankie Gallagher for a start. She could visualise her parents reaction. There was that dreadful woman Nellie Gallagher! The very thought of her and that habitual drunk of a husband becoming related to the Steeles by marriage would be simply too much to bear. The very thought would terrify them!

The problem was a real worry for Peggy and the question still occupied her mind, but she didn't hear any voices offering any answers.

Nor was she aware of the person that silently approached her across the grass until he spoke. "Hello Peggy, I thought it was you. Enjoying your little nap?" She was startled into awareness at the unexpected interruption, her eyes blinking in the bright sunshine at the newcomer. "Mind if I join you?" asked Dave Parker, settling down beside her on the grass without waiting for her response.

She sat upright, her dazzling smile evidence of her pleasure as recognition dawned. She leaned familiarly towards him, brushing his cheek with her lips in welcome. "What are you doing in Roath Park, David – and on your own too," she added noting that he looked every bit as handsome as ever, perhaps even more so in his neat short-sleeved white shirt, well-fitted khaki shorts and leather sandals.

He sat forward, elbows resting on his knees, hands clasped, absorbing the vivaciousness of the young woman sitting facing him. "I might ask you the same thing, Peg. No boyfriend today?" he enquired in a slightly mocking tone. She studied his face, a slight smile emphasising her dimples.

"No David, not today. Frankie and I have an arrangement. We see each other twenty four hours a day, six days a week." She leaned forward, touching his arm. "Today is my day off."

Dave acknowledged her slight rebuke with a sheepish grin, then stood up. "What do you say to a stroll and a cup of tea at the cafe by the lighthouse," he suggested, offering her his hand by way of reinforcing his invitation. She nodded, brushing off bits of grass from her skirt as he helped her up. They exchanged small-talk, bringing each other up to date on gossip as they walked across the large expanse of newly-mown grass, its scent pervading the air. It was, they agreed, a really beautiful summer evening.

They walked, content in the pleasure of each other's company along the wide tarmac path that encompassed the entire oval-shaped lake. The two mile-long waters, some two hundred yards wide, were set among a tree-lined park bordered by large houses in which some of Cardiff's wealthiest citizens live. Donated to the city by the local landed gentry, Roath Park and its Lake, now populated by dozens of swans, ducks and moorhens, provides days of fun for boaters and their lovers. At its southern end, nearest the city, a large white painted lighthouse stands, topped by a four-sided clock. A large plaque commemorates Captain Scott's departure from Cardiff Docks on his epic journey to the Antarctic.

As they strolled, Peggy learned that Dave had one girlfriend with whom he spent more time than others, but 'nothing is cast in concrete' as he put it. Anyone she knew? He didn't think so.

In the Lakeside Cafe, they sat facing each other across the table, both knowing inwardly they had something needing to be said to the other. Dave Parker was the first to speak. "I know it's quite some time since we left school and we have tended to go our separate ways Peg, seeing little of each other except for the occasional party or dance." He paused and she could sense what was coming. "But you know that I've always had very strong feelings for you, even in school. You do know that Peg, don't you and seeing you again today has brought all these feelings flooding back."

He again paused, searching her face and eyes for signs of the response he craved for before continuing. "I know you've been involved with Frankie Gallagher, but deep down inside, really deep down, I've always believed that there was a place for us together. It's something I've always wanted to happen." He studied her eyes, a voice inside his head screaming, "say you believe it too, Peg! Say it!"

She squeezed his hands then held them gently in hers. She braced herself. "There's only one way to tell him," she thought "and that's to come straight out with it." She spoke quietly. "Although we met purely by chance today Dave, I'm glad we did because there is something very important I have to tell you."

Dave's heart leapt. Peggy's heart pounded. She took a deep breath. "I'm pregnant," she said, almost in a whisper. "It's Frankie's baby," she added, letting her pent-up breath out slowly.

His hands fell away from hers as he sat right back into his seat, total disbelief disfiguring his face. "Pregnant! Pregnant!" he exclaimed. "By that scum Gallagher?" The rising, raw anger in his voice dismayed her, even frightened her.

She hadn't expected his congratulations but a perhaps a sympathetic response might have been forthcoming. They had, after all, enjoyed a long-standing friendly relationship. But from his frightening, angry reaction, she now knew he had never regarded their friendship as platonic but something much more intense. Why, oh why had he never expressed these feelings to her before? Some things might have changed in both their lives.

He slowly pushed his untouched cup of tea away and stood up. "If what you say is true and that's what you want, there's not much more to add, is there," he grated through clenched teeth. "You've just said it all!" He called the waitress over and threw a handful of coins onto the plate.

Peg felt the tears welling up in her eyes and then noticed with surprise that his eyes too were brimming as he fought inwardly to control the depth of his emotions and his barely-contained anger. "I'm sorry Dave," she whispered. "I truly am, believe me," her tears now openly coursing down her pale cheeks.

He hesitated briefly then patted her on her shoulder. "Look Peg, I've got to go now," he said huskily. "I'll see you around sometime" – and with that he was gone.

Peg sat there, slowly stirring her unwanted cup of cold tea, her eyes blanking out to her surroundings. She was completely oblivious to the comings and goings of the other customers as she replayed the events of the previous half hour over in her mind. A troubled thought occupied her as she rose to leave the cafe. "If Dave Parker reacts like that when I tell him I'm pregnant, what on earth are my Mum and Dad going to think?"

Dave Parker left Roath Park Lake and headed for the nearest tram stop but as he walked, nothing around him seem to register. He strode past the tram stop shelter, not noticing those waiting for the tram, nor other passers-by as he continued walking – his mind numbed by Peggy's news of her pregnancy.

He knew now, by God he knew that he'd made a big mistake allowing Frankie Gallagher to make the running when it came to courting Peggy for her affections back in their school-days. Even when all three had left school for good, his failure to maintain other than a friendly relationship with her had allowed Gallagher numerous opportunities to cut him out of Peg's life while strengthening his own claims. If he hadn't realised before how detached he had become, how truly foolish he'd been, he certainly knew it now as the truth hit him like a sledge-hammer! She was having

Gallagher's baby! Oh, how I hate that rat, he inwardly fumed. But he just couldn't rid himself of the thought that Peg had let him down – very badly indeed!

Peggy didn't need it spelt out to her either. She had long known she had acted in a manner that would hurt the people closest to her. It was only a matter of time before her pregnancy became apparent so she had no other choice than to confront her parents with the truth. She had already decided to live with the stigma of an unmarried pregnancy and the inevitable whispers of disapproval from her neighbours and workmates. But Dave Parker's reaction had really shaken her to the core.

Yes, she had some fence-mending to do with him and truths to be told to her parents. The prospects that immediately lay ahead suddenly had taken all the pleasures out of what had started as a beautiful summer's day. It was the autumn and winter that was to follow that depressed her as made her way homeward.

Chapter 6

The unmistakeable stench of petrol was overwhelming as Frankie struggled to clear his befuddled mind. His head felt as if it had been split wide open, the pinpoints of flashing lights only reinforcing the pain that seared through his eyes. "Where the hell am I? This has to be a nightmare," he groaned. "Let's hope that I'm going to wake up soon – the sooner the better, for Christ's sake." His disorientation was replaced by the numbing realisation that he was cold – freezing cold. At least it couldn't be Hell he thought grimly.

He lay there in the gloom of the winter night for what must have been another ten minutes or so, although he had no way of knowing. His uncertainty was pierced by an awareness of a comforting warmth suddenly trickling across his frozen face. The warm fluid, for that's what is was, trickled into his mouth. Its bitter taste, a taste he couldn't identify, stirred him into a misty awareness that gradually cleared as his eyes slowly focused.

The large scruffy dog stood over him, snuffling noisily, first in the shallow layer of snow, then around him as it again explored the crumpled human heap sprawled on the frozen grassy roadside verge. It lifted a hind leg and repeated the dose as it again urinated with even greater emphasis into the face of the stranger that had invaded its territory. The urine by now had mingled with the blood seeping into his mouth from the gashes on his forehead and right cheekbone.

Its initial inspection now over, the dog cocked its rear leg yet again and completed its ablutions by pissing over his less-caring boots. Frankie spat out the unwelcome cocktail with disgust but the sour, bitter taste persisted. Sharp, stabbing pain burned through his back and neck as he attempted to sit upright. Given the pain and the effort it caused, he had to settle for a while resting on one elbow.

The hissing noise a couple of yards to his left, gradually registered on his increasing awareness of his surroundings. Steam was still blowing from the ruptured radiator of the wrecked vehicle, now lying on its side, the front end very badly damaged by its collision with the huge, black tree that dominated the narrow country lane. The fresh scars on its gnarled layers of bark, now oozing with sap, were visible even in the dim light,

The dog by now had shifted its attention to the second person lying motionless several yards ahead of the stricken vehicle. It was then the real horror of the crash came flooding back.

"Peggy! What's happened to Peggy?" he moaned, his voice rising with fear that welled into his chest as he screamed at the dog inspecting its next target. The unexpected noise in the stillness of the night had the desired effect, the startled dog loping away into the early morning gloom.

Frankie gritted his teeth, his mounting fear generating the strength to force himself first to sit up, then rising gingerly to his feet, swaying unsteadily, shivering in the chill wind. His own concerns had by now been forgotten, replaced by sheer dread as he moved slowly to where Peggy's crumpled body lay.

She had been catapulted through the windscreen glass, the remains of which were scattered over the thin covering of frozen snow. Frankie stumbled to where Peggy lay silent, mercifully unaware of the lacerations that now disfigured her beautiful, young face. He knelt, wincing at the difficulty of the movement then carefully, softly cradled her head in his arms. A sudden flow of tears burned his cheeks, creating pale channels on his bloodied face.

The dog had now returned, just standing there, weighing up its chances, looking at the stricken pair. A series of shouts, gradually becoming louder penetrated Frankie's numbed mind. The dog, which had returned to foraging, excitedly exploring the different smells of the two strangers and their damaged vehicle, bounded away to greet its owner.

The farm worker quickened his pace, the powerful beam from his torch flooding the crash area with its jerky glow. His face creased with concern as he took in the sight of the badly-damaged car and the injured couple. "Is the other person still alive? Are you OK?," he called out as he approached. He bent over the unconscious Peggy, feeling for her pulse.

"It's very faint," he announced. "We're going to need help – and quick. She looks as though she's in a really bad way. Will you be OK with her for a while?" Frankie nodded his assent, incapable of anything else as the newcomer turned his attention back to Peggy.

Frankie tried to ease himself into a more comfortable position without disturbing Peggy. Less than an hour earlier they had been discussing their plans for their new baby, due in two months. But the horror of the seconds that led up to the crash and what followed would scar his memory for the rest of his life.

The bend in the unlit country lane was much tighter than he had anticipated, causing him to wrench at the steering wheel. Unable to cope with the rapid change of direction on the frozen surface, the car swerved drunkenly, skidding out of control. It glanced off a heavy wooden fence and with no room to manoeuvre in the narrow lane way, he couldn't prevent it smashing head-on into the huge tree on the other side of the road. Peggy's scream of terror as he clung on to the steering wheel was the last sound he recalled before blacking out as the front end of the car crumpled sickeningly under the force of the collision.

The farm worker stood up, shaking his head dubiously. "There's hardly any traffic comes this way of an evening sir, so I don't expect we'll see many passers-by if any. There's a local police house across the fields and he's got a telephone. We'll get some help from there. I'll be as quick as I can," he added, trying to sound reassuring. He removed his duffle coat, motioning Frankie to take it. "Here, have this to cover the young lady. I'll pick up some blankets for you on my way back."

With that, he turned and scrunched his way across the frozen layer of snow. His dog hesitated for a last backward look at the strangers before loping away in the same direction as they both disappeared into the darkness.

Frankie arranged the stranger's coat as best as he could to protect Peggy from the chilling wind before drawing her gently to his chest He thought briefly of trying to pick away several shards of glass embedded in her deathly white face, then desisted realising that his shaking hands might cause even further injury to her shattered face.

"Why, oh why did this have to happen to us and our baby," he groaned inwardly but as guilt flooded his mind, he realised he had answered his own question. He gently kissed Peggy's forehead, ignoring the bloodstained state of her matted hair. "Please God, make them come back quickly," he whispered. "I don't want my Peggy or our baby to die."

Even as he uttered the words, he couldn't suppress the pangs of guilt that persisted. He couldn't remember the last time he had given any thought to God. He was still nursing Peggy gently thirty minutes later when he saw the first flashes from the rescuers torches. The dog led the way, confident of its sense of direction and eager to resume its examination of the injured couple.

A different, deeper voice broke through Frankie's numbed thoughts. "How is the girl? Is she still breathing?" The uniformed policeman shone his torch at the couple. The signs of their facial damage forced an involuntary sharp intake of breath from the burly officer. He felt for Peggy's pulse. "She's still with us son but only just. And we don't know yet if she's sustained any internal injuries." He stood up. "Let's hope she's a strong girl and can hang on until the ambulance arrives." He leant closer, looking at Frankie's injuries. "You've collected some damage yourself, young fellow. How do you feel?"

Frankie nodded. "I'm OK. It's Peggy I'm worried about."

The policeman reached behind him, producing two blankets from a rucksack which he draped carefully over the crash victims. "Can you manage a drop of hot tea?" he asked, motioning with the flask to Frankie. The look in Frankie's eyes prompted the policeman to pour the steaming liquid into the flask's bakelite cup.

Frankie released a supporting arm carefully from under Peggy, taking the proferred cup, handle first as he did so.

The policeman then gently cradled the young woman's head and shoulders. Certain he had her safely, he eased one hand away and placed a gauze pad over the deep lacerations in her right cheek to prevent any further dirt entering her wounds. The slight medicinal smell assailed Frankie's nostrils. He took several deeper than normal breaths, sensing the sharpness of the chill evening air. A myriad of thoughts raced through his muddled mind as he lay, waiting for the warmth and comfort of the help on its way.

Frankie touched the policeman on his arm. "Peggy is pregnant – seven months. Do you think they'll be alright and survive this?" The policeman shrugged his shoulders. It was a question he couldn't answer but he understood the young man's reasons for asking.

"Let's get you out of here first, then we'll see."

Frankie eased his pain-wracked body back onto the ground. As he did, the sound of the approaching ambulance grew louder. His mind filled with a thousand thoughts as the vehicle, lights blazing, slowly scrunched to a halt several yards away on the crisp snow. But there was only one thought that really burned through his consciousness as they were transferred to the warmth and safety of the ambulance. Just one thought to cling to. "At least Peggy and I are still alive – and while we are, that gives our baby a chance."

By the time the ambulance drew up outside the Accident and Emergency unit at Cardiff Royal Infirmary, A & E personnel had already been briefed that the female passenger was in a coma – and pregnant.

A detailed examination of Peggy revealed that the impact of the collision had smashed her skull leaving her with brain injuries and a shattered spine. On the positive side, the examination had revealed that the unborn child was unharmed, but the crash had left Peggy in a comatose, vegetative, state with virtually no brain responses – a condition normally considered to be permanent.

Determined to allow the unborn child to develop as much as possible within safe parameters, Peggy was kept alive in an intensive care unit – but alive only in the medical sense. Throughout the three weeks she remained in her suspended state, Frankie's injuries had responded sufficiently to allow him use of a wheelchair. The medical staff informed him that they were considering their chances of delivering Peggy's child, given certain conditions.

The turning point came when she eventually started to breathe unaided. The hospital's gynaecology specialist and clinical director of obstetrics considered that if any time at all was appropriate, this was the time. Baby Elizabeth was successfully delivered – the name the lovers had decided upon if it was a girl – weighing just under four pounds The infant survived after spending the first week of her new, miraculous life in a special baby-care unit.

Frankie's intense feelings of guilt and responsibility for the accident were compounded by burning feelings of grief when Peggy subsequently died, from kidney failure, three weeks after giving birth to their new child.

Peggy's death had a profound effect on her parents, already reeling from the shock at the extent of the injuries she had sustained in the crash. They had lost their daughter in the most tragic of circumstances, having earlier endured coming to terms with news of her pregnancy to of all people, Frankie Gallagher. But out of their pain and bitterness was forged a determination to win custody of the infant and bring her up as their own child.

Frankie too was equally intent to hold on to the most miraculous affirmation of his love for Peggy – their very own child. The battle for custody was intense but brief. The magistrate agreed with the child's grandparents. While there was irrefutable proof that Peggy was the child's mother, there was absolutely no proof whatsoever to support Frankie's claim that he was the father, other than an inconclusive blood test.

"It could be said," the magistrate pointed out however painful it was to the Steele's ears, "that anyone of half a dozen men could possibly make the same claim. And furthermore, the criminal tendencies of the Gallagher family including the alleged father Frankie Gallagher, precludes him from being granted the custody of the child."

Peggy's funeral was a quiet affair. A dozen of the Steele's closest family attended, but her parents made it very clear to Frankie that they didn't want to turn it into a mini-circus by having to cope not only with their grief, but the Gallagher family numbers as well. In their opinion, he had already caused enough strife by his attention to their daughter for several years, despite their resistance to their daughter's unwelcome association. While conceding to their wishes regarding members of his family, Frankie insisted on attending. As far as he was concerned, he had as much right as Peggy's family, given the circumstances. There was also another person among the mourners. Dave Parker's discreet presence went largely unnoticed at the grave side during the vicar's final address. Unnoticed to many that is, except Frankie.

They studiously avoided each other, but the inner feelings betrayed on Parker's face left Frankie in little doubt that he had created a real enemy that one day would seek retribution.

With the distress and grief of the funeral now behind them, the Steeles reacted quickly and positively. Determined to rid the child and themselves of the Gallaghers' corrosive influence, they moved out of Cardiff to settle in an unknown destination somewhere in southern England.

There would be an inquest to attend in Cardiff at some future date to determine the cause of the accident and Peggy's subsequent death. But at least they had taken the first important step to create a new start in life for themselves and the child.

Chapter 7

Dave Parker's feelings of bitterness towards Frankie Gallagher had slow-burned ever since their school-days but Peggy's death fanned the smouldering embers into a white-hot fury waiting to erupt.

During the weeks that followed, Parker arrived at a decision that would change his life. His present job in the City's accounts department demanded little of his abilities and for several months he had already considered looking for a new challenge. Now he believed he had found it.

He reasoned that to really settle the score with Gallagher, he could hardly beat him to within an inch of his life as punishment for his part in Peggy's death. He would certainly risk massive retaliation from the Gallagher family – or even the law. If, on the other hand he became part of the system that upheld the law, he would have every legitimate right to pursue Frankie Gallagher in particular and his family if need be, for their law-breaking activities. It would be sweet revenge indeed. His application to join the city's police force followed the very next day.

The competitive nature of his new colleagues and the disciplines involved in training ideally suited Parker's temperament. But after only several months into his new career, his life and that of young men and women throughout Britain came to a juddering halt.

The clouds of uncertainty over Europe had grown following the election of a new German Chancellor with expansionist ideals, six years earlier. Adolf Hitler's rebuttal of Britain's demands for restraint led to a declaration of war against Germany.

Hitler responded by letting his military hordes loose in Europe, sweeping aside the ineffectual resistance of Poland, Belgium, Holland and France.

As Britain rallied to meet the challenge, impending military conscription provided the country's young men and women with their first real opportunity to venture beyond the suffocating boundaries of their urban lifestyles, among them Dave Parker and the six Gallagher brothers old enough to enlist. Parker was accepted by the Royal Marines while the Gallagher boys followed in their father's footsteps by signing on for the Merchant Navy.

To Nell Gallagher the news that she was about to hand over six of her sons to the service of their country filled her with dread. She had already suffered the early deaths of three of her children and those painful memories had never left her.

Her husband Charlie took the news somewhat differently as he glanced at her across the large kitchen table. Two mugs of tea were accompanied by freshly-made toast, whose aroma filled the room. Charlie took out his handkerchief and prepared to blow his nose. "I see the boys are signing on for the Merchant Navy, Nell." He blew his nose. They've made the right choice, following their old man."

Nell remained silent for a while, then raised her head to look at her husband and snorted in derision. "Yeah, that's right – you did eight years on the coasters in peacetime. But my boys will be working on ships that will be facing God knows what kind of danger from those bastard Germans." She again lapsed into silence while Charlie, deciding that no further comment might be preferable, dipped a large piece of toast into his mug of tea and stuffed it past the gaping hole in his teeth and into his mouth with relish.

Nell sat there, shaking her head. "I'm worried Charlie, I really am," she uttered tearfully, her tears now spilling unashamedly down her plump cheeks. She looked at him again. "They're my boys, my lovely boys and I don't want to lose any more," she ended, barely audibly. Charlie pushed his chair back, walked around the table and put a comforting arm around his wife's shoulders. "There,

there, Nell. They can look after themselves and when it's all over, we'll have a party to end all parties. You'll see!"

Nell was speaking but he couldn't catch her words. He leant closer, as she turned to face him. "Mary, mother of Jesus," she whispered. "I'll pray every day until they do come back – that's what I want more anything, for them to come back when it's over."

———

The freezing spray from the savagely whipped-up waves searched for Jack Gallagher's face – the only part of his body not protected by his heavy wet-weather clothing. As he adjusted his oilskin head-gear to provide more protection to his rapidly-freezing face, his clumsy gloves made the relatively simple task substantially more difficult. The severe pitching of the battered cargo ship prompted him to tighten the belt on his safety line.

"What the fuck am I doing here on forward watch somewhere in the north Atlantic? I'm supposed to be the fucking cook on this rust-bucket," His silent question received a bellowing reply that was instantly whipped away from his lips into oblivion by the fierce wind. "Because you volunteered for it, that's why, you arsehole!"

He struggled to keep his balance, while in his mind, he went over the dramatic events that had occurred earlier the day before. Cut off from the rest of the convoy by temporary engine trouble eventually repaired, the ancient vessel battled its lone journey across the North Atlantic. It provided an easy target for the German aircraft, which, settling on a line for its bombing run, released a stick of four bombs at its victim.

The first two fell just short into the raging sea, the explosions causing a concussive effect on those crewmen in the lower decks. The third for some reason, struck part of the upper deck and failed to detonate as it glanced off into the sea. But it was fourth time lucky for the aircrew as it struck home, instantly killing five crew-men sleeping on bunks in their cramped cabin. "Some Christmas for them," Jack Gallagher thought grimly. The damage was patched up but left the vessel limping and easy prey to an enemy marauder of which there were many in the Atlantic.

He tensed the muscles of his body in a bid to ward off the numbing cold, but it had little effect in the howling, freezing wind. He didn't become aware of the presence of his brother Bobby until the youngster tapped him on the shoulder. "My turn on watch Jack," Bobby mouthed silently, conversation being near impossible in the fearsome conditions. Jack nodded vigorously, only too happy to swap places. He signalled 'OK' with a thumbs-up sign, unhooked himself from the safety lifeline belt and handed it to Bobby who secured it around his waist and crutch, then took up Jack's former position.

Descending the narrow steps carefully, Jack struggled against the wind as he forced open the door to their sleeping quarters. His success as it swung open brought a stream of curses from the huddled figure occupying one of the three small bunks in the cramped cabin. "Shut that sodding door for Christ's sake, will you! It's not time for my watch already, is it?"

Nick's grumbling tone served to remind Jack that all three Gallagher brothers had not only survived yesterday's bomb attack but the previous eleven months on North Atlantic convoy duty. His bulky, oilskin-clad figure stood there awhile, allowing the water to drip off his protective clothing. The steam rose from his body as he stripped off, adding to the variety of sweaty odours in the cabin that were their daily companions. "Relax Nick. Bobby's just relieved me so you've still got a few more hours in your pit." Now it was his turn to enjoy a few hours of rest as he eased himself gratefully into his narrow bunk.

His eyes roamed around the walls of the cabin, noting the pictures and illustrations of impossibly curvaceous women, all torn out of American magazines. But it was a larger, cardboard sign stuck to a cabin locker door that brought a smile to his face. The words, 'The Three Musketeers' were accompanied by a cut-out picture of Douglas Fairbanks and his faithful companions. That's what the rest of the 28-man crew called the Gallagher brothers. Well, it had been twenty eight until yesterday. Jack's return hadn't proved any barrier to Nick's desire to sleep. He was soon snoring and noisily passing wind as he slumbered.

Jack was considering giving himself a bucket bath before finally getting his head down. He should have had one before he'd got into his bunk.

The rolling and pitching of the ship and the rhythmic thump of the engines were instantly forgotten as a terrific explosion rocked the vessel, sending a massive quiver shuddering through its structure. The lights went out leaving a faint emergency light operating that couldn't compete with a candle. Both Jack and Nick tumbled out of their bunks, Nick roaring in pain as he cracked a shin against the bunk leg. "What the fuck was that?" he yelled as they blundered around in the confined space between the bunks.

The smell of thick oily smoke partly answered Nick's frantic question. "Torpedo! Was that a bloody torpedo?" yelled Jack as they strained to throw on some clothes before they laboriously made their way to the upper deck. Huge flames, driven by the freezing wind, burst out of the gaping, jagged hole amidships where the torpedo had sliced through the steel hull like paper and exploded. Jack grabbed his brother. "See if you can find out where Bobby is," he yelled against the wind. Nick nodded, his face strained as he pushed his way past several crewmen frantically trying to launch one of the four lifeboats, each one capable of carrying eighteen men.

Jack made his way to the radio room but found the door jammed from the explosion. He smashed his boot repeatedly against the metal door until it gave way. In the dim glow from the emergency lighting, he located some radio equipment, stuffed it into a water-proof sack along with two pairs of shoes and a couple of blankets to blunt the sharpness of the wind. Nick appeared in the doorway of the room, his face reflecting his fear and anxiety.

"Some of the blokes said they saw Bobby in one of the boats but don't know if it got away over the side," he said through clenched teeth. "It's time we did the same Jack before this bloody crate sinks under our feet." Nodding his agreement, Jack grabbed the big sack with one hand and his brother with the other, leading them to the fourth lifeboat already crowded with fearful faces and shaking limbs.

As it was winched downward to the cruel, unsympathetic sea, another huge explosion from the doomed ship rent the air, to send the lifeboat lurching into the path of a massive wave as big as a waterfall. The huge swell completely soaked the lifeboat's occupants before it finally bounced down with a crash onto the foaming water. Another wave following in quick succession, spun the lifeboat away from the stricken ship's heaving side, leaving two of its occupants struggling in the wild, freezing water as it swept them out of sight.

With two men to each oar and the apprentice officer taking charge, the ship's carpenter, an old Shetlander, steered the lifeboat clear, keeping it head-on to the waves. The oarsmen pulled strongly, desperate to put as much distance as they could between themselves and the stricken ship, now getting lower in the water by the minute. Finally, with only its stern visible in the growing light, the doomed vessel gave several more groaning, grating rumbles signalling its death throes before disappearing in a cauldron of hissing steam and wild water.

The stunned, numbing silence of the lifeboat's occupants as they stared at the empty, unforgiving sea was broken by the apprentice officer, intent on asserting his authority. He cupped his hands over his mouth. "Has anyone seen anything of the other boats? Does anybody know how many got away from the ship," he yelled. The shaking of heads of the survivors, still shocked by the dramatic recent events confirmed their worst fears.

It looked, at least for the time being, that they were on their own, some four hundred miles west-north-west of Scotland. To his credit, the young officer acted positively. "We'll need to work the oars on a rota basis and on bailing out water." He turned to the Shetlander. "These boats should be OK for rations so I want you to check what food and water we've got on board in the storage compartments."

Their plight became infinitely more serious as the search revealed that someone on board their ship had earlier removed or stolen most of the rations stored in the emergency lockers. All that remained was some pemmican dried meat, hard tack biscuits and drinking water in the tanks. Another blow was that the medical supplies had also gone, so the wounded survivors on board would have to grin and bear it – or face the consequences.

Jack and Nick made sure they pulled on the same oar when their turn came, giving them the chance to talk. One thought was uppermost in both their minds. What had happened to Bobby? "I hope to Christ he made it," uttered Jack through chattering teeth as both men clung to the hope of their brother's safety. The dread that young Bobby might have failed to get clear of the sinking ship gnawed away at their restless minds, both fearing the worst, both fearful of putting their thoughts into words.

Although everyone in the lifeboat was soaked to the skin and suffering further from the freezing water they were shipping into the boat, the effort needed to row helped to generate some body heat and there was no shortage of volunteers when it came to taking turns on the oars. Luckily for Jack and Nick, the blankets Jack had grabbed helped them to ward off some of the bone-chilling cold even though they were wet, but the harsh conditions were taking their inevitable toll. By the fifth day, four men had died – the survivors struggling to tip the bodies overboard without capsizing the boat.

Several other blankets and bits of canvas brought from the ship were shared among the men, the neediest taking priority. Even though the blankets were always wet, they helped to keep out some wind and cold. On the seventh day, the tough old Shetlander spotted a ship. The despair, pain and hunger of the past week faded as the men on the oars, urged on by their companions, added extra effort to their rowing despite their aching muscles, fearful their saviour would sail out of sight.

As they neared the vessel, which they recognised as a British merchantman, their euphoria at the prospects of rescue and safety was subdued by the stillness and silence of the stranger. It was unnerving. There was absolutely no sign of life aboard. Having secured the lifeboat to the strange vessel, they scrambled wearily aboard and to their surprise, the only one to greet them was a cat. It soon became evident that the ship had been abandoned following an attack.

They explored the eerie silence below deck and were rewarded with the discovery of ample supplies of food, drink – and every bit as welcome – a cabinet of medical supplies. It didn't take long

for the two Gallagher brothers to sort out a cabin to share and col-
lapse on the bunks as stiffness and sheer exhaustion took over
their aching bodies.

It was twelve hours later before Nick woke – a bath or shower his
first priority. It came as a shock when he saw that his feet, which
by now were quite swollen, had turned an odd purply colour. He
inspected his feet more closely, pinching his toes to test their feeling. To his horror, the tips of the first two toes came away in his
fingers. He stared in horror and disbelief, sucking in his breath,
repulsed at the sight. He had seen something like this before, but
that was on somebody else, a shipmate who had later been dis-
charged from the Merchant Navy. It was frostbite.

He leaned over to Jack, shaking him roughly by the shoulder and
again as Jack at first failed to respond. "Jack! Jack! Wake up will
you, for fuck's sake!" His urgent tone slowly roused his brother
into awareness. "What's up, our kid. Wassa marrer," he slurred,
his mouth tasting and feeling absolutely foul.

Nick grimaced, not from pain. He couldn't feel any. "Jack, look!
I've bloody well got frostbite. Look!" he cried, a hint of hysteria
creeping into his voice. His brother swung sideways to his feet
from the bunk, peering closely at Nick's discoloured ankles and
toes. "Christ, I think you're right Nick. It certainly looks a bleeding mess," gasped Jack. "How did it happen?" In response, Nick
held out his hand, the bits of toes looking like lumps of wax on
his palm. "I've tried the other foot," said Nick as he eased himself
slowly back onto the bunk, "and they look OK, I think."

Their grisly conversation was interrupted by excited shouts coming from the upper deck. The clamour of noise was prompted by
the sighting of a small ship flying Swedish colours. It was headed
their way. The sheer relief of the stricken crewmen was clearly
evident as several unashamedly cried, no matter what their mates
might have thought!

With the British survivors transferred to the warmth and safety
of the Swedish ship, medical treatment for the walking wounded
and the more seriously affected was arranged without delay.

As for Nicky, it was some treatment – and only just in time! His
rescuers took him to a cabin where they sat him in a chair and eased

his injured foot over a washbasin. Two Swedish crewmen held him down, while a third poured surgical spirit over the injured foot. The fourth person, the skipper of the ship, selected a scalpel from a small tray and proceeded to cut away the discoloured flesh a piece at a time. Nick felt nauseous, his stomach retching drily, not liking one bit what he was watching. He didn't want to but somehow he felt compelled to watch in a macabre fashion.

He turned his head to one of the crewmen. "Do you have a shot of whisky or brandy, mate," he said, not knowing whether the fellow understood a word. The crewman looked at his skipper, who nodded. The fiery spirit caused Nick to gag as it burned its way down his throat, unused to the power of the drink. Coughing and spluttering, he finally managed to speak. "Well, I asked for that, didn't I, but it was a bit stronger than I expected." When Jack heard of the spartan treatment meted out to his brother, his query was met with an apologetic shrug – and an explanation from the skipper. "Your brother was in such a weakened condition, we couldn't risk giving him any anaesthetic."

Over the next two days, the process of removing flesh from Nick's foot was repeated until the skipper declared himself satisfied he had done what he could to save Nick's foot.

It wasn't too long before the British survivors were put off at the Faroe Islands where they heard that their families had been informed of their rescue and return to dry land. The bad news was that nothing had been heard of the whereabouts of seven of the sunken ship's crew, including young Bobby. It was news certain to upset Nell as she continued to pray for his safe return. Nick meanwhile and several of his shipmates were transferred to a hospital where they gradually recovered. It was a further two weeks before Nick, Jack and the rest docked at their home port of Cardiff, with Nick requiring more hospital treatment. It was several months before he could wear socks again.

It was at this point that Nell's hopes for Bobby were finally shattered. Along with two other seamen, he had died from his injuries sustained in the later explosions on their ship. It was a cruel homecoming for Jack and Nick and a foretaste of the tragedy that was still to come for Nell and the rest of the Gallagher family.

Chapter 8

It wasn't only those serving their King and Country that faced up to the demands of war in Britain. Along with hundreds of Cardiff families left behind at home, several of Nell's girls worked in a local factory contributing to the war effort. They were employed at the John Curran works who switched from its peace-time production of pots and pans to making shell casings as it had done in the 1914–18 Great War.

Of the 13,000 people employed by Curran's, around 5,200 were women. The employees received a huge boost to their morale five months after the war started when on the 9th February 1940, King George and Queen Elizabeth visited the factory on what was supposed to be a secret visit, but the news leaked out. For days afterwards, the Royal visit was the main subject of discussion around the Gallagher dinner table with Katie basking in the glory of the King and Queen's visit. Later, on the evening of the Royal trip, Nell's impatience was clear as her girls excitedly discussed their day.

"Come on Katie," said Nell. "You said you spoke to the Queen. Well, what did she say to you? She did speak to you, didn't she?" insisted Nell, in a tone of mounting exasperation.

Katie giggled nervously. "I was so scared Mam, I nearly died when she stopped by my machine and asked me what I was making." Katie gulped and continued. "I could hardly speak at first and once I started, I couldn't stop! She's really lovely Mam, you ought to see her!"

Nell's face beamed with pride and delight. Fancy one of my girls

49

meeting our Queen. "I hope you bloody well curtsied. You have to show you've been brought up proper, like," she added as the food was ladled onto their waiting plates.

Charlie Gallagher was also doing his bit for the war effort. He headed a five-man ARP team on fire-watching duties in his district of the city. His steel helmet and canvas knapsack occupied pride of place hanging on a big hook next to the kitchen fireplace. During air raids, his team patrolled the streets at night on fire-watch duties based on a rota system.

Katie's meeting with the Queen earned him more than one bottle of ale or a pint of beer from mates eager to discuss the details, usually embellished a little by Charlie for extra effect. On the nights when German bomber raids were expected, the family and many of their neighbours sheltered behind the massive walls of Cardiff's impressive Castle, occupying pride of place right at the heart of Wales' capital city. Wooden shelving had been installed alongside inner walls, on which to bed down with blankets and pillows, while the bombs rained down outside, usually onto the docks or inner city areas. The castle provided a safe haven where spirits were high among those gathered, especially those out of a bottle.

On an evening expected to be free of air raids, Nell and her husband were enjoying a drink in one of their local pubs when George Davies strolled in, glanced around, nodded to various customers and made his way over to their table. "Evening both," he greeted them. "Mind if I sit down?" which he did without waiting for a reply.

Charlie took a pull at his pint, then looked over the rims of his spectacles at their visitor. Nell stared at him, her dislike evident. Davies leaned forward, addressing Nell. "I hear you've set up a nice little gambling club at your house Nell. You don't need me to tell you that it's illegal, do you?" His comments were accompanied by a smile that wasn't a smile.

Nell looked at him, sipped from her glass before replying. "Are you in here for a drink or just passing through, Mr Davies," adding, with a nod in the direction of the bar, "there's plenty of room over there."

Charlie leaned back in his chair, content to let the exchanges flow without any contribution from him. He took another swig from his glass.

Davies ignored Nell's polite invitation to piss off. "Some of my people with an ear to the ground also tell me that you and that admirable bunch of folk residing in your house are fencing stolen goods around some of the pubs down the Bay. You don't need me to tell you that's not legal either, Nell." He pushed his chair back and stood up to leave. "Don't be surprised if you get a visit sometime soon." Nell caught his sleeve. "Those people of yours Mr Davies are nothing more than a bunch of lying grasses who need to watch their asses. You don't need me to tell you that, do you Mr Davies?" He shrugged his burly shoulders and went over to the bar, spoke to the barman and then left.

Charlie got up and crossed to the bar. "What was all that about Gerry? Was he asking you about me and Nell?"

The barman finished polishing the glass in his hand, put his cloth down, leaned under the bar and brought up two bottles of Mackeson stout from a crate and handed them to Charlie. "Yeah, Charlie, he did mention you. He said to give you and Nell these two beers and to put them on his tab."

Charlie looked at the barman in bemusement. "He said that, did he Gerry?" The barman nodded his assent. "Yeah, just that. Nothing else." Charlie returned to his seat, eager to satisfy Nell's curiosity. "What went on over there with Davies at the bar? Tell me Charlie," she urged. Which he did.

The following morning, Charlie walked up the steps of the Police Headquarters situated in Cathays Park, entered and spoke to the policeman on the duty desk. "Can you make sure that these two bottles are handed to Mr George Davies and tell him from Nell Gallagher to shove 'em. He'll know where to put them." With that, he hitched up his trouser belt, adjusted his cap to its usual jaunty angle, leaving a puzzled policeman staring at the bottles on his desk.

The following day, Cardiff experienced several hours of continuous torrential rain. For Nell and her battalion of young troops it was a windfall not to be passed up. As it was too wet to go out, most were gathered in the kitchen. Nell bustled into the room. "All of you. Get the bogeys out into the road and start collecting the blocks that are loose. You'll have to hurry up because the Council men will be along to check the tram lines and it'll be too late then!" They scattered, for when Nell gave her orders like that, you moved!

The road surface in many areas of Cardiff comprised a layer of thick wooden blocks, heavily tarred over to secure the tram rails embedded among the blocks. Over time, the vibration and jolting caused by the heavy trams loosened many blocks to such an extent, they became loose. The heavy rain did the rest. The Gallagher kids rolled out their bogeys from the cellar like a squadron of Spitfires taking off to do battle with the enemy.

Their bogeys were constructed of a thick plank of wood five or six feet in length with a pair of old pram wheels nailed or better still, bolted onto the underside at each end. With a piece of rope tied to the left and right hand side of the axles for steering, the bogey was propelled by another person pushing it and its pilot from behind with a broom handle or pole.

They worked furiously, tugging the heavy blocks free and loading them onto the bogeys. Another ten minutes or so and the Council men would be along. As each bogey was fully loaded with blocks and with Nell keeping a watchful eye on proceedings from her front window, the bogeys and their valuable cargo disappeared into the bowels of the Gallagher household, never to see the light of outside day again.

As the rain eased off and the floodwater subsided, the tram lines lay exposed, shining their appeal for help, as the gaping holes around them signalled their vulnerability. The maintenance men took the best part of the day to repair the road surface, watched by the block raiders from the safety of their front windows. The blocks were heavy and they smelt of tar, but they burnt furiously on the Gallagher fire providing much needed warmth – and they were free!

It wasn't the only thing that was free. To help needy families in hard times, a local scheme known as 'the Parish' was founded, providing a form of support paid for out of the city's rates. A committee of 'guardians' comprising local business people administered the fund, to which needy families could apply.

The guardians would assess the merit of applicant's claims and if successful, the family would receive boots, shoes or clothing. In the case of boots and shoes, the part of the undersole in front of the heel was 'branded' with a motif that could not be removed to prevent them being sold on for a profit by their new owner! Some cash was occasionally added to the family kitty by collecting large empty corned-beef tins – the eight pound variety – from local butchers and grocers shops.

Usually imported from Argentina or the United States, the extra-large tins were opened by 'keys' that were anchored to the tins by big blobs of solder. The blobs could be melted down into small lumps and then sold to the local plumber. It was painstaking work providing little reward. It was no small wonder they later turned their attention to easier ways of making money.

The use of Cardiff Docks increased dramatically as the south-eastern ports of Britain came under heavy attack from German air raids. Hitler responded by switching his attacks to the big dock areas on Britain's western coastline, concentrating on Plymouth, Cardiff, Swansea, Barry, Newport and Bristol. January 2, 1941 was one such night with Cardiff the prime target.

Charlie Gallagher patrolled with his team of ARP wardens, when the districts of Riverside, Grangetown and Canton took a terrible hammering. Landmines dropped by parachute devastated large areas killing more than 150 people. The rescue teams, along with the Fire Brigades worked themselves to a standstill day and night pulling bodies, some still alive from the carnage. The many hours spent on duty by the Home Guard relieved the pressure on regular soldiers desperately needed elsewhere during the nightly onslaughts.

Always a close family, the bond between the Gallaghers is strengthened by their common plight of facing up to war at home and now, five brothers away at sea. Bobby's death last October still leaves Nell grieving over his loss, now ever more fearful for her other sons at sea. Lydia too, has to come to terms with the absence of her husband Alec, who volunteered for the Welsh Guards regiment the day after war broke out on September 3rd, 1939. They were indeed a family at war.

Elsewhere, Dave Parker's outstanding qualities soon single him out from many of his colleagues in the Royal Marines. Considered ideal material for the Commandos, his transfer is followed by many months of tough, physical training on which he positively thrives. Every day, so it seems, he thinks "If I have to be somewhere, this place is as good as any."

Though the balance of the war starts to swing slowly in favour of the Allied Forces, Nell and her family still share tough times along with the rest of Britain's population. Those of the Gallagher family at home are still finding money in short supply. Nothing has changed there. To offset this, Nell takes a number of young women in as lodgers whose on-street activities leave little to her imagination.

To put them in the picture, she summons them to a noonday meeting in the kitchen. – family style. It's the prelude to Nell laying down one of her 'golden rules'. "Whatever you do on the outside is your business," she announces. "But whatever you do in this house is my business. I don't want – and won't have – any men in my house. It's not a bleeding brothel," she roared. "Anyone – and I mean anyone that breaks my rule will be out on the street on their fannies double quick. Got that!" It wasn't a question, it was a command.

They got the message and she had their undivided attention. "There's something else you'll need to bear in mind," she rasped. "Your rooms will be kept spotless and you'll do your own laundry and cooking. My girls are not a bunch of skivvies, so show them respect." She dismissed them with a nod of her head, reached for the gin and poured herself a measure as they trooped out of the kitchen. Any doubts that may have lingered about who ran the household had been well and truly squashed.

Chapter 9

George Davies had never shared the view that he and his police colleagues would have an easier time of it because many of the local villains had either volunteered for the Armed Services or had been called up at the outbreak of war. Far from it. In their absence and with the increasing importance of Cardiff Docks, hundreds of strangers, mostly foreigners, were now working in and around the docks area presenting the local police force with many different problems.

The huge Cold Store building was now bursting at the seams with frozen meat, a third of which was distributed throughout various parts of the UK. Literally hundreds of the smaller consignments were disappearing, the result of organised gangs. Davies' latest briefing to his officers was to nail the bastards who were not only thieving, but depriving the local population of their badly-needed meat rations. It soon became clear that anything that wasn't screwed down disappeared in a flash – an indication that new people and different outlets for fencing were being used.

Davies turned these problems over in his mind as he took a brief break, strolling from Police HQ in Cathays Park towards Kingsway. His thoughts were distracted by the group of people leaning on and looking over the two sides of the cast-iron bridge parapets that spanned the canal that ran under Kingsway. As he approached the bridge near the Evan Roberts family store, he could hear splashing and the cheers of spectators throwing coins into the water to be retrieved by a number of youngsters diving either off the bridge or from the canal bank. A silver sixpence or threepenny piece was rewarded by a dive from the bridge, whereas a copper coin earned a dive from the canal bank.

It provided great fun for spectators, among them a number of American servicemen stationed at a nearby airfield and was a welcome source of pocket-money for the kids. Later, fortified by a pint of Brains Dark beer and a Clarks meat pie, Davies made his way back to the office.

As he studied the latest reports on the Docks thefts, a knock on his door announced one of his detective constables who handed him two folders. "There's some info you've been waiting for sir, some of it from one or two of our local snouts." Davies nodded his acknowledgement and as the detective made to leave, he hesitated at the door. "Oh, one other thing sir. Frankie Gallagher was seen in town last night. Apparently he's on leave from his ship – it's a coaster I believe. It's only for a few days." Davies sat upright, his interest aroused. "Frankie Gallagher, eh? Even if it is only for a few days, tell our boys to keep an eye out for him and report anything of interest to me."

The young man nodded. "Right sir, I'll let them know," and left, closing the door behind him. Davies leaned forward, elbows on the desk, staring at the wall. "Just like always, that Frankie. He's a lucky bastard getting aboard a coaster. He's hardly likely to run into big trouble dodging up and down the coastal ports. Not like his brothers on the Atlantic run."

Those were prophetic thoughts indeed. Less than a month later Nell Gallagher was once more plunged into misery and grief when she received that most dreaded and unwelcome of communications from the Merchant Navy authorities. It informed her that her sons Jack and Nick, both of whom had only recently returned to active duty on the Atlantic Run following their previous sinking by a U-Boat, had been killed at sea along with most of the crew.

Their ship, hit by two torpedoes from yet another of the deadly wolf-pack of German U-boats hunting 24-hours a day in the North Atlantic, blew up and sank almost immediately, with the loss of many seamen's lives, along with vital munitions and weapons supplied by the United States of America to their British allies.

Nell had always feared that her sons at war might not come back but in her heart had prayed for their safe return. First it was young Bobby. Now, the shock news of Jack and Nick's deaths were a tragic double blow to her and the rest of the family resulting in weeks of heart-breaking distress and grief. Even George Davies was moved enough to send her a note of condolence – a gesture this time she didn't reject. Nell's personal pain at her triple loss never fully faded away over the remaining war years. Her grief remained unfulfilled by her inability to bury her sons and close a traumatic chapter of her life. Now, after six weary years of deprivation and the painful absence of her beloved sons, the eagerly-awaited declaration of peace followed.

The Gallagher family and many around them now have to focus on re-shaping their disrupted lives in a peacetime Britain suffering from the most dreadful shortages of many of the essentials just to stay alive. It was time for a fresh start.

Faced by the hardships they experience, it's not long before Nell and her family realise there are plenty of easy pickings to be had exploiting the shortages of the early post-war years. She calls a meeting, chaired by herself, with her husband Charlie taking occasional notes. The boys straggle in and take their places around the large kitchen table of many uses. The air is filled with the hanging haze of cigarette smoke, bottles are opened, glasses are at the ready.

Nell cleared her throat noisily. It was the signal for their undivided attention." There's a lot of money to be made out there on the streets and I want us to get our share of it. Agreed?"

Heads nodded. They agreed. So she continued. "I don't want anybody going off half-cock on some poxy little job of their own." She paused for another cough. "Everything has to come through me first so we can co-ordinate our efforts. That way, we can plan better and have less chance of being pulled in by the rozzers. Any objections? Or better still, any ideas?"

Chaz was first to respond. "What if I see a bike asking to be knocked-off which I can sell for a few bob. Do I have to check with you first, Mam?" Nell sighed and glared at Chaz. "That's just the thing we don't want, you daft gett! That's the sort of arse-brained idea that could bring the rozzers swarming around here making enquiries just when we don't need them!"

Chaz looked anywhere except his mother's eyes. "I suppose it was a bloody daft idea" he thought as he squirmed on his seat.

Frankie leaned back in his chair, before speaking. "I think Mam's idea is absolutely spot-on. We need to be organised and I'm all for that." He shifted his position on his chair, leaning forward for emphasis. "There's going to be a lot of shysters out there pulling jobs right off the top of their brainless heads, without even thinking where their next meal's coming from. They'll be leaving trails a mile wide that'll lead the rozzers right back to them. We don't want that!" he snapped.

Nell folded her plump arms, one arm comforting the other as she spoke. "We need to run our side of things like a business, for that's what it will be – a business." Her husband Charlie, who meanwhile had been sitting away from the table taking in all that was said, broke his silence. "There's one thing we just have to sort out or the bloody business will go belly up – and that's the question of farming out the stuff to some good and I mean really good fences."

As he had their attention, he explained further. "We all know somebody who's been a 'grass', so don't forget that these grasses will be dealing with the same fences as us. So selecting the right fence will be crucial." He'd said his piece so he returned to his notes, pencilling in several names that might fit the bill. Nell shot an approving glance at her husband. "Your father's right, so pass on any names that you think will be OK and he'll check them over."

An exchange of ideas followed, among them the setting up of a protection racket. The Gallaghers would pick the targets with hired hands supplying the muscle. While this proposal had the merit of making plenty of money, the idea of promoting fear among small shopkeepers and their families didn't go down at all well with Nell. She'd dealt with many of them on a regular basis for years. The suggestion was promptly dropped, once and for all, never to be raised again.

Meanwhile, Dave Parker's successful period of military service stood him in good stead when it came to resuming his civilian career as a policeman. It was no secret that he aspired to greater heights and in the year or so that followed, his track record was impressive enough for his senior officers to take note of the rising star in their midst.

⸻

Two years passed during which Nell and her sons streamlined their 'business' selecting the most promising targets, using surveillance to check out their strong and weak points and noting the comings and goings of staff. They scored several notable successes using only members of the family for security reasons.

The appearance of more 'organised crime' on George Davies' patch brought a strong police response, but it was the 'hit and miss' villains that were getting scooped up in Davies' net. It was galling for the police knowing that the Gallaghers must be involved somewhere down the line but were unable to make any charges stick. Frankie and two of his brothers made several court appearances but had to be released for lack of evidence. In fact, Frankie's good looks, flashy clothes and string of girl friends led to some form of celebrity status, with newspaper crime reporters referring to him as 'Frankie the Gent'.

Nell's finances meanwhile, had improved to such an extent that she bought her own house and the run-down place next door, providing the family with an ideal base from which to operate. The extra accommodation enabled some of the Gallagher boys to 'shack up' with their current girlfriends – a move greatly appreciated by those concerned as it was regarded as a sign of their increasing maturity for the degree of privacy it provided. As for Nell, it suited her purposes, for it meant she could keep a closer eye on the women with whom her sons were sleeping, enabling her to run a tighter ship.

Meanwhile, George Davies' success against the local villains enforced a period of inactivity for the Gallaghers. It was during such a lull that Frankie told his mother he had made the decision to move to London – and two of his brothers, Danny and Joe would be going with him. He made out his case for their moving whilst driving Nell to a local hospital to visit a friend of hers recovering from an operation. "It's something I've wanted to do for some while now. Mam. It was just a question of choosing the right moment." He glanced across briefly at his mother. From the look on Nell's face, this obviously wasn't the right moment! "You do understand don't you Mam? There are some really big opportunities in the 'Smoke' and I don't want to pass them up."

His announcement, though not entirely unexpected, still upset Nell at the thought of losing close contact with Frankie, Danny and Joe for goodness knows how long. She sighed deeply in resignation, while acknowledging their right to determine their own lives. "There's never a right moment for splitting up the family, Frankie. We've been so close, for so long. It'll be a terrible blow to me, your father and the rest." She slumped down in her seat as he sought to lighten the effect of his decision.

"We've been doing well for a couple of years now Mam and you're set up better than you've ever been from the money angle and the house." He pulled the car over into the hospital car parking area, stopped and switched the engine off. Nell turned to face him. "Don't get out yet. I need to know when you plan to leave. After all, it's going to seriously affect how we run things after you, Danny and Joe have gone."

He took her plump hand, smoothing it softly, in a show of affection. "You've always known we love you more than anything Mam and wouldn't do anything to hurt you." He leaned across and comforted her, taking a deep breath, knowing there was something else he had to tell her that wouldn't go down too well either. "It'll be about three weeks before I'm away because I need to take care of another job – one that doesn't involve the family." There – he had said it! He was determined to press on despite her look of surprise and concern.

"I've set up a job with Benny Driscoll and two of his mates for the week after next. When that's finished, I'll be away." As soon as he spoke, he knew he had touched an exposed nerve! Just look at her face!

Nell's expression of disbelief was soon replaced by anger as she gave vent to her feelings. "Since when the hell do you make decisions to go outside the family for business – and without consulting me!" She was really working up a head of steam now. "And who the fuck are these arsehole friends of Driscoll's? And anyway, that bastard's not to be trusted as far as I could kick this bleeding car," she fumed, sweeping into the hospital entrance like a battleship under full power. It proved to be an uncomfortable couple of hours for Frankie before he dropped her off at the house. Telling her about London had been tough, but the prospects that lay ahead more than compensated him for that. All he had to do now was prove it!

Back in the Cardiff Docks area, the duty sergeant walked slowly from the kitchen tucked away at the rear of the Bute Town police station, concentrating on not spilling a drop from the two cups of steaming hot tea he carried. He walked over to the main desk where a constable sat writing a report.

"Anything special going on at the moment Fred?" asked Sergeant Billy Rees, carefully placing both cups on the beer mats provided to prevent unsightly circles appearing on the carefully polished woodwork. He blew on the steaming contents of his cup long enough to cool it, enabling him to take several careful sips.

PC Fred Evans looked up from the log book, laid his pen down and sat back in the round-framed wooden chair, easing the tension of his neck muscles by massaging them with both hands. "Not much really Sarge – just a bit of bother with that crowd of young buggers from that youth club." He took a swig from his cup before continuing. "But Griff Matthews sorted them out, so that should keep them quiet for a while."

Sergeant Rees eased himself into the only comfortable chair in the office – nobody else dare use it when he was on duty. A wry smile creased his face as he absorbed what his young constable had said. Police Constable Griff Matthews was built like the proverbial brick lavatory and standing at six foot six in his socks, had his own way of having a quiet chat with the area's lively gangs of white and mixed-race wayward youths.

With the help of a colleague, he'd bundle four or five of them into the back of the station's Black Maria police vehicle – a large van normally equipped with bench seats on either side, used among other things for transporting prisoners. This van – Griff Matthews' van – occasionally served a different purpose. No seats, just a bare inner area without any means of support for its passengers who were obliged to crouch in a cramped position or lie on the bare metal floor.

Once loaded with its occupants and the rear doors securely locked, Matthews would drive the vehicle down the arrow-straight, mile-long, Bute Road at speed, only to jam on the brakes fiercely every hundred yards or so. He would then accelerate away once again at speed. The accelerating, braking procedure was repeated several times with the van's passengers shouting in alarm as they were hurled from side to side, crashing into each other or the metal walls of the vehicle.

This continued for five minutes or so, up and down the same road until Matthews was satisfied that his passengers fully understood his point of view – all achieved without a single finger being laid upon them. The tangled heap of youths, now sporting a bruise or two, brought a grim smile to Matthews' lips as he unlocked the rear doors of the van.

"Right you lot, now bugger off and keep your noses clean – that's unless you want another free ride in a police van." Matthews stood there, hands on hips as his passengers disembarked and made their way past him gingerly, proceeding until they were out of sight around the nearest corner.

"That bastard Matthews," snarled Joey Castrano, the oldest of the dishevelled gang as they took temporary refuge, now well out of Matthews' sight. "One day, I'll get that big-headed bastard and do him for good – you'll see!" The rest looked at their leader as he spat out the words. "Yeah, we'll all do him – one day Joey," chorused the bruised, scruffy band – their fragile confidence gradually returning with every extra yard they put between themselves and the object of their threats, who was now totally out of earshot.

"Yeah, one day," they all yelled in unison, their bravado now fully restored as they drifted homewards. Their swaggering body-language gave evidence of their claim to their territory They were back, so look out everybody! But as they continued their parade of territory ownership, Joey couldn't help taking a quick, nervous look over his shoulder – just in case, but there was nobody there. Yeah, he'd give that fat copper Matthews a real beating one day in front of all his gang. One day... Well. erm, someday – or other.

Chapter 10

It was warm, very warm, in the parked car. The driver shifted his cramped position for the umpteenth time since he had stopped and switched off the engine of the unmarked police car. His discomfort reminded him that his trousers and his sweat-soaked buttocks were firmly stuck to the seat.

DS Dave Parker glanced at his watch, shielding the ivory-coloured dial against the bright sunlight that slanted through the partly-opened side window. Ten past twelve. It was little more than thirty minutes since he had driven into the dusty, run-down back street, identical to dozens of others in Cardiff's dockland area.

He had coasted to a halt for no reason other than a highly-developed copper's instinct for sniffing out trouble. His sighting of smalltime local burglar Benny Driscoll's red and yellow Ford parked outside number 187 Maria Street was reason enough. The house was owned by a Maltese pimp named Delgado. As far as he was aware, Driscoll and Delgado weren't all that well acquainted.

By now perspiring freely, Parker considered moving over to the unoccupied passenger seat to gain the benefit of the shade on that side of the car. He dismissed the idea almost immediately. That kind of movement might attract unwelcome attention, especially from the seemingly unoccupied front rooms of the terraced houses whose net-curtained windows silently looked onto the litter-strewn street. Parker stared ahead, trying unsuccessfully to blink away the perspiration that insisted on finding its way into his eyes.

An under-fed, motley-coloured cat picked its way slowly across

Parker's line of vision, certain of its safety on its own territory. The policeman's vigil had been so unobtrusive, the cat appeared unaware of his presence – or his sticky discomfort.

Despite the dusty silence, broken only by the sounds of ships' sirens and distant dockyard traffic, Parker could sense unseen eyes watching him – watching. What, he pondered, was Driscoll doing there? He wound down the side window, grateful for even the slightest breath of warm air that drifted into the car from the street.

Parker's discomfort reminded him of his mistake in wearing a woollen suit to work that day. He liked to set an example for smartness to his colleagues. Especially the younger ones who had missed out on the war. It was a legacy from his time spent as an officer in the Royal Marine Commandos on active service.

He felt yet another trickle of sweat slowly running down into his collar but a sudden movement from the shaded doorway of the house he was watching instantly checked his wandering thoughts. A man emerged. It was Driscoll. He was followed by a second man. Both paused, briefly glancing left and right before stepping across the pavement to the car.

As Driscoll opened the car boot, the watching policeman's senses tingled as he recognised the second man. Well I'll be buggered, he thought. Frankie Gallagher! If that bastard's involved, there's definitely something going on.

Parker instinctively slouched lower in his seat without shifting his gaze from the activities of the two men. Frankie's head emerged briefly from the depths of the car boot. He again glanced briefly up and down the street before hauling out the tools of his trade. The oxy-acetylene welding torch was accompanied by a length of twin rubber hose and a welder's protective helmet. As Frankie returned to the house, Driscoll slammed the car boot door shut, a heavy metal cylinder balanced awkwardly on his shoulder. Delgado then appeared in the doorway, quickly checking out the street. Apparently satisfied, he too retreated inside, closing the door, leaving the dusty street to return to silence.

Parker picked up the car radio handset microphone and spoke. The response from the Docks police station was prompt. He spoke quietly but clearly into the mouthpiece. "I'm onto to something here at 187 Maria Street. There are at least two of our regular customers, possibly more involved inside, in possession of safe-breaking equipment. I'm going to need some uniforms, so move it, but don't bloody well charge in like the US cavalry. We don't want to scare them off."

Parker waited with growing impatience. He checked his watch for the umpteenth time since his call to the station. Where the hell were his colleagues, he fumed. Deciding to wait no longer, he opened the car door and slipped into the shady sanctity of the nearest doorway. Moving with an athletic tread despite his cramped vigil in the car, he reached the doorway of number 187 into which his quarry had disappeared.

He paused, then pressed an ear against the scarred, scruffy door panel. Unable to distinguish anything coherent from the mumble of voices, Parker took one step backwards thinking "here goes" and knocked the door firmly with four sharp raps.

The mumble of voices ceased, followed by more silence. He knocked the door even harder a second time. More silence. Then the sound of footsteps echoing on the passageway's stone-tiled floor. Parker braced himself as someone slipped the catch on the other side of the door.

At first, the door stuck, then slowly eased open several inches to reveal the pockmarked face of the pimp in the narrow gap. Delgado's eyes dilated in fear as recognition flared. "For fuck's sake it's Parker!" he yelled, head screwing backwards as he simultaneously struggled to close the ill-fitting door.

The powerfully-built policeman smashed a brawny shoulder against the weather-beaten door panels, splintering the top one in the process. A second charge and the barrier between the two men gave up the unequal struggle. Parker heaved the door inward, causing Delgado to stagger backwards, before stumbling in fright the length of the passageway.

The pimp plunged through the partly-opened door at the end of the hall, his hoarse yelling startling the room's four occupants into action. Hearing Parker shouting "there's more coppers at the front," they scattered. Two jumped through the open kitchen windows, the others bolted through the rear door before clearing the low garden walls like hurdlers as they sped to the safety of the back street lanes.

Parker charged into the kitchen, stumbling over the steel cylinder, then cracked his shin on the security safe that lay on the floor. His gasp of pain was quickly forgotten as he saw the safe. He took a quick look through the kitchen windows. There was no sign of any of the room's earlier occupants – or his colleagues!

"The bastards," he muttered between gritted teeth – a sentiment directed equally at the low-life that had escaped the scene and the non-appearance of his fellow officers. A sound behind him caused him to turn, too late to avoid the heavy blow aimed at his head by the attacker hiding behind the door.

Roaring in anger, Parker struck out blindly, catching Delgado with a heavy punch to the face. Blood spurted from Delgado's mashed nose. The pimp collapsed in a heap, his face distorted, his mouth gasping for air. Parker added to Delgado's misery by planting a heavy kick to his crutch and another to his stomach.

The pimp would have screamed in agony if he could have mustered the breath – his only response being a low, choking groan, his blood forming a small puddle on the quarry stone floor. Ignoring the throbbing from the blow to his own head, Parker looked down at his victim without pity before hauling him to his feet by his greasy shirt collar.

He thrust his face in front of Delgado's. "You'll pay for that wallop you little shit," he snarled, slamming the wretch in front of him against the wall with a bang and adding another blow to his stomach for good measure. "You'll have to do for now," he said grimly, "but I'm going to flush out the rest of the rats you call your mates and you're bloody well going to help even if I have to kick ten colours of crap out of you."

The commotion in the hallway heralded the belated arrival of his uniformed colleagues from the station. The grim-faced Sergeant looked apologetically at Parker. "Sorry we couldn't get here any earlier Dave, but we had problem with the car. It seems like the other villains have scarpered, is that right?"

Parker ignored his question and pushed the bloodied wretch he was gripping towards the Sergeant. "Look after that arsehole. I'll tell you later what the charge is." He poked a finger at one of the two constables. "You! Check the back and the lane. See if anything has been left behind that may be of help to us." He turned to the other. "Get on to the station and get a team down here to give the place a good going over." The Sergeant, sensing a bollocking coming his way from Parker for the delay in responding, tried to redress the balance. He pointed to the safe. "This could be the peter stolen from the trade union offices in Newport Road last week, As you had a good look at the villains, there shouldn't be any problems fitting them up for that job, should there, Dave?"

Parker wiped the sweat from his forehead with the back of his hand. "Yeah, you would think so wouldn't you, but this lot have one of the best briefs in town on their payroll, so it's certainly not cut and dried."

With that he turned on his heel and made for the hallway, calling out over his shoulder, "I'll see you back at the station at three o'clock. Do you think you can get there on time?"

Just before three o'clock, Dave Parker pushed open the door of the interview room at the police station. Sitting at a table immediately facing the door, Delgado looked up, his startled face still looking pale but bloodied from his encounter with Parker's fist. Dave Parker addressed the constable sitting some three yards from the table, his back against the wall.

"Has he said anything yet, anything at all?" he asked as he eased himself into the chair opposite Delgado. "Nothing yet, except to ask for a cup of tea," explained the constable. "He's been sitting there ever since the doctor left about twenty minutes ago."

"The pimp's nose certainly looks a mess – probably broken," thought Parker as he relaxed back into his chair. He looked at the dejected wretch in front of him. "I suppose you're going to tell me that you know nothing about the safe or the villains that brought it to your house, right?"

Delgado stared at his tormentor, his bleary eyes shifting repeatedly from Parker's face to the table top and back again. "That's right Mr Parker," he said finally. "I don't know anything about that safe or why they brought it – honest!" The lump of white cotton wool in Delgado's hand had turned crimson as he continued to mop his tender nose, grimacing with pain as he did so.

Parker continued to scribble a few notes on the pad in front of him before resuming. "You know we could turn you over for running prostitutes and a brothel, right, so don't mess me around Delgado. You could also go down for aiding and abetting in a burglary with known criminals."

Parker leaned right across the table into Delgado's face causing the pimp to sit back fearfully. "You can make my life a lot easier," Parker continued, "by telling me who was with you at the house besides Frankie Gallagher and Benny Driscoll." The detective paused. "And I can make your life a fucking misery if you don't!" Delgado's face glistened with perspiration, his eyes dilated with fear as rivulets of sweat ran down his unshaven cheeks.

He sniffed nervously before replying. "Even if you know about two of 'em Mr Parker, the others will know I grassed on them and their mates will be after me. My bloody life won't be worth living – it won't be worth a cockle!" He dropped his head into his hands, his shoulders shaking. Parker eyed him coldly. "Your life won't be worth living anyway if I've got anything to do with it." He pushed his chair back and stood up. "You've got ten minutes to cough up before I charge you, so make your mind up. Tell the constable when you're ready."

Parker returned to his office. Less than five minutes later his telephone rang. It was the constable. Delgado was ready to squeal and confirm the names of all four men. He also said he would give evidence against them when the case came to court. Parker replaced the receiver on the handset, a broad smile crossing his face. He had waited a long time for this moment – the chance to collar Frankie Gallagher and put him where he bloody-well belonged. Doing time in the nick.

It was a moment of intense satisfaction and yes, revenge for the pain Gallagher had put him through when Peggy died all those years ago. He left his office to continue his interrogation of Delgado. There was work to be done and he wasn't going to waste any time getting the ball rolling.

Delgado's co-operation and signed statement, though reluctantly given, was the spur needed by Parker. Following the subsequent briefing to the team of officers on the case, Parker instructed them to bring in the four alleged burglars named on the arrest warrants. As expected, Benny Driscoll, Frankie Gallagher, (Big) John Griffiths and Harry McAllister had all gone to ground. It was another three weeks before they were taken into police custody, Delgado's inside information proving to be priceless. Nell and half a dozen of her family attended the court sessions at Cardiff Crown Court to eventually hear the verdicts handed down by the judge.

Frankie and Benny Driscoll each received two years, McAllister and Griffiths going down for eighteen months as their accomplices. As for Delgado, his contribution in shopping his co-villains earned him twelve months and a fine for keeping and running a brothel. But his problems weren't over yet. Word had been conveyed to him that he faced a very tough time in gaol from the other inmates. If there's one thing they detest, it's a grass – and he was about to pay plenty for squealing.

Outside the courthouse, Nell made her way carefully down the dozen, wide stone steps, a willing daughter on either side supporting her. As she waited for her taxi, the inevitability of Frankie's guilt and gaol sentence still rankled. His return and that of two of his brothers relatively unharmed from their wartime service at sea, had been joyously welcomed with numerous parties to celebrate.

Now just two years later, she was going to lose her Frankie again for another few years and for that she blamed just one person, that self-righteous bastard Dave Parker. Frankie's return to his former ways after the war was deemed perfectly normal to Nell's way of thinking. It was his way of life – his career, so to speak. Her life too, if she had ever stopped to think about it.

But it almost seemed like fate the day Frankie told her outside the hospital that he was going to throw in his lot with Benny Driscoll for one last job before leaving to live in London. Now it would be a few years before Frankie would be able to live that dream.

Parker had again cast his shadow over the family. Nell's simmering anger welled up again. It's a pity somebody doesn't take him out of circulation, she thought gloomily as her girls helped her, huffing and puffing wheezily into the back seat of the taxi. But you never know, she mused. Stranger things have happened..."

Chapter 11

The slightly-built young woman approached the front door of the Gallagher home, pushed the fingers of one hand through the heavy brass letter box and felt for the piece of string attached to the inside of the door. She retrieved the key, opened the door, returned the key and let herself in.

Lydia made her way down the darkened passageway and entered the large kitchen that doubled as a lounge. Two of her younger sisters sitting at the large wooden table scrubbed white by years of elbow grease, rose to their feet smiling a welcome. "Hello Sis," they chorused, enveloping her with enthusiastic hugs.

Katie held onto Lydia's hands in greeting. "If you've popped in to see Mam, you've missed her. She's gone into town," she explained before returning to the mound of vegetables scattered on the table. Lydia understood their keenness to get on with the job only too well. Many times in the past she had felt the weight of Nell's heavy hand as punishment for taking too thick a peel off the potatoes. She noticed with a wry smile that today's peelings were as wafer thin as ever.

At that point the scullery door leading off the kitchen opened as her father Charlie entered, towelling his monk-like fringe of grey hair vigorously, still damp from its recent sluice under the cold water tap. "Hello Lydia, my love. Are the kids OK?" he enquired, giving her a quick peck on her cheek. "Take the weight off your feet, my love. I'll get you a cup of tea."

He took the teapot off the hob on the black metal fire grate and poured two cups, added milk to both, one spoonful of sugar to Lydia's cup and four to his own. "Can't stop now love. I'm off to town to meet your mother at the Cambrian for a gargle," He patted her affectionately on her face and left the room, carrying his cup with him.

Lydia settled down on one of the wooden chairs facing her sisters, sipping her tea. "How is Mam, anyway? She must still be finding it a bit quiet at the moment." she ventured, taking another sip of steaming tea.

Her younger sister answered without raising her head. "Mam's OK except for a cold. Doctor Cohen says she should go to bed for a day and stay there until she's rid of it, but you know Mam, you can't tell her anything." She looked up at Lydia. "Everybody else is out," she added, returning to her task.

Lydia nodded. She had wondered where everyone was, except that is, the quartet of brothers who were otherwise occupied. Gerry was still doing time in Cardiff gaol for breaking into a cigarette warehouse – and getting caught, while two of his younger brothers were improving their social skills in the Borstal corrective institution located at the near-by village of Dinas Powis. But the weekend after next promised to see the family in a real celebratory mood.

Frankie was due out of gaol in ten days time, having completed his sentence for his part in a safe robbery and his sisters had planned a big party to welcome him home. "That will liven the place up," grinned Kate gleefully as she cleared up some of the pile of peelings and put them in a bucket at her side. "Fancy another cup of tea, Lyd?"

Lydia hesitated. "No thanks, Kate. I've got to be going as Alec has a half day off from work and we're going to Pontypridd Market. Maybe we'll pick up a bargain there."

She rose to leave. "Sorry to have missed Mam. I hope she feels better soon. Give her my love, will you?" She moved around to the other side of the table, gave her sisters a brief hug and a kiss each. With that, she left.

Lydia settled back on the hard seat of the tram, reflecting on some of her earlier life spent in that large, grey house she had just left. She and her husband Alec had made the right choice when deciding to move out of her mother's house after their marriage. They had found and rented their own small house across the other side of the city in the decent area of Roath. The rent was affordable and she had made it into a comfortable home for her, Alec and their two children.

The neighbours were friendly enough and she didn't have to carry the burden of the family reputation either. At least, not for the time being. No, she didn't have any regrets and had been only too happy to pass on the housekeeping tasks in that big place to her younger siblings.

Lydia stared absently at people as they got off the tram and others got on as it rumbled its way across the city. Yes, money was tight for her and Alec so they had to keep a watchful eye on how they spent it, but they enjoyed what they had she thought, as the tram lurched and squealed its way towards the familiar landmarks that meant home.

Charlie meanwhile, had chosen to walk into town for his regular lunchtime drink. He breathed in deeply, savouring the breezy air sweeping up the River Taff from the sea as he crossed the cast-iron Taff bridge near the famous Cardiff Arms Park rugby stadium. His walk took him past the city's main railway station, across St Mary Street and straight in to one of his favourite local pubs, the Cambrian.

There were several pubs nearer his home than the Cambrian, but he preferred drinking there as several of his closer fellow imbibers frequented the place. It also stood on the fringe of the city centre, providing the perfect jumping – off point for a pint in several other pubs nearer the city centre, especially the Old Arcade which also served one of the best pints in town.

Few people really knew much about Charlie. His earlier life as a young man in Edinburgh, the son of respectable parents with their own business for whom he kept the books, came to an abrupt end when he was discovered embezzling the company's cash. His attempt at creative bookkeeping, from which he was the sole beneficiary, led to his father kicking him out of the family home.

Undeterred, he drifted around picking up casual work that kept him in cigarettes and booze. Drawn to the south, he utilised his accountancy skills to assist a number of shopkeepers on a part-time basis with their books. Eventually, he arrived in Wales via Liverpool put his roots down in Cardiff and it was here that he met Nell – the woman he was to marry.

Charlie walked into the pub with his usual rolling gait. Was it a legacy of his years at sea? It was a habit frequently misconstrued as a swagger-factor that really got up some people's noses from time to time, especially if they'd previously had a few drinks.

He made his way down the floor of the lengthy bar, its newly-sprinkled layer of sawdust barely disturbed at this early lunch-hour by the scuffling of its patrons' boots and shoes. There was something else about Charlie that tended to upset the other customers-and he didn't disappoint them on this occasion either.

As he reached his favourite corner with its round wooden table and small bench seat, he turned and addressed the other customers, several of whom were total strangers to him. "I'll fight any man in the house," he bellowed, tossing his well-thumbed, greasy cap onto the floor with a flourish.

He repeated his challenge, more stridently as they cast their eyes over the old soak making all the noise. "Any takers, then? No? I thought so you gutless lot," he muttered as he wheezily retrieved his cap, brushed off the sprinkling of sawdust, slapped it across his fleshy thigh and replaced it at a jaunty angle on his bald, shiny pate. That Charlie. He really could be and often was, a real pain in the arse!

The other regulars, too busy drowning their own sorrows and knowing Charlie of old, ignored the old bastard. His challenge however had not gone entirely unnoticed by three strangers standing at the bar, all of whom had no previous knowledge of Charlie's usual boastful babblings.

He continued to drink alone, wondering why Nell hadn't turned up. She said she'd be there, hadn't she, the cow! When "time" was called, to herald the afternoon break, he was well and truly oiled.

By dint of relentless practise, he negotiated an unsteady route out of the pub, made it to the tram stop and eventually found his way home. His dutiful daughters had prepared lunch for him but he opted instead for the comfort of a large couch, sleepily unaware that his belligerence had once again sown the seeds of reprisal. How long it would take to surface, only time would tell.

Chapter 12

Eddie Gallagher waited impatiently outside the popular Kardomah Coffee Shop in Queen Street, glancing every few minutes at the large clock above the jewellers shop opposite. His eyes constantly scanned the ebb and flow of people going about their business in one of the city's busiest shopping areas as yet another tram clanged its way past Eddie's vantage point before squealing to a metal – grinding halt some thirty yards distant.

A slight shiver ran through his body as he picked out the smartly dressed pretty brunette that appeared among the several passengers leaving the tram. As she neared the Kardomah, her eyes widened in recognition as Eddie cut down the distance between them, his arms spread in welcome.

"Hiya Julia. It's great to see you. I thought you might have changed your mind," exclaimed Eddie, the relief evident in his tone. Julia briefly embraced him by way of response and took his arm. "Shall we go on up," indicating the stairs to the upper lounge of the coffee shop. Having settled themselves in a booth as far away from the other customers as space allowed, their coffees, reputed to be the best in town, soon arrived.

Eddie couldn't take his eyes off the elegant young woman seated opposite. Not only was she absolutely gorgeous but she dressed and spoke like a well-groomed, privately-educated nineteen year-old daughter of one of the city's top barristers – which is precisely what she was.

Her dazzling smile revealed white, perfectly even teeth as she leaned forward to speak. "Why did you think I might have changed my mind, Eddie? Or was it you that may have had second thoughts after last night?" The memory flashed through his mind.

Yeah, last night. He couldn't believe his luck to have met this gorgeous girl and fixed up this morning's date at their first ever meeting at the Regal dance hall.

He hesitated before replying, trying to choose the right words without scaring her off. "Well, you're not exactly the sort of girl that fancies a bloke like me, coming from the other side of Cardiff like I do. So when we danced and then you agreed to see me again this morning, I was surprised – very surprised. I was sure you wouldn't bother to turn up," his words tapering off, his uncertainty clear to see.

Julia's captivating laugh served to further enhance her attractiveness. "I didn't agree to see you this morning just because I took a passing fancy to a bit of rough. I did so because you are very good-looking, you have a nice sense of humour and I find you good company too. What more could a girl ask," she ended, her eyes feigning innocence.

"Money?" he suggested after a short pause, causing them to giggle like a couple of school-kids. They sipped their coffee in synchronisation, like they had been doing it all their lives, their eyes locked together in mutual appreciation.

Eddie replaced his cup before speaking. "How do you fancy coming with me to a family party on Saturday? My brother Frankie has been away from home for a few years and this is his homecoming do. I'm sure you'll like it and my mam will just love meeting you – she really will!" He was in full flow now, striking while the iron was hot. "There'll be loads of food and plenty of booze – erm, I mean drink," he ended lamely.

Julia's long pause convinced him he'd overstepped the mark. "Oh Christ, that's done it," he inwardly winced. But she flashed that wonderful smile again, nodding her agreement enthusiastically. "I would love to come Eddie. It will give me a chance to say 'hello' to your family and friends. I'm sure they are very interesting."

She took his hands in hers, the contact sending shivers of pleasure coursing through his body.

"They're interesting, all right" said a silent voice in his head, as they set about letting their newly-discovered attraction for each other take its natural course.

The silent voice continued speaking. "I just can't wait to show you off to my brothers. They'll be as sick as pigs!"

———◦◦◦———

The local church hall was abuzz with noise and activity as the Gallagher girls busied themselves with the final tasks of laying out the food, paper napkins, party hats and cutlery on the several large trestle tables erected at one end of the hall. The other end was for dancing and there was plenty of that on the agenda.

Nell, as usual was directing operations from her command post. She sat on a sturdy, circular wooden chair next to the table on which several bottles of Gordon's Gin and a case of Guinness took pride of place. Everyone knew that was Nell's private stock, so keep your hands off! Her husband Charlie, equally well-schooled in the ways of Gallagher parties, had placed his equally sturdy chair next to the six 72-pint barrels of real ale and dark beers supplied by the S.A.Brains local brewery. There were also a number of bottles of whisky and brandy within arms length – just in case.

The pianist hired for the occasion turned up and after slaking his initial thirst, went through a few of the old favourites in his repertoire just to warm things up. 'Knees up Mother Brown', 'Danny Boy', 'Nellie Dean' and the 'Hokey Kokey' figured prominently, He was obviously saving his best numbers for the dancing to come.

The clamour increased as guests arrived, their children earning a wallop over the head for running around wildly and sliding across the polished wooden floor to the good humoured annoyance of their elders.

Eddie and Julia's arrival soon set the tongues wagging among a group of other female guests, lined up like latter-day Robespierre's hags at a Paris execution.

To her credit, Julia looked absolutely stunning in her pale blue tailored suit, white blouse and white shoes and was immediately surrounded by Eddie's sisters throwing compliments at her like confetti.

While this was going on, Eddie took the opportunity to check out his brothers' reactions and was cock-a-hoop at their unbridled envy. He could tell they were impressed. They even put their pint glasses down for a moment to introduce themselves.

It was left to Nell to offer Julia a Gallagher welcome, smothering her inside her oversized bosom while running through a list of fulsome adjectives describing the newcomer's beauty and refinement, causing Eddie's neck and face to redden with acute embarrassment.

Suddenly, everyone's attention was drawn to the main door, when, to a rendering of 'There's no place like home' from the maestro on piano, Frankie made his entrance, accompanied by his brother Chaz who had met him at the gates of Cardiff Prison, earlier in the day.

Now freshly bathed, suited and booted and wearing his newly-purchased flash suit and open-necked white shirt, Frankie looked just what he was – the guest of honour at his homecoming party.

The piano player, determined to earn his money, switched the tune to 'For he's a jolly good fellow' as Frankie, acknowledging the handshakes, kisses and embraces, pushed his way through the throng until he finally reached Nell's 'throne'.

He flung his arms around her and with a surprising show of strength, lifted her to her feet. They hugged and squeezed each other repeatedly as Nell planted a series of kisses on her favourite son's face, before regaining her seat, panting from the exertion of her welcome.

As for Eddie, he couldn't wait to introduce Julia to Frankie who was bowled over by her well-spoken, well-groomed appearance. But she was intrigued by his smiling comment that he had run across her father once or twice in the past while he was practising his profession in court!

It was the signal for the tempo of the party to increase by several notches. The music and chatter increased in direct proportion to the booze consumed while the buffet disappeared with astonishing speed.

Suddenly, with the merrymaking in full swing, the proceedings were interrupted by a series of thunderous knocks on the church hall doors, followed by someone seemingly trying to shake the doors off their hinges.

Frankie excused himself from his shouted conversation with his father, threaded his way through the throng on the dance floor and pulled open one of the double doors. He certainly didn't like who and what he saw.

He glowered at the nearest man standing in the door entrance. "What the fuck are you trying to do Bailey? Rip the fucking doors off their hinges?" Stan Bailey, fronting a group of six, maybe seven other local ruffians, stood his ground.

"Welcome home, Frankie. Nice to see you out of the nick," he sneered, attempting to push past the guest of honour.

"Hey! Hold it there Bailey." Frankie emphasised his instruction by pushing his hand firmly against the unwanted visitor's chest, preventing any further progress. "This is a private party and you and your lot are not invited. So fuck off. Now!"

He again emphasised his words with a shove of his hand against the big guy's chest and stepped forward to further bar their way.

The exchanges at the door were quickly relayed to Nell's command post. She beckoned to Danny and Chaz. "It looks like we've got trouble at the door. Frankie's over there but he's going to need help. Get the rest of the boys and get over there now!"

She barely had time to finish her warning when Frankie was bundled through the doorway by sheer weight of numbers as the unwelcome visitors forced their way into the hall.

The piano player, a veteran of many local family festive occasions, stopped playing and immediately took cover behind the piano. Stan Bailey, followed by his companions, swaggered over to the food and drink-laden tables, scooping up handfuls of sandwiches and grabbing whole bottles of spirits. It was at this point all hell broke loose.

Eddie caught Julia by the arm, leading her to a corner behind Nell's chair. "I want you to stay here with Mam and don't move. I'll be back in a few minutes." With that, he ushered the startled Julia into the safety of the corner and dashed over to join his brothers, who by now were furiously trading punches with Bailey's gang. As flailing punches found their targets, bodies hurtled onto carefully-prepared trestle tables scattering their contents onto a floor already awash with spilled drinks and squashed sandwiches.

The women, not to be outdone by their menfolk, added a kick or a wallop with a bottle at the unwelcome raiders, tearing at their shirts with talon-like nails, reducing them to shreds.

Nell, meanwhile, having restrained Charlie from bellowing out his usual pub challenge and making him sit down with a bottle of whisky for company, was screaming out a torrent of abuse at Bailey's increasingly battered men, overlaid with hoarse encouragement to her boys. She also found time to calm any fears that Julia was experiencing at the mayhem that had erupted in such strange surroundings.

It was clear that the tide of battle had clearly turned in favour of the Gallaghers as shouts of "let's get the fuck out of here" came from a crumpled heap on the floor, struggling to get to his feet. Bailey and his followers decided they'd had enough and retreated in confusion to the exit, helped on their way by the scruff of their necks and a few well-placed kicks up the arse.

A big cheer rang out as the party-goers checked that their assailants really had departed. There was hand-shaking and pats on the back all round as Frankie slammed and re-locked the doors before turning to face his family and guests.

He beamed a huge smile and called out, "Right then everybody, lets clear up this mess as best as we can – and get on with the party!"

Making his way over to the piano, Frankie leaned over the instrument and smiled at the cowering pianist. "You can come out now maestro. It's all over, so let's have some lively music and get this party going again!"

There wasn't one single shirt worn by a party defender that had escaped being torn – some to absolute shreds – or bloodied. Pieces of the cotton material were used to stem blood flowing from battered noses and an interesting variety of cuts. Some ugly bruises enhanced the colourful scene.

It was a scenario made-to-measure for Nell. She took immediate charge, despatching a couple of her daughters back to the house to rustle up antiseptic, bandages and sticking plasters.

No serious damage had been caused such as broken bones, so proper medical attention could wait. As for her boys, they ignored whatever damage they had sustained, preferring to wear their cuts and bruises as badges of honour.

Eddie went to where his mother had returned to her seat. Nell was making soothing noises and stroking Julia's hands. "She'll be alright in a minute, Eddie," she croaked. "It's just that she hadn't seen anything like that before and it upset her a bit." Julia retrieved her hands from Nell's gentle touch and hugged Eddie in sheer relief.

"I'm alright Eddie," she whispered in response to his searching look. "It's just that for a moment, I thought I had been caught up in a Wild West cowboy film," she murmured, snuggling in even closer.

Eddie blew out a long sigh of relief. "I'm sorry about that Julia." He gave her another squeeze. "It doesn't happen at all our parties, but I told you that it would be interesting meeting my family, didn't I?"

And so ended another happy weekend in the social life of the Gallagher family.

"I still think they were very lucky! You just wait till we get them at Twickenham next year and then you'll see how rugby should be played!" Charlie's beer-induced assessment of the England rugby team's performance barely made the short distance from his lips to Alec's straining ears in what passed for conversation amid the bedlam inside the jam-packed pub.

Swollen to its seams with Welsh and English supporters, the noise bombarded the senses as they argued the respective faults and merits of that afternoon's game at Cardiff Arms Park, won 9–6 by England. It was a difficult pill to swallow for the Welsh who cherished high hopes of a win in the first international match staged between the two old adversaries since the end of the war two years earlier.

Alec mmmm'd his agreement rather than replying, choosing to down his pint before rejoining the scrum at the bar for two refills. He returned, thrusting the brimming glass into Charlie's ready hand – and his mouth nearer Charlie's ear. "Yeah, you're right," he concurred. "We were unlucky today, seeing how we were the best team on the pitch." Alec's comments revealed him as a fully-paid up member of that band of Welsh rugby followers who need to see their team really hammered before conceding defeat.

He took a generous pull of his pint, wiping the excess froth from his mouth with the back of his hand. "Me and some of the blokes at work have already been saving up for next year's game at Twickenham. I love it up there in the 'Smoke'. We have a bloody great time! The only trouble is, I've spent most of it on beer this afternoon," at which they both burst into fits of raucous laughter.

A couple of pints later, Alec prepared to finish what remained of his beer, before beckoning Charlie closer. "There's something important I want to speak about to Frankie." He glanced around briefly. "I don't want to say anything here in the pub, in case some nosey bastard is twigging." Charlie's bleary eyes lit up in expectation as Alec leaned closer. "Ask him to meet me here on Monday, say about 'erm, one o'clock." He gripped his companion's arm. "You won't forget now, will you – it's very important."

Charlie waved his caution away. "Don't worry about it, our kid. I won't forget." He fumbled in his pocket, feeling for some stray coins, but Alec stayed his hand. "Not for me Charlie – I have to be off or Lydia will kick up hell if I'm late and my meal is ruined." He patted the swaying figure in front of him on the shoulder. "You understand don't you. After all she's your daughter and she can be a real Gallagher when she wants to be."

Charlie nodded knowingly, having been responsible for plenty of ruined meals in his time.

Alec pushed his way through the crowded bar to the door only to find just as many drinkers milling about good-naturedly on the crowded pavement. The trams were also crowded, but he eased his big frame past several strap-hangers to find standing space further down the tram. As it rattled its way through streets crowded with supporters and their flashes of red and white colours, he mulled over his urgent need to speak to Frankie.

There was no point in deluding himself. Despite his own respectable record as a civilian with a good job and as a former Welsh Guardsman with a fine record and several wartime medals won on the battlefields of Europe to his credit, he was about to reveal the details of a golden opportunity to his in-laws, the Gallaghers. An opportunity to rob a bank under conditions that were never likely to occur again. It had to take place soon, or the chance would disappear, in all probability forever. The thought filled him with apprehension and suppressed excitement in equal measures.

Alec again turned the idea over in his mind. He wouldn't be taking part in the actual robbery although he would be providing the information and the means that would make it possible.

If Frankie and his brothers pulled this one off, they would move up into a much bigger league. For Alec though, the time had arrived for him to bite the bullet.

Chapter 13

The muffled voices and occasional laughter of the pub's occupants could be heard from twenty paces away, even above the noise of passing traffic and electric trams as they rumbled by in the busy city centre street.

Frankie paused in the saloon bar entrance, peering through the thick, ornately decorated plate glass door with its heavy oak frame and polished brass handle. He inspected those of the pub's lunchtime customers in view. It was several seconds before he spotted his brother-in-law sitting alone, glass in hand, drinking deeply from a pint of his favourite draught bitter.

Frankie thrust open the heavy door, the volume of sound increasing instantly as conversations mingled with the chink of glasses. Most of the bar's customers noted his entry without even a suspicion of a glance in his direction or even the lifting of an eyebrow. But they saw him alright.

There wasn't much this poxy lot missed, thought Frankie. The tobacco smoke from sickly, sweet smelling briar pipes mingled with countless brands of cheap cigarettes, created a hazy, ever-changing blue-grey cloud that came courtesy of the customers.

Alec downed the remnants of his pint at his brother-in-law's entrance then rose to his feet as Frankie approached the table. They shook hands. "Same as usual Frankie?" he asked, more in confirmation than a question as his companion sat down.

Alec duly returned, carrying another pint and a large brandy. His rough hands betrayed evidence of many years of manual labour.

His trade as a plasterer explained his heavily muscled arms, barrel chest and broad shoulders. He had a physique that had served him well as an infantryman in the wartime Welsh Guards. These days it was put to use working for the council's maintenance section.

He had lost most of his dark curly hair. What remained was slicked back with hairdressing oil. A craggy face reflected his rugby-playing days.

Frankie, ignored the stuffy atmosphere, concentrating instead on the contents of his glass. He savoured the fiery liquid, rolling the brandy around his tongue before speaking.

"Right then Acker, what have you got for me. My father said he thought it could be big."

He settled back on the hard wooden bench, refusing his brother-in-law's offer of a cigarette. Although having already checked that no one was within hearing distance, Alec still leaned closer. "We're working on a flooring repair job in Queen Street. It's in the Council Rates office. It just so happens that the room is sitting right on top of Lloyds Bank."

He took a long pull at his pint, replacing his glass carefully on a cardboard beer mat, before glancing at his brother-in-law trying to gauge the effect of his news.

Frankie stared at his companion, digesting what he'd heard.

"Go on Acker, let's have the rest."

Alec leaned forward again. "I expect you'll be wanting another brandy. I'll have a pint while you're at the bar."

Alec's insistence on a refill at this point irritated Frankie but he concealed his feelings as he rose to comply.

Alec took the opportunity to relieve himself in the gents, toilet, slumping heavily into his seat upon his return.

Frankie sat there, waiting, his barely-concealed impatience and curiosity evident in equal measures.

Alec continued. "Remember last week's heavy storms? Well they caused some water seepage from the damaged roofing in the Rates Office, so we were called in to repair the damage." His eyes were rarely still as he continually checked out the ebb and flow of the bar's occupants. "We had to take up a wooden block floor to get at the mess underneath. Then guess what happened?"

He treated the quizzical raising of Frankie's eyebrows as an invitation to carry on. "One of our blokes got a bit heavy-handed and put his pickaxe right through the floor so that you could see into the room below. Do you know what room it was? It was the bank's safe deposit vault, that's all! Would you believe it? The bank people went bleeding potty. It nearly caused a fucking riot!"

It was Frankie's turn to lean forward. "When was this? What are the bank security people doing about it – the hole I mean? How long is it going to take to repair the hole?"

The questions tumbled from his lips, his manner now hoarsely urgent, his laid-back approach noticeably less evident.

Alec sat back, satisfied at the effect of his news on his brother-in-law. "It happened last Friday morning – the day before the rugby international. They are leaving us to fix the damage to the floor and the vault ceiling below. It'll take about two or three or days to fix and we are going to start on this Friday."

He took another pull on his pint. "You haven't heard the best yet Frankie," he said with a grin. "When we went through to the vault, none of the alarms went off. They only operate if anyone goes in through the vault's main door. Can you believe that? You'll be able to go in through the ceiling and out again this weekend before we finish the job. I tell you, it'll be a fucking cinch."

The two men studied each other's faces in silence, before breaking into a fit of suppressed laughter, their shoulders shaking. Sideways glances in their direction from the other drinkers were an instant reminder sufficient to restore their earlier desire for relative anonymity. Nobody missed a trick in this pub.

Alec took another pull at his pint then continued, the level of his voice returned now to one of caution. "I can get you into the Rates Office. After that, you can get to the hole above the vault and then you're in!"

"You can do the safes, deposit boxes or the bloody lot if you think you can handle the weight of the money."

"All you need to do then, is get out of the bank the same way you got in." Alec sat back as Frankie savoured the startling prospects opened up by his revelation, absent-mindedly rubbing the scarred tissue above his right eyebrow – the legacy of a success-ful amateur boxing career.

Frankie puffed out his cheeks in admiration at Alec's scheme. "It's a once in a lifetime chance Acker – maybe even better than that but we still have to crack the Rates Office before we can get at the vault. That's a big problem because even the small-time pick-pockets in town know that the Council's Rates offices are protected by some sort of alarm system or other."

His companion nodded his assent. "You're dead right Frankie. Of course there's the usual alarm systems which trip when you go in either through the front or back of the Rates Offices. The only dif-ference is," and he paused for maximum effect, "I've got a duplicate set of keys to the Rates office rear doors which will make cracking the bank a real cinch. But I've saved the best bit 'til the last."

He stopped to take another mouthful of beer – the pause caus-ing Frankie to grip his arm. "For Christ's sake Acker, what are you holding back?" Alec's face tried not to betray his excitement as he calmly announced, "I've also got a set of copy keys for the safes inside the vault. It's going to cost you £500 for these keys but it's going to be worth every bloody penny!"

Frankie stared in sheer disbelief at the prospects opened up by his brother-in-law's information, trying to grasp the full signifi-cance of the rewards on offer. "Jesus Christ Acker, this has to be the pot at the end of the rainbow!"

His companion nodded in silent agreement. "Don't forget Frankie that it's going to cost you £500 for the keys, but it'll cost you a bloody sight more for my contribution. The £500 is for the bloke on the inside of the bank who took the impressions but the shit is really going to hit the fan in there once they discover what's hap-pened." Alec paused for a swig, then continued. "As for me, don't forget you'll owe me a very big drink – a real slice of whatever you get from the bank."

His second brandy still untouched, Frankie scanned the bar's occupants in confirmation that they were still unaware of the details of their conversation. "Do you or your contacts have any idea how much money is in there at the moment?"

Alec slowly finished his pint, replacing the empty glass on the beer mat just as precisely as before. "I can't be certain but they reckon it could be as much as two hundred thousand quid. Can you imagine that? It's one hell of a lot of cash! A bloody fortune!" Alec again lowered his voice. "One of my nephews works for the bank in one of its district branches in Rumney. Every week he has to deliver a big leather bag of used banknotes to the main branch in Queen Street – the one we're looking to knock over."

"He says the bag is secured to his body by a long chain that goes from the handcuff on his wrist, up the sleeve of his jacket, down to his waist where it's fitted like a belt and then locked. If you wanted to steal the bag, you'd have to chop the poor bastard in half!"

His companion shook his head, the prospects of untold riches seemingly evaporating before his eyes. "There's not going to be much money in one bleeding bag Acker, no matter how big it is, right?"

But the big fellow hadn't finished yet. "Yeah, you're right. I thought the same when he mentioned the bag, but then he explained that there are forty or fifty couriers doing exactly the same thing from their district banks on the same day every week. They use different routes as often as they can to put any robbing bastards like your lot off the scent."

Frankie's white, even, teeth flashed in a grin as he savoured Acker's description of his family. "Yeah, robbing bastards – I like that."

Alec was well into his stride now. "I haven't got a clue how much is going to be in the vault, but my nephew said that all the takings from a load of pubs, petrol stations and the local political clubs are deposited there over the weekend-for safety's sake – and that's a bleeding good 'un," chuckled Alec.

"What with the hole and this weekend coming up it couldn't be better timed. There's got to be an absolute fortune in there." With that, he sat back enjoying the effect of his words on Frankie.

A grin spread slowly over Frankie's face. "You know Acker, this could be the really big one we've been looking for. If we can pull this one off – and you'd have to have shit for brains not to – then you're definitely in for a big score and no mistake."

He stared ahead, his brow furrowed as he calculated their chances of pulling off the job. "We still need to work out the best way to get clear of the bank and then out of the city. If anything – even the slightest thing – goes wrong, we could be right in the cacky and doing mailbags for the next thirty five years." He paused as he considered their getaway options.

"There's only three main routes in and out of Cardiff and if anybody knows that, it's the bleeding rozzers. They can bottle up the city as tight as a duck's arse if we have to make a run for it."

Frankie's face momentarily betrayed his nagging doubts despite the golden opportunity that had been dropped in his lap.

"It helps that we'd be in and out by the early morning and that's got to be in our favour," he said somewhat thoughtfully.

The big fellow opposite leaned forward and patted Frankie's hand. "Stop worrying – I've cracked that as well."

He leaned closer. "The last place the rozzers will think of sealing off is the canal feeder that runs right past the back of the bank." Alec was clearly enjoying every moment as he unfolded his ideas.

It was evident to Frankie as he listened attentively that his companion possessed a much sharper mind than he'd thought.

But from Alec's point of view, his army training had provided plenty of opportunities for planning attacks on targets – and the bank was just another target – albeit a rather special one!

Alec continued. "The canal feeder flows past the back of the bank, then disappears under Queen Street, OK? Then it swings right and flows into the new tunnel under Churchill Way. From there, it goes right through to the docks. You'd be there in say, forty minutes at the most using a small boat to carry you, the team, all the gear and the money downstream."

He sat back. "Don't you remember Frankie? We were always swimming in the canal feeder when we were kids and some of us even made it to the docks for a dare. With a boat, it would be plain sailing," said Alec, amused at his unexpected pun.

Frankie visibly relaxed, the obstacles lessening as the overall picture became clearer, his mind racing as he envisaged the tasks ahead.

"We'll have to use a folding boat – say of canvas, but big enough to carry four of us and our gear, yet small enough to get in the back of a van. I can fix that with a pal of mine down the Bay, but he'll have to be paid off to keep his mouth shut."

He hesitated as he again considered their options.

"We'd have to launch the boat quite a way upstream, away from the council offices, probably near Blackweir playing fields."

Alec nodded his agreement. So far so good.

Frankie continued. "That way, if anyone spotted us in the boat on the canal we'd still have time to call it off, but I hope to fuck it doesn't come to that." Still keeping his voice low enough not to be heard by their fellow drinkers, Alec now gave vent to his doubts.

"You're still running a bloody big risk travelling the best part of a mile downstream before you get to the council offices aren't you?" Frankie looked at him, a smile slowly creasing his face. "Acker, if the money's big enough, it'll be worth the risk. Don't worry we'll be careful – we'll make damn sure we are."

With that, Frankie drank his brandy and stood up. "We're going to have to move fast before you and your blokes get going on that hole. I'll get Mam and some of the family together and meet you at our house tonight at around, say, eight o'clock, OK Alec?"

The big fellow nodded. "Yeah, that's alright."

Frankie by now was so enthused with Alec's scheme, he could barely contain himself. "We'll need to go over every last detail to make sure everyone knows exactly what they have to do. We'll also need a folding ladder, long enough to reach down into the bank vault with something to spare."

"Oh, and yeah, I'll need those keys of yours, or copies at least. Without them we'd be absolutely knackered."

Alec looked at his empty glass, but it was clear Frankie was ready to leave. "I'll bring a few flagons of beer along – but remember Frankie, you'll have to supply your own brandy – and the rest of the booze."

The faint light from the lamp on Alec's old bicycle barely provided enough illumination in the fading evening gloom to see where he was going but it was only switched on to prevent being stopped by some over-zealous policeman on his beat.

The wheels complained constantly with a high-pitched squeal from lack of oil as he pedalled slowly to his rendezvous with his in-laws. The squeals were accompanied by an occasional 'clinking' from the three large flagons of beer jammed into his former army rucksack strapped to the bike's crossbar. Now the khaki-coloured bag did duty as a 'bag of all trades' in its civilian disguise. He free-wheeled the last twenty yards or so arriving to see young Chaz peering out of the front room window.

"He's here," he called out to the rest as he hastened down the hallway to open the front door. Alec motioned with the heavy bag. "Grab this will you," handing him the bag. He wheeled his bike into the hallway, leaning it against the anaglypta paper-covered wall, trimmed three feet above the floor with a two inch wide border, both painted in the fashion colour of the day – a dark brown gloss paint. 'What a bloody depressing sight,' thought Alec as Chaz urged him on. "Go on through Acker. We've been waiting for you."

Alec pushed open the door, careful not to trip as he stepped down the single stone step onto the quarry-tiled floor of the all-purpose room that served as the family kitchen come lounge come living room.

The haze of smoke that hung in the still air reminded him of a gambling joint, which come to think of it, was just what it was at times. The tiles gleamed from hours of elbow grease, not Nell's, but from the elbows of her many daughters.

The large, oblong-shaped room featured a vast, black cast-iron fireplace topped with a thick wooden mantelpiece upon which were displayed a gallery of family photographs, occupying pride of place. There must have been twenty of them.

The room was lit by a very bright, single bulb, screwed into a green-painted metal lampshade hanging from the centre of the ceiling.

Nell sat at one end of the table holding court, while awaiting Alec's arrival. The number and variety of bottles and glasses on the table gave evidence of the way they had passed the time.

Being far too plump to rise without difficulty from her high-backed wooden chair with its circular armrests and comfortable cushions, Nell remained seated, beaming a cheerful welcome, two gold teeth in an otherwise full mouthful of teeth glinting through the smoke.

Alec greeted her first, not just out of courtesy but also of respect. "Hello my lovely. Come here Acker and give us a kiss," she wheezed, her powerful, plump arms extended. Alec knew what was coming next as he surrendered to her all-embracing hug. He was trapped between her soft, ample breasts in a hug that lasted fully a minute. Then followed the barrage of wet kisses on both cheeks. Nell never did things by half, especially when it came to greetings. She was, after all, part gypsy and he was, after all, part of the family. Nell finally released him. "How's my beloved Lydia and my two gorgeous grandchildren, then?"

Alec eased himself into the one vacant chair, acknowledging the five Gallagher brothers present with a smile and a nod of the head. "They're all fine thank you Nell and the kids send lots of love." Nell beamed her pleasure and waited while Danny topped up her empty glass.

"We've got the place to ourselves Acker," she continued. "All the girls have been sent upstairs and told to stay there until we've finished. They know something's on but don't know what, or how big. You've done a really great job, my love."

Nell cleared her glass with one swallow, refusing a refill from the attentive Danny, then wiped her lips with the back of a podgy hand. "From what Frankie tells me about the problems at the bank, it looks as though we could clean up if it comes off. We've been talking about nothing else since he told us."

At this point, Frankie started to fill Alec in on what progress had been made in the short time that had elapsed since their meeting in the pub.

"Mam's organised the boat for the canal – a folding one like the Navy use – and I've sorted out the bloke that will take me across the Bristol Channel to Weston." At this point Chaz broke in. "A friend of Mam's will pick up Eddie, Danny, me and the boat when the job's over and drop us off back here. It's his boat," he added by way of explanation.

Eddie, who hadn't yet contributed to the conversation, decided to make amends. "How are we going to split up the money once we've nicked it?" It could well have been a question on most lips but none had dared to voice it. As soon as he uttered the words, Eddie knew he'd dropped a bollock. Nell leaned forward, her eyes narrowing.

"I'll decide that when we've got it and no one else, understand?" The tone of her voice and the menace in her eyes left no room for any conjecture on the subject. "Now why the fuck did I say that?" thought Eddie, wishing he could disappear through the floor as the disapproving eyes around the table turned to mock him.

The drinks flowed as the details of the planned bank robbery were discussed at length, each one at the table contributing, except Eddie, still feeling a right stupid bastard. His brothers often thought he was just that anyway!

Nell cleared her throat. It was a gargantuan effort lasting ages but it had the desired effect as the others realised she required their undivided attention.

"There are two important things we need to sort out – very, very important." They hung on her words as she paused. Whether it was for effect or the phlegm trapped in her throat, they weren't sure. She leaned forward, arms folded on the table. "If we pull this job off – and Jesus, Mary and Joseph I hope we do, then we are going to need cast iron alibis for the time just before, during and just after it happens." She waited for her words to sink in.

Frankie nodded his agreement. "You're dead right Mam. When the bank people and the rozzers find out what's happened, they'll go fucking spare and the first ones they'll want to talk to is us! They'll be down on us like a ton of bricks, so we have to be ready for 'em. Right everybody?"

The rest nodded their agreement, spending the next ninety minutes proposing and counter-proposing different options until they were satisfied they were good enough to withstand the expected police interrogation.

Nell took a long drag on her cigarette and sat back, slowly easing herself into a more comfortable position on the chair. Nobody spoke, leaving Nell to break the silence.

"Personally, I prefer to go with the alibi we thought to be the best, where we were all here playing cards from Sunday lunchtime onwards and carrying on well into the early hours of Monday morning." While the proposal seemed a bit far-fetched, it was up to the police to disprove it.

If that was good enough for Nell, it was good enough for the rest of them. They nodded their agreement and as they did so, the enormity of the job before them suddenly took on a different dimension. It wasn't just the thrills of the caper anymore – this was for real!

Alec picked up a flagon, pouring himself a full glass of beer.

"You realise that the rozzers probably know I'm married to a Gallagher girl. It'll take them about five minutes to find out that I'm also the foreman in charge of the Rates Office repair job. Even those thick bastards will be able to put two and two together and come up with five and then my arse is in a sling, so I'll have to be extra careful as far as alibis are concerned. But don't worry, I'll sort it out, watertight like."

He took a swig from his glass and glanced at the clock. "I'll have to be going soon, as Lydia will be getting worried. She doesn't like me being out on the bike in the dark after I've had a few bevvies."

Frankie stood up. "Look boys, for Christ's sake. This is a fantastic opportunity and all we've got to do is to stick to our stories and rely on each other." He circled the table, grasping the shoulders of each of his companions in turn as Nell stayed silent.

"Now you all know what my alibi is. I'll be in London from Saturday onwards staying with Hetty at her house, where she uses one of the three floors as her own flat and I won't be back for a few days. The rest of you will have to stick to your stories like shit to a blanket." He continued circling the table, the centre of attention. "If we've got cast iron alibis, the rozzers will be able to do fuck-all about it. Just stick to your stories and they'll be running round in bleeding circles."

He returned to his chair and sat down. "Oh, and remember," he continued, "none of you know Hetty's address. That way they can't hassle me until I get back and I'll be able to handle it from there. You know something Mam," he added, "I was dead lucky to meet a girl like Hetty on that weekend I spent in London last year. She's a real cracker and owning her own house is a huge help for us."

Nell, who had remained silent while Frankie spoke, nodded her agreement before returning to her second point of importance. "It's not a problem yet, but it will be if we cop on for the money from the bank." She continued, directing her remarks in particular to Eddie. "You were asking how the money was going to be split up when we've got it, but when we do get our hands on it, we won't be able to spend it for months. Yeah, that's right, Eddie – months!" she grated.

Even Danny and Chaz looked chastened as all three younger brothers saw their anticipated spending sprees evaporating before their eyes by Nell's seemingly unnecessary caution. But any lingering protest that might have been germinating in their young minds was instantly squashed when Nell continued to hammer the message home.

"I hope we all understand just what's at stake here so we don't fuck up by anyone being bloody careless. Otherwise, we could all end up in the bleeding pokey! Well, that looks like it for tonight then, boys."

Alec checked his watch this time, pushed his chair back and stood up. "Right, I'm off. I'll check back with you Mam and Frankie on Saturday morning to make sure nothing's changed. I'd also like to hear sometime what plans you've lined up for the cash once Frankie reaches Weston, OK?" A final sloppy kiss from Nell, and with quick handshakes from the rest and a "see you again" to all, he was away.

As he cycled homewards, Alec considered the evening's events. They seemed to have wrapped up most things nicely. He pushed harder on the pedals as he contemplated how he and Lydia would spend the prayed-for windfall that he hoped was coming their way. They'd need luck – a lot of luck, but it was a nice warm feeling, it really was, he concluded as he added extra energy to his pedalling.

Chapter 14

The two men stood just inside the entrance of the bank's large strongroom, the huge circular door dwarfing them by comparison as they examined the damaged ceiling of the vault. The strongroom, located on the same floor as the bank's main business and customer areas, was cool but Ian James' manner was anything but cool as he fretted at the delay in completing the necessary repairs.

He turned to address his colleague. "When did the Council's maintenance people say they would finish repairing the damage Jeff? They seem to be taking one hell of a long time."

His deputy Jeff Brown shrugged his shoulders, shaking his head slowly as he searched for a response. Eventually he spoke.

"I talked to the foreman before we left here last night and he said it would be sometime on Monday. They seem to be dragging their heels though." He sighed. "But as it's Saturday today and the bank will be closed until Monday, I suppose it could be worse, Ian, don't you think?"

The manager blew out his cheeks in exasperation. "Hardly," he muttered through gritted teeth, then turning on his heel, he stepped out of the vault. He waited impatiently for his deputy to follow suit. The pair combined their efforts to swing the massive door shut then headed for the corridor that led to the main banking hall.

As they made their way, Ian James spoke over his shoulder to his colleague. "By the way Jeff, I want you to check with security that they're satisfied the Rates Office will be fully secured over the weekend. You would think I was to blame by the fuss they're kicking up at Head Office," he added as they walked along the corridor to his office. "Monday morning can't come quick enough for me," he sighed as he slumped into the large chair behind the even bigger oak desk. "Nor me," thought Jeff Brown as he departed to dial the security officer's internal telephone number.

Worried they may have been, but if they had known that the very same hole in the bank vault ceiling was the subject of intense discussion elsewhere in the city, they would have been very agitated men indeed.

Alec again turned up as promised at the Gallagher household, satisfied he had made a significant contribution to the family's planned assault on the bank later that weekend. As expected, Nell gave him her usual smothering welcome.

"Frankie will be here in a few minutes luv," she explained as Alec settled into a chair. He rummaged briefly in his ex-army rucksack, then fished out a bunch of keys and placed them on the table in front of Nell. "They're the ones I promised you. With them, the job should be a real cinch."

He then pulled out a large, folded sheet of paper, spread it out on the table, smoothing out the creases with his large, rough hands. "I've drawn this sketch of the Rates Office layout. It'll help you to know your way around."

Nell leaned forward, scanning the drawing with a practised eye. "You've done a fantastic job here Acker," she croaked, her voice not yet having come to terms to the morning's relatively early hour. "I see there are just two doors to open – then we're into the Rates room above the bank vault." She prodded the drawing with a plump index finger. "There's the outside alarm bell you're going to fix Chaz," adding for Alec's benefit, "Chaz has all the stuff needed to take care of the bell, Acker, as well as the sacks and the folding ladder." Chaz nodded his assent in response to Alec's enquiring glance. "Everything's set up Acker – the folding boat and Frankie's lift across the Bristol Channel to Weston. The bloke that owns the boat and the lockers in Weston is one of Mam's cousin's, so he can be trusted."

At that point Frankie opened the kitchen door, acknowledged Alec with a grin and a brief handshake before sitting at the table and inspecting the Rates Office drawing. "Christ Acker, this is just what we needed. And the keys are going to make this job into a school milk run." He settled back into his chair, his eyes glinting with excitement. "Boy, are those bank people and the rozzers going to get a bleeding shock when they turn up for work on Monday, eh Mam?"

Nell's face creased into a huge smile, her raucous laughter setting off the others as they savoured the prospects ahead of them. As their laughter subsided, Frankie sipped from a steaming hot cup of tea handed him by Chaz. Each person was now occupied by their own private thoughts as they contemplated the sheer audacity of their plan. Their musings were interrupted by Nell as she heaved herself forward, her fleshy forearms supporting her weight against the circular arms of the sturdy wooden Windsor chair. She directed her remarks to Frankie.

"One thing you can be dead certain of is that the rozzers will come down on us like a ton of bricks after the job is discovered – especially you Frankie." Nell paused to light a cigarette before continuing.

"It makes sense for you and the other boys to lie low and not do anything stupid for a few days or so – and that also means staying sober," she added glancing meaningfully at each one in turn. Nell took a long, slow drag on her cigarette, satisfied she had everyone's attention before continuing. "I've set up a card game for tonight with some of the family and a couple of friends. We'll need to get some extra booze in – and some ciggies for me. You can see to that Chaz, OK?" He nodded several times in compliance.

"Sure Mam, but I'll need some cash as I'm skint," while meanwhile thinking "why does she treat me like a little kid? For Christ sake, I'm nineteen," he silently fumed, his face not daring to betray his rebellious thoughts.

Nell noisily cleared her throat of phlegm before continuing. "As long as we stick together on our story about playing cards here until Sunday morning around 5 o'clock – and you being away for a few days, Frankie, that should be enough to keep the rozzers guessing and off our backs for the time being. Then we'll see what develops."

Frankie rubbed his nose then looked at his companions. "Got that straight everyone? Right then." He motioned to Chaz. "Give me a refill, our kid, will you?" handing his cup to his younger brother, who was still miffed at his junior role in the proceedings.

Suitably refreshed, Frankie continued. "After the job, I nip across the Channel to Weston with the gear and stow the bags away safely in Mam's cousin's boathouse. He's got some steel containers in there that he normally uses for stowing spare boat gear, right Mam?" Nell nodded her assent, motioning Frankie to continue. He eased himself into a more comfortable position in the hard wooden-backed chair.

"Once I'm there, I stash the gear and then change the locks just in case some nosey bastard has a spare set of keys to the original locks. Mam's cousin then gives me a lift in his car to Bristol Temple Meads railway station where I catch the early morning train to Paddington." Frankie paused for another swig from his cup.

"I should get to Hetty's flat in Ladbroke Grove, say about ten o'clock on the Sunday morning and stay there for a few days, then catch the train back to Cardiff, say on Tuesday."

He stood up to stretch his back and legs. "When the rozzers want to know where I was at the time of the bank job, I can place myself at my girlfriend's flat in London over the whole weekend." He grinned as he thought of the runaround the police would have over this one. "Hetty is going to back up my story that I've been there a few days and I'll get rid of the rail ticket from Bristol to London so that it can't be traced to me." He added a drop of brandy from a miniature bottle in his pocket, to his tea. "The rozzers won't know where to turn next, the poor bastards, especially if we have watertight alibis."

He raised his cup high. "Cheers everyone. Here's to Lloyds Bank and the money they're going to donate to our worthy cause tomorrow."

At this point, Nell reached under her chair and fished out a bottle of Scotch whisky. "The job's not done yet and it may be a bit early to celebrate, but I reckon a toast to good luck and our future success won't go amiss, will it boys?"

Before Nell could unscrew the cap from the bottle, the front door bell rang, followed by a series of sharp knocks on the door.

Nell removed the cap from the bottle and placed it on the table. "Get some glasses Chaz – and Eddie, you go to the front door and see who it is." Chaz rose with a sigh then called out loudly for the benefit of those at the door, "Eddie, have a look who that is before they knock the bleeding door down, will you?"

The sharp raps at the door were repeated impatiently just as Eddie opened it. He was confronted by DS Dave Parker and another, older person whom Eddie didn't recognise. "We'll need to come in Eddie," said Parker, moving to push past him. Eddie may not have been born the quickest thinker in the business, but he instinctively blocked Parker's way. "Hey, hold on a minute Mr Parker. Tell me what you want and I'll see if Mam is out of bed yet. By the way, I suppose you've got a warrant?" With that, he closed the door firmly on the two detectives and virtually ran down the tiled hallway to be confronted by Nell and the rest who hadn't heard all the earlier exchanges at the door.

"It's Parker, Mam and a bloke who looks like another rozzer," Eddie blurted out hoarsely as he stumbled into the kitchen. By this time everyone was on their feet, the fear of discovery evident on their faces. Their celebratory mood had disappeared now, completely forgotten because of the threat at the front door.

Nell was first to react. She folded up the Rates Office plan, picked up the bunch of keys and stuffed the lot into a cupboard that was fitted with a false front situated next to the large open fireplace. She then turned to Alec. "You'll need to go out the back way and over the wall into the lane, Acker. We don't want them to see you here if they insist on coming in." Alec needed no further bidding. "I'll be in touch Nell, when the job's over." With that, he left.

Frankie took a deep breath. "I'll attend to these two, so stay nice and relaxed." With that he left the room and made his way through the long hallway and opened the front door to confront the two detectives. "It's a bit early for you lot, isn't it," he said, his distaste for the two callers evident as he leaned against the door frame, arms folded. "So, what do you want? Unless you have a warrant you can stay where you are. I suppose you're both pulling in some double-time wages over the weekend, yeah?" But despite his casual and contemptuous manner, Frankie's nerves were jangling.

Dave Parker didn't shift his steady gaze from Frankie's mocking eyes. "There was a job pulled at a petrol station in Canton last night," he said evenly. "We're making enquiries about who was where when it happened." Frankie returned Parker's unblinking stare. "If all you lot have to do is hassling us about a poxy job like that then you can fuck off back to your office and play with your paperclips." Parker stood his ground, his companion silently looking on, unmoved by Frankie's outburst.

"Where were you and your lot last night, around midnight, between ten o'clock and one pm? Can you account for your movements?" Parker responded calmly. "Around midnight, you say and my movements?" said Frankie thoughtfully as he considered last night's activity. "Midnight, yeah. I remember now. I was fucking a new girlfriend and it went on for hours. We like it that way."

Parker studied Frankie's taunting face. He nodded his head slowly. "We won't come in right now, but stick around because we'll be needing another of our little chats before long."

At this point, Frankie seized the opportunity to plant his alibi for the weekend firmly in Parker's mind." You're lucky to find me in because I'm off to the Smoke this morning to look up another girlfriend. If anything, she's an even better screw than the one I had last night. See you around fellows but don't make it too soon." With that, Frankie slammed the door shut, then leaned thankfully against the passageway wall, a shudder rippling up and down his spine. "Christ, for a moment, I thought that bastard Parker had cottoned on to our job at the bank. He really gave me the shits for a while."

His heart was thumping like a sledge hammer as Nell's voice rang out from behind the partly-opened kitchen door. "Frankie! Hey Frankie! Have they buggered off yet? What did they want? Are we OK?" Frankie took another deep breath and rejoined his family. "Don't worry Mam, everything's kosher," he said, exhaling a long-drawn out breath of relief. He slumped thankfully into the chair recently vacated by Alec. "They were checking on us to see if we knew anything about a petrol station robbery in Canton last night." He laughed derisively. "As if we'd tell them anything anyway, the thick bastards. I told them to push off and shuffle the papers around on their desks if they were looking for something to do."

The whisky bottle still beckoned on the table. Nell leaned across and picked it up, a broad smile creasing her fleshy features." I think we need that drink now to settle our nerves and anyway, after tomorrow, we'll really be celebrating."

Chapter 15

The near-full moon reflected ever-changing silvery patterns on the slow moving waters of the dark canal as it penetrated the gaps in the overhanging branches of the trees lining the canal bank. The dense foliage provided ideal shadows of cover for Frankie and his three companions, none of whom were in any mood to appreciate the eerie beauty of the cool autumn night. The chances of the foursome being visible among the shadows were even less likely with all four wearing black zip-up overalls that covered them from below their chins right down to their shoes.

The former naval canvas boat in which they had slowly drifted nearly a mile downstream between the high banks of the canal rocked unsteadily as Eddie awkwardly manipulated the wooden paddle to bring the boat alongside the grassy bank. They paused silently as one, listening intently to the strange muffled sounds of the night which duly confirmed their lonely presence. The occasional early morning noise of passing traffic reminded the foursome that the main central roadway curving past the City Hall and Cardiff's impressive civic centre, was just one hundred yards away, with the city's Central police station as its brooding, well-lit neighbour.

Frankie leaned towards the grassy verge, grasping a low hanging branch. He tugged the boat the last few remaining feet to the bank before stepping unsteadily onto the safety of the small wooden staging at the foot of a series of rough steps, formed by a number of old railway sleepers. Quietly beckoning his brothers to follow, he touched Danny on the shoulder. "Tie the ropes at each end of the boat to those branches." His whispered command brought a nervous response as Danny fumbled his simple task. "Let's have the bags and be careful how you handle them. We don't want to drop them in the bloody water before we even start." Again Danny's twitchy reaction as he transferred the bags from the boat to his brothers exposed the tension he was experiencing, though they would be the last to admit they were feeling jumpy too.

Danny handed a pile of empty bags to Chaz and a separate one containing a folding ladder. The final bag betrayed its contents by the clunk of metal upon metal. "Careful Chaz, this one's heavy," warned Danny. Chaz handed the spare bags to his brothers, hoisting the heavy bag over his shoulder. "They must think I'm a fucking donkey," he groaned inwardly.

Again pausing long enough to check the night's noises, Frankie then led the way up the steps, bringing them up to the level of the employees entrance at the rear of the Rates office. They halted, confronted by eight-foot high iron railings topped with sharp spikes, a barrier that ran the length of the darkened building. Frankie turned to Eddie. "You know the drill. Make sure you keep your eyes peeled and if there's even the slightest thing that seems suspicious, let's know – and I mean fast! You got that? Have you checked your two-way radio?" Eddie nodded. "You can rely on me Frankie, you know that."

Despite his young brother's assurances, Frankie still felt uneasy. Chaz moved to the railings, placing the heavy bag on the ground. Unzipping the bag, he pulled out an oil-operated car jack which he placed sideways between two of the railings. Slowly, he pumped the handle, building up the oil pressure. At first nothing happened, then as he continued pumping, the bars slowly gave way until the space between two of them was big enough for them to clamber through.

Their rubber-soled shoes enabled them to make silent progress across the tarmac pathway leading to the heavy, oak panelled rear door of the building. "It really is quiet," thought Frankie, "too quiet." He was right. The silence was suddenly shattered by Danny who lurched sideways, colliding with Frankie, cursing as he stumbled.

"What the fuck was that?" Danny's unexpected outburst startled his companions, all of whom froze where they stood.

The surprised squeals of the large rat that had run into Danny's foot were replaced by its screams of pain as he lashed out, kicking the rat against the wall, the blood from its brains and head spattering the wall as its skull fractured by the impact. It lay there, its body twitching as it tried to summon the strength to crawl away to some kind of safety. Danny shuddered. "God, I hate those bastards. They really give me the creeps," he uttered through clenched teeth. Frankie was the first to regain his composure. "You scared the shit out of us then, but for Christ's sake let's keep the noise down, rats or no rats. There's plenty of them around anyway on the canal bank." Although he hadn't uttered a word, Chaz's spine tingled with cold shivers. He couldn't stand rats either. In fact they scared the shit out of him too but he wasn't going to admit it in front of his brothers.

Still shaken by his unexpected encounter with the rat, Danny took a deep breath and then shone his shaded torch onto the six stone steps that led up to the door. He flicked the light further upwards, searching for the circular, red painted, burglar alarm bell located some twelve feet above the steps. It was where he expected. Would the bastard go off even though Chaz knew how to stop it? Its malevolent look of silence would shatter the night air with an almighty bloody clanging if his brother got it wrong. "Here goes," he thought. His struggle to extricate the lightweight, four-piece folding ladder from its bag brought an exasperated gasp from Frankie, the tension reflected in his voice.

"For Christ's sake Danny, let's have the fucking thing out of there." Stifling the urge to respond, Danny freed the sharp-edged ladder from the bag, handing it to Frankie. Unfolding the sections, Frankie carefully placed the ladder against the wall. "Okay Chaz, you know what to do so let's get going."

Even in the darkened night, Chaz agilely climbed the ladder, pausing as he reached the level of the heavy metal bell. Steadying himself on the narrow metal rungs of the ladder, he rummaged in the pockets of his black dungarees, producing several pieces of thick cotton waste.

A further rummage in his pockets produced a roll of black adhesive tape. He was about to remove his gloves to carry out his task, aided by his brothers' torchlight, when Frankie's voice from below stopped him in his tracks. "Keep your gloves on you arsehole. We don't want to leave our calling card for the rozzers, do we?" Frankie's reminder irritated Chaz, knowing he had just forgotten their golden rule. "He must be a bleeding mind reader," he fumed silently, inwardly thankful for his brother's timely warning.

Easing the metal hammer head away from the bell, Chaz wrapped it carefully in the cotton waste. When it was fully covered, he then wound the insulating tape around the wadding until he was satisfied there could be no movement of the bell striker if was tripped. The slim torch he had gripped between his teeth for several minutes made his jaw ache, despite the fact that several of his front upper teeth were missing, having been smashed out in a particularly nasty street fight several years earlier. Still, his occasional girlfriends didn't seem to mind and the gap made a perfect place to secure the torch.

"How's it going up there?" Frankie's hoarse whisper was ignored by Chaz, the torch now causing him quite some pain in his lower jaw. He stepped off the ladder, removed the torch, flexed his jaws, opening and shutting his mouth several times. "It's OK," he finally replied, still feeling the effects of his efforts up the ladder.

Danny eased the ladder away from the wall, lowering it to the ground and this time, folding it effortlessly to replace it in its canvas bag. "We're going to need this again quite soon," he offered, as Frankie shone his torch on the colour-coded set of duplicate keys he had fished from his pocket. He concentrated on the earlier briefing they'd had from Alec – 'Red for the outer door, blue for the inner door'.

He inserted the red key into the lock and turned it. The tumblers of the lock opened smoothly. "Hmmm. So far, so good." No alarm bells He gingerly pushed the door open. It moved no more than two inches, before the alarm bell tripped. But instead of a nerve-jangling clanging in full throat, there was no more than a slight, soft vibration of the dreaded hammer on the red bell. With a final check to Eddie to maintain a watchful vigil, the rest gathered up their bags and stepped into the dark passageway. Frankie flashed his small torch, selecting the blue key. Seconds later, all three moved into the main administration area of the rates office.

The low-level night lighting provided so thoughtfully by the local council was enough to get their bearings. They moved quietly through to the small side office where the night-watchman spent most of his working life. With a forefinger to his lips cautioning silence, Frankie peered slowly around the doorway into the night-watchman's domain. Jack Watkins lay slumped, chin on chest, his ample frame filling the wide, circular-armed, red painted wooden armchair. A tea mug sat on the desk keeping the local evening newspaper company. The partly-completed crossword revealed how Jack spent at least some of his nights of vigil.

Chaz poked his head around the door frame. "Is he asleep?" he enquired anxiously as Danny pushed him aside to view the results of their efforts to nobble the night-watchman. "If he's not, then we're in the shit," whispered Frankie looking back towards the floor area that was the real focus of their attention. "I was told that stuff his tea was laced with was good enough to put him out for at least eight hours, so let's get cracking and bring the bags with you."

They moved into the main accounts office, standing silently looking at the seemingly innocuous cordoned-off floor area that could just be the source of previously undreamed-of riches. It was just as Alec had described.

Frankie broke into their silent contemplation. "We're going to have to take up the temporary flooring they've nailed over the hole in the wood block floor." Taking this as his cue, Chaz selected a short-handled pickaxe and a crowbar from his bag of tools. Ducking under the thick paper tape that hung at chest height around the repair area, he knelt down and forced the flat chisel end of the crowbar under the thick sheet of nailed-down plywood. Within seconds, he had gained sufficient leverage to ease several inches of the plywood sheeting off the wooden blocks. He continued, gradually moving around the outer edges of the plywood, watched intently by his brothers.

"Once this boarding is removed I should be able to get at the concrete ceiling panels in the bank vault," confirmed Chaz as he continued using the crowbar to good effect. Frankie nodded his assent, before being aware that Danny was missing from the scene.

He flashed his torch around the room, further illuminating the darkened corners not covered by the emergency night lighting.

"Where are you Danny? What the fuck are you doing?" Not receiving any kind of response, he crossed the wide floor, skirting several desks in the process. Now he could see the darting beam of Danny's flashlight as it illuminated an office on the far side of the room. "There's a safe here," explained Danny as Frankie entered the room. "It might have some cash or something else worth nicking." Frankie stepped forward, pulling the kneeling Danny to his feet. "We're getting out of here because it's not what we came for. Anyway, there's probably peanuts in there."

Frankie stifled his brother's protests by closing the palm of his gloved hand over his mouth. "Let's get back in there, our kid is waiting."

They returned to the main office where Chaz's efforts had enabled him to lift the sheet of plywood away from the damaged floor area. "Where the fuck have you two been? That panel was bloody heavy and I could have done with a hand." His aggrieved tone struck a guilty chord as they both hastened to make amends. "Sorry Chaz, it was my fault," explained Danny as he knelt down to inspect the task ahead of them.

His brother pointed to a number of flat concrete panels that were now exposed. They rested on the lower flanges of parallel steel girders that supported the ceiling of the bank vault. "You can see from the hole that Alec's team made right through the floor that there's a fairly thick layer of plaster covering the bottom side of the panels, that's the actual ceiling surface of the vault."

His explanation, though accurate, was too lengthy for Frankie's liking. "Forget the building lesson Chaz. Let's get on with it or the bleeding staff will be clocking on for work."

Chaz returned to his task of levering up the wooden blocks until a four foot square area of the concrete panels lay exposed. The first panel, damaged by the maintenance team, was difficult to shift at first, but eventually gave way under his persistence. Loosening the other panels by using a rocking motion, they gave way, causing lumps of plaster and white dust to fall onto the floor of the vault.

The unexpected bleep of the radio phone jammed in Frankie's pocket startled all three into alertness. He rose to his feet, shushing his brothers as he did so. "Yeah, what's wrong?"

Frankie's hoarse whisper reflected the anxiety in his voice. In the stillness, Eddie's voice was heard by all three. "What's happening there? Why are you taking so long? It's giving me the flaming creeps being out here, especially as a rozzer's van went by a few minutes ago." Frankie's heart was still pumping quickly in alarm as he replied. "Eddie, I told you not to contact us unless we had trouble and you being afraid of the dark is not trouble, so stay off the fucking phone unless it's necessary. We'll be finished here as soon as we can. That's it!" He switched the handset off, shaking his head at his brothers.

"Eddie can be a daft bastard at times." They nodded their agreement, returning to the ever-widening hole in the vault ceiling. Chaz handed a another panel to Danny. "I reckon that will do it," he announced, sitting back on his haunches, his knees now aching, having straddled two of the girders for some ten minutes without respite. He rose stiffly, massaging his knees as he straightened. "Christ, I'm glad I don't have to that for a living," he groaned. Ignoring his self assessment on the state of his knees, his brothers began the process of unfolding the ladder.

"I'll go down first," declared Danny easing the ladder down into the black void of the vault. A satisfying thud on the vault's floor showed they still had a couple of feet of spare ladder. He stepped carefully onto the first rung. "We're in, so let's get among that money." It's not me that's afraid of the dark, he thought as he descended, his small torch clenched awkwardly between his teeth. It was about the only time he rued not having a gap in his teeth like Chaz. Frankie's voice came from above, urging him to locate the light switches in the vault.

Suddenly the whole vault was flooded with light, its brilliance causing a seemingly solid shaft of light beaming up through the hole in the floor, illuminating the room above to an alarming degree. It was a massive contrast to the earlier gloom.

"Jesus, I hope that light can't be seen from outside because if it can, we've got problems." Frankie's concern worried Chaz. "What are we going to do Frank, pull out?" His brother stepped onto the ladder. "We're in and we're sitting on the bleeding jackpot, so let's get stuck in." With that he disappeared down the ladder to be followed shortly by his brother.

As his brothers joined him in the vault, Danny waved his arms wide in triumph. "Just look at this lot. Have you ever seen anything like it before?

His question was unnecessary in the circumstances. They were confronted on one side by a wall that was covered with row upon row of chrome coloured safe deposit boxes each measuring about nine inches by four inches. There must have been at least two hundred of them. "I've only ever seen this kind of thing in the pictures where Hollywood gangsters rob banks," said Chaz, clearly overwhelmed. "Well what the fuck do you think we're doing now? That's just what we are doing. We're robbing a bank!" Frankie burst out laughing, caught up in the sheer fantasy of their situation.

Slowly at first, then as relief replaced their earlier caution, his brothers joined in, hugging each other and bouncing around like a couple of school-kids. Frankie brought them quickly back to earth. "Have you checked that lot on the other side," he said, motioning to the eight large steel safes embedded in a single row in the wall opposite. "It's not those boxes we should be wasting our time on. It could take us a week to jemmy that lot." His words caused his brothers to glance over their shoulders, turning as they did.

"They look like a hard bunch of bastards," snorted Danny as he stepped forward and tested one the handles with a firm twist. It didn't move, not even a fraction. "You're right, they are just that, a real hard nut to crack," responded Frankie, moving forward to the first safe on the left. "What you don't know is that Alec did a deal with one of the bank messengers who managed to get a copy of the keys to these safes."

If he had said the Empire State building had just collapsed, it wouldn't have had greater effect. "Christ Frankie, this job is going to be a cinch, when Danny and me thought all along we might never pull it off, although we never mentioned anything to you," said Chaz.

As Frankie tried the key in the lock of the first safe, his brothers eagerly crowded forward. The door didn't budge at first, but then swung open slowly as Frankie twisted the handle.

The unmistakable sight of piles of neatly packed banknotes literally took their breath away. Less then two feet distant and now completely unprotected, sat thousands of pounds of used banknotes, giving off that musty smell that was sometimes offensive when it was just a single, crumpled note fished from your pocket. But when they sat there in neat piles, in their thousands, their whole attraction suddenly changed – and bollocks to the smell.

Frankie pushed his brothers back. "I'll pass the bundles out. Danny can do a rough count on how much is one of the bundles and you Chaz can put the cash into the bags." Frankie deftly emptied the first safe, discovering a second layer of banknotes behind the first. "There's about a grand or maybe eleven hundred quid in each bundle. They're all five pound notes," announced Danny, passing his bundle to Chaz who continued to stuff the bundles into a bag. "There's forty five bundles here, or was it forty six, I'm not sure," he said, adding, "anyway it's a lot of bloody cash."

By now, Frankie had opened the second safe. It revealed that it too was packed with banknotes. Encouraged, he went along the line of safes unlocking each one in turn. He pulled open the door of the eighth and last safe. It was bare.

"This bastard's empty!" he snarled. He moved on to the seventh safe. It was also empty, so was the sixth. "What the fuck's going on here," he hissed in exasperation, moving on to the next safe door. He swung it open. It wasn't empty but contained two cardboard filing boxes. He wrenched them from the safe, hurling them on the floor. "Check what's in those, somebody. Anybody!" he yelled.

Danny knelt down, examining their contents. "It's just a pile of poxy old papers," his disappointment clear. Chaz then twisted the handle of the nearest unopened safe. "This one's got money in it," he yelled, to the huge relief of his brothers. Danny stepped forward and tried another of the unopened safes. He gave the handle a good twist. "So has this one." There was a pause as he tried the next." This one's full too – and so's this one," he echoed as he moved down the line of safes.

His success immediately cushioned their disappointment. "We've got a right whack of cash here which isn't bad for a night's work," he added. "Right, let's get the cash into the bags and piss off out of here," grunted Frankie for despite the rewards, the claustrophobic atmosphere of the vault was getting on his nerves. He glanced to his left where the massive, steel door of the vault presented an impenetrable barrier. "Christ, it would have bleeding impossible if we hadn't come through the ceiling," he mused, gathering up two of the bulging canvas bags. Even though he knew they'd be weighty, he hadn't reckoned on them being that bloody heavy. "Jesus, have you copped on to the weight of these bags yet?" he queried as he struggled to cope with his load. "We'll have to be careful going up that ladder, because I'm not certain it'll take more than one of us and one bag at a time." He dropped one of the bags onto the floor.

"Any idea how much we got?" enquired Danny to nobody in particular as he eyed the rows of unopened safe deposit boxes lining the opposite wall.

Whatever was bothering Frankie was clearly fraying his patience. "Forget the bloody boxes – they'll take all night to jemmy and we have to get going – now." His rising tone of intolerance warned Danny not to persist. "Check we've left nothing behind that can be traced back to us. We don't want to signpost our address to the rozzers. And don't forget the ladder!"

Danny sighed. "As if I would, bighead," he mouthed to himself.

Gripping one of the bulky bags, Frankie turned to Chaz. "I'll go first and you can pass the others up. With that, he tested his weight on the first rung then after a pause, continued his ascent. His head and shoulders soon reappeared, framed in the dark hole as he leant downwards ready to take the next. Chaz handed him the tool bag. They repeated the exercise until all the bags were stacked on the floor of the administration office.

But now came one of the most important phases of their assault on the bank vault. Chaz's earlier work on the vault ceiling had created a substantial covering of plaster dust on the vault floor.

With their work clearing out the safes now completed, they needed to erase evidence of their shoe prints and other scuffles clearly visible on the vault floor.

Danny removed a small but powerful electric vacuum cleaner from the haversack slung over his shoulder. Straightening out the flex, he plugged it into the nearest electric point. The noise of the cleaner as it burst into life sounded so incredibly loud in the confined space of the vault, that Danny and Chaz were convinced they were about to be caught red-handed!

Nevertheless, Danny set about the task diligently until all traces of the minor debris and plaster dust had been cleared.

He switched the cleaner off and returned it to the haversack before handing it over to Chaz.

"Don't forget to switch the lights out," warned his brother as Danny took a final look around to check they hadn't left anything that could put the finger on them. Chaz scaled the ladder, resisting the reaction to remove his gloves.

He had barely stepped into the upper office, when the whole area was suddenly plunged into total blackness as the vault lights went out. Their vision was gradually restored as their eyes became accustomed to the office emergency lighting. A muffled curse came from down below, followed by Danny's emergence from the hole. "What's up with you – another rat?" Frankie's sarcasm went unnoticed as Danny rubbed his tender shinbone, skinned by his fall off the blacked-out ladder. He hauled it up out of the hole, carefully folding it down before replacing it in its canvas bag.

At this point, all three removed their shoes and stuffed them into the same haversack that contained the vacuum cleaner. After all, they didn't want to leave evidence of their shoe sizes via any dusty imprints left on the Rates Office floor.

"How's the watchman doing Chaz," enquired Frankie.

"I've already checked on him – some bleeding watchman – and he seems OK but he's still out cold."

"I hope the old sod's not dead," said his brother, a hint of concern evident in his reply. Frankie heaved two bags over his shoulders. He made his way across to the exit hallway. Chaz and Danny followed suit. Frankie re-locked the inner door. They made their way to the heavy outer door. All three listened carefully, Frankie pressed an ear to one of its panels. The stillness and quiet from beyond encouraged to him unlock it, easing it open gently. All three emerged into the cool night air. Frankie finally locked the outer door, his brothers waiting at the foot of the stone steps, adjusting the weighty bags for a more comfortable grip.

"Where's Eddie?" enquired Danny softly, peering into the darkness. "Christ knows but he'd better be around to let us know what's been happening," murmured Chaz. Motioning them to be silent, Frankie listened intently, his ears straining to catch the slightest sound, his eyes now accustomed to the gloom, searching for his young brother.

A rustling noise, seemingly coming from the undergrowth and some short bushes near the grass verge, was followed by silence. Then the noise again. A sort of hissing sound. "If I didn't know any better, I'd say he was having a piss over there in those bushes," whispered Chaz. The three remained frozen in mutual silence until a shadow emerged from the bushes. It wasn't until Eddie had finished zipping up his flies that he saw his brothers. "You been there long then? I was wondering when you'd be back," the relief evident on his young countenance. By way of explaining his temporary absence, the 'shadow' explained, "I needed a slash, I was absolutely busting. Did you get the gear?" The questions tumbled from his lips. "You look as though you struck lucky there," pointing to the bulging bags.

"Everything's OK Eddie," replied Frankie tersely, the tension still evident. "Let's be on our way. You can fill me in when we're in the boat."

The foursome padded quietly back to the gap in the railings. A shaded torch provided sufficient light as they descended the wooden steps down to the boat. Eddie grasped one of the tethering ropes to steady the boat as his brothers loaded all their bags but one into the vessel.

There was one final piece of evidence of which they had to dispose – their overalls. All four carefully removed them and thrust them into the bag containing the fold-up ladder. This last bag was then loaded into the boat along with the others. One by one they clambered aboard carefully, unused to the bobbing motion caused by the downstream current.

Danny released the front tie rope. Eddie did the same with the rear rope, grasping the paddle to push the boat out into midstream. Using the paddle alternatively as a rudder and an oar, he guided the boat into downstream.

Chapter 16

Despite the time spent in the Rates Office and the bank's strongroom, the early morning gloom still provided the four marauders with sufficient cover to thwart all but the keenest eyes of any one in the immediate vicinity as they approached the first of six low bridges under which they would pass on their way to the docks and the open sea.

Eddie's warning of "Keep a lookout and mind your heads," was a timely reminder. The bridges seemed a lot lower than they remembered when they regularly swam in this canal as schoolkids. The canal swung almost at right angles as it gurgled its way south to the docks.

They were approaching Queen Street where the open canal routed its way underground for the next half a mile or so as it passed underneath the newly-constructed Churchill Way. The new road had been formed by placing massive blocks of steel reinforced concrete a yard wide and seventy feet in length across the two narrow roads running either side of the canal. When it was covered, a new road surface was laid on top of the blocks to provide a dual-carriageway that linked the city's central and eastern main shopping and entertainment areas of Queen Street to Bute Terrace and the Butetown area leading to the docks.

"Here's the first one," warned Eddie as they glided past the rear of the prestigious Park Hotel and into the blackness of the canal aperture beneath Churchill Way. Apart from the occasional bellows of early morning drunks and the odd motor vehicle, their passage had been fairly quiet. But for all four, this part of their journey was a new experience as none had ever travelled the long, black mildew-encrusted tunnel under the roadway.

"Christ, it's creepy," murmured the boat's forward passenger, Danny, who despite the large flashlight he shone ahead of them took the brunt of the cobwebs and slimy tendrils that festooned the tunnel's low ceiling.

"You can say that again," agreed Chaz, clutching on to his heavy canvas bag like grim death. Thought of the bag however reminded him that they still had the tools and overalls they'd used on the job. "What do you want to do with these tools Frank," he enquired, rattling the bag for emphasis.

After a slight hesitation, Frankie turned, speaking over his shoulder. "Dump the lot in the water. Nobody will ever find them there. Just make sure you dump the right bloody bag."

Chaz shone his torch on the bag between his knees. Unzipping it, he inspected the contents, checking that all the tools were there. He zipped the bag shut, lifted it over the side and let go. It instantly disappeared as the boat continued on its way, aided by the downstream current. He hadn't seen it sink but it must have done, he reassured himself.

A few pinpoints of light appeared ahead in the blackness. They eventually grew larger, more defined, to reveal themselves as street lights at the end of the tunnel. A collective sigh of relief went up from the boat's passengers. "Apart from the other small bridges it should be plain sailing from here on," said Frankie, unaware of the unintended pun. Now the bank-side shapes changed, the sharp shapes of small canal-side factories and workshops replacing the earlier blackness of the long tunnel under the road.

The thoughts that raced through Frankie's mind however did not concern his immediate surroundings. He felt safe enough from any prying eyes, the darkness being a reliable partner in tonight's crime. His mind was focused on the next stage and the one beyond that of their night's activities. Once they cleared the canal, they would be faced with the problem of hauling the boat and its contents over a lock that barred their progress to the sea. At this time of early morning, the tide would be rising but there was still a drop of around eighteen feet to the mooring area for the fleet of small boats that bobbed on the sea, tethered to their moorings or lying tilted on their sides on the mud of the bay exposed by the low tide.

He only hoped that the transfer of himself and the heavy bags from their canvas boat to the small power boat he had hired to take him across the Bristol Channel to Weston-Super-Mare went without a hitch. Though considering how it had gone so far, he permitted himself a pat on the back. Why not, for Christ sake – it was the biggest job anyone had ever attempted in this part of the country. The bank people and the rozzers would go fucking spare when it was discovered.

They had been travelling parallel to Bute Street for some time now when the canal swung slightly to the left and the Pier Head. Within minutes they arrived at the huge gates of the lock.

Eddie stepped out of the swaying craft, tethering the rear end rope to a metal stanchion on the stone bank leading to the lock gates. One by one, they stepped from the boat, carefully retaining firm grips on the heavy bags. Eddie then untied the rear end rope from the stanchion and with two men taking hold of the ropes at each end of the boat, they lowered it into the water on the other side of the lock. Eddie retained a very firm grip on his rope as his brothers made their way down the slippery stone steps descending from the top of the lock gate to the incoming tide water level. As Danny was leading the way, he tugged the boat around until he could grab the front end rope trailing in the water. He secured this to a large steel ring embedded in the dock wall side, before stepping into the boat.

Frankie turned to Chaz. The brothers squeezed each others' shoulders before shaking hands. "We'll be waiting to hear from you in a day or so once you've sorted something out in Weston." Frankie nodded his confirmation. "Danny will be about half an hour before he gets back from the other boat. Remember, the three of you will have to get home as soon as you can. The bloke we paid to lend us his boat will drop you off in his van."

"You're due to meet him outside the Ship and Pilot pub in about an hour's time. Just leave the boat folded down and stick it in his van. After that it's up to him. Is that clear?"

They nodded their assent.

"One other thing, the most important of all," added Frankie. "Make sure you've got your alibis absolutely straight because the rozzers will be down on you and the family like a ton of bricks when the shit hits the fan. OK?" With that he stepped into the boat. It didn't take long for the boat, its two passengers and valuable cargo to disappear in the early morning gloom as Danny's muscles strained to their task.

Chaz made his way back up the stone steps to where Eddie waited. "Got a fag?" It was only then that he realised he hadn't had a smoke since they started out on the bank caper. Eddie, who'd had plenty of smokes while keeping lookout despite Frankie's warning not to, fished a crumpled packet of Woodbines from his chest pocket. "You're lucky," he replied. "I'm down to my last two."

Handing one to his brother, he stuck the other between his lips. Although one of the youngest in the family, Eddie smoked more ciggies than anyone else except his mother. It probably caused his ever-present cough. He cupped his hand around the match as it flared. His brother leaned forward, sucking deeply until the cigarette burned brightly. Eddie lit his and sat on the low harbour wall, flicking the spent match away into the canal.

Chaz caught him by the arm, pulling him down into a sitting position below the level of the wall. "There could be all sorts of people sniffing around here right now," he warned. "Better lie low until Danny returns." Eddie nodded in silent agreement then spoke. "I wonder how much money we nicked tonight. I've been so screwed up coming down that bloody canal, I nearly forgot about the money."

Chaz took a long pull on his cigarette. "You won't believe just how much it is, Eddie. Go on, have a guess." Eddie paused, hesitating to suggest too low a figure. "About thirty grand?" he finally ventured. "Yeah. You're right about the thirty grand, but it's more like two hundred and thirty grand," exclaimed Chaz gleefully.

Eddie puffed out his cheeks in disbelief, his astonishment visible even in the dim early morning light. "You have to be kidding!" he snorted. "Two hundred and thirty grand? That's a fucking fortune. We can live like millionaires on that," he whooped, the frailty of his arithmetic failing to raise any comment from his brother. "We could do with a drink right now to celebrate," he added, "although there's no bleeding chance of that." Chaz flicked his cigarette butt into the dark water below his feet.

It was followed a minute later by Eddie's exhausted butt.

"What are you going to do with your share of the money, Chaz?" he asked. The next twenty minutes was spent fulfilling their wildest fantasies from the seemingly inexhaustible supply of money coming their way. "We'll have to be careful though, Eddie," cautioned his brother. "Frankie has warned us before about flashing too much money about. It'd be a dead giveaway to the rozzers. We'd be inside before our feet touched the ground."

Eddie nodded his agreement, then rose quickly to his feet. "Did you hear that Chaz? I think it might be Danny. Can you see anything?"

Chaz joined his brother at the water's edge, peering intently into the murky, early morning gloom. Again the sound of splashing pierced the night silence. Both of them heard it this time, no doubts. Less than a minute later the shadowy figure of the canvas boat materialised, its shape and substance strengthening by the second.

Eddie leaned forward, grabbing the bow of the boat, pulling the vessel parallel to the dock wall. "The other boat was there, right? Did Frankie make it OK with the stuff?" His anxiety faded as Danny stepped from the boat, his teeth bared in a huge grin, both fists clenched in a gesture of triumph. "It went like bloody clockwork and Frankie's well on his way to Weston by now," enthused Danny, his exhilaration shared by his brothers as all three pummelled each other in sheer delight. As their high spirits subsided, Chaz brought them back to reality. "We have to get over to the Ship and Pilot pub right now. We may be cutting it fine as it is."

Eddie and Chaz hoisted the boat clear of the water, then collapsed it until it was small enough to fit into its original bag. Danny motioned to Eddie to pick up one end of the bag while grasping the other end. Elated by the success of their night's work, they barely noticed its weight as they set off on the journey to their rendezvous.

Their familiarity with the area made it easy for them to move confidently through the darkened streets. The approach of an occasional car, headlights blazing forced them to seek the refuge and shadow of nearby doorways. Satisfied, they moved on, silently crossing the road to the popular Butetown pub that dominated the street corner on which it stood. Still seeking the shadows of doorways, they waited.

Although their progress to the pub had been cautious, it had not gone unnoticed. Some two minutes elapsed, then a solitary figure stepped from the deep well of a side doorway, waiting in silence on the pavement. Danny was the first to react. "Are you the bloke Frankie saw about the van?," he queried in a stage whisper. Too bad if it wasn't. It was too late now if the shadow was a nosey copper on his dock-side beat. The stranger nodded his assent, saying 'follow me'. The foursome made their way across to the imposing Coal Exchange building, a massive elegant monument to the turn of the century period when Cardiff had dominated the world's exportation of coal.

They skirted the vast building, making their way to the rear, where a van normally used for the carriage of beer and spirits was parked. "It'll be easier if you got in the back out of sight," said the stranger as he unlocked the rear doors. They heaved the boat into the van then clambered in. There was no seating of any kind, just a pile of rough canvas sacks. "It smells just like a bloody brewery in here and I could just do with a pint right now," said Chaz.

His remarks helped to lighten the tension still present from their night's activities. The doors slammed shut leaving them in total darkness. "I hope he knows our bleeding address," offered Eddie. "Anybody got a fag?" He regarded his brother's silence as a 'no'. Suddenly the engine roared into life. They were on their way to Tudor Street in Riverside – and home.

Chapter 17

The small but powerful fishing boat coasted silently to its regular berth in the marina, its engine switched off some fifty yards away from the jetty. Weston-Super-Mare was as still as a grave at this time in the early morning. Just as well. Frankie and his mother's boat-owning cousin Reg, who was also Frankie's second cousin by some distance, didn't want any prying eyes to witness their movements as he manoeuvred his boat into the narrow space between two other moored vessels.

Reg stepped up onto the causeway, securing the boat in a practised manner. "Let's have the bags one by one," he urged quietly. Frankie complied, taking care not to drop any of the heavy bags into the dark water.

Reg gave Frankie a helping hand out of the boat before turning to the large, corrugated iron boathouse and unlocking the sturdy double doors. Frankie caught his companion by the arm. "I'll need those keys Reg. I know we're all family but I can't take any chances. I'm sure you'll understand." Reg grinned, then passed the keys to Frankie. "It's part of the deal and Nell's promised me enough readies to buy myself a thousand locks and keys. They're yours."

With the job completed to Frankie's satisfaction, they were on the road to Bristol within fifteen minutes, negotiating the village of Congresbury with only an early-morning milkman in sight. Temple Meads railway station was busier with post and newspapers being loaded from vans onto trolleys, then onto trains.

Frankie got out of the car. "Thanks for all your help Reg. We'll be in touch, soon." A quick handshake and he was away to the railway ticket office.

Frankie settled back on the dusty, hard-cushioned seat of the railway carriage, briefly taking in the faded, brown photographs of local seaside resorts, in their equally tatty frames, screwed to the carriage walls. His mind raced over the hectic activities of the previous twelve hours, his memory striving to recall even the smallest detail. It was, he reminded himself, the small details that often mattered on these occasions.

He shifted his position several times on the hard, unyielding cushions in a bid to seek out hidden comfort, then gave up the unequal struggle. The monotonous 'clackety clack' of the train's progress caused him to succumb sleepily to the dreariness of the carriage. His body ached for no apparent reason. "Could it be the tension of the previous few days? Could tension have that effect on your body?" Maybe it could. After all, he pondered, he felt like he had just been run over by a fucking truck! He dozed off, without resistance.

A sudden lurch in the train's progress jerked him fully awake. He looked at his watch. "Not long before I get to Paddington." His luck was still in. Nobody had checked his ticket to see if he had paid. "Too early, I suppose." The juddering of the train and the squealing of its brakes heralded the train's arrival at Paddington, the capital city's western outpost. Frankie pulled on the thick, brown leather strap, which with its holes, looked like a belt. He released the strap from the thick brass studs, allowing the window to open. He leaned out through the window, pulling at the handle. "Christ that's stiff," he muttered, but it eventually gave way and the door swung open.

He stepped down from the carriage, glancing along the platform. Not many passengers. He quickened his step to join them. Once clear of the station, he walked briskly, safe in the knowledge that Ladbroke Grove was literally just minutes away.

To his surprise, Hetty answered his push on the doorbell in seconds. A brilliant smile of welcome accompanied by a squeal of "Frankie," a brief embrace, a very long kiss, an even longer and slower fondle of her extremely feminine parts and minutes later they were enjoying the comforts of her extra-large bed, still warm and smelling fragrant from her earlier presence.

Whatever the adverts proclaimed for this particular make of bed, they had never ever mentioned the kind of erotic pleasures enjoyed that morning by the newly-reunited couple in Ladbroke Grove. Who knows? If they had, they might have enjoyed record sales.

"I really don't feel like cooking today. Fancy a spot of lunch out, say Italian around two o'clock?" said Hetty as she leaned over Frankie, running her hand through his already tousled hair. She kissed him several times on his cheek then longer, more purposefully on his lips. He rubbed his eyes, blinking in the daylight that slanted through the tall, arched windows.

"That sounds fine to me Hetty, but there's something that needs seeing to first."

Their lovemaking that followed was more leisurely than earlier that morning following his arrival from Bristol. While they relished the subtleties of their intimacy, Frankie felt unusually jaded. It must be the stress and tension brought on by the robbery and his getaway to London that made him feel so washed out. "Yeah, I do fancy an Italian right now," he mocked, the double meaning amusing them both as he swung out of bed and headed for the shower.

As they sat chatting at their restaurant table, enjoying the subtle herby aromas drifting in from the kitchen, a waiter bustled over, delivered their drinks and took their order. Hetty touched Frankie affectionately on his arm. "Remember I told you that I wanted to rent out one of the floors in my house – the floor above my own flat? Well I've agreed a deal with two people I know who are regulars at the pub where I work part-time." Frankie looked up from the card he had been studying, listing the forthcoming events at the restaurant. "Mmmm you have, have you?" What are these blokes like? Do you know much about them?" he queried.

She smiled. Was that a hint of jealousy from Frankie? she wondered. "Oh yes, I know them, but I don't think you'll have much to do with them other than to say good morning from time to time.

They're involved in a nightclub near Marble Arch. They seem nice enough and appear to be well-off for cash," she added. "They've also given me three months rent in advance, so I agreed."

Frankie replaced his spoon on the soup plate and wiped his mouth with his napkin. "A night club, you say? What's the chance of meeting them while I'm here in town?" Hetty pouted prettily. "It sounds like I might be getting some competition from a nightclub if you get your way." Frankie smiled warmly. "You never know do you, but the sooner I can meet them the better."

She patted his hand. "They're certain to be at the Lord Nelson tonight and although I don't normally go there when I'm not working, I'll make an exception in your case."

At around seven o'clock that evening, Frankie held the lounge bar door open for Hetty, noting the greetings of recognition from customers and staff alike as they entered. She made her way to an empty table. He soon returned from the bar with a large brandy and a gin and tonic. He sampled his drink, rolling the fiery liquid around his mouth, enjoying the flavour. Hetty added some tonic to her gin. "It seems like you and your two brothers have made up your minds to come and live in London." She took a sip from her glass. "When you do, I'll expect you to move in with me. Your brothers could have the ground floor flat, so you'll all be nice and cosy." She looked at him invitingly, awaiting his reaction.

He sat back, studying the attractive, auburn-haired woman sitting opposite. She's a good-looking woman, with a nice body and she's good in bed. Now she's asking me to move in with her! Jesus, I could do worse – a lot worse! "Yeah, you're right about me and the boys," he agreed out loud. "I've earned some big money lately and now I'd like to invest some of it in a business here in the Smoke." He paused, "and seeing you're offering a place to live, I suppose it's better than dossing down in the Salvation Army Hostel!"

She banged her small fist on the table. "Ooh! You can be so maddening at times Frankie Gallagher," she said aggressively, her face changing from mock anger to pleasure almost instantly. At that point, the door of the lounge bar opened and two men entered, glancing around as they made their way to the bar.

Their entry caught Hetty's eye. "There's the two chaps I was telling you about. Do you want me to call them over?" Frankie caught her arm as she prepared to get up from her chair.

"No, not just now. You didn't mention that one of them was black, not that it matters. I just like to be kept in the picture," he exclaimed. "Wait until they've been served and settled down – then you can say hello."

Frankie's attempt to dissuade her was wasted as the shorter of the two men caught sight of Hetty and made his way to their table.

"Hi there Hetty, howya doing babe?" he greeted her cheerfully, giving her a quick peck on her cheek, meanwhile looking expectantly at Frankie. She flashed the newcomer a dazzling smile. "Mal – this is Frankie. He's staying with me for a few days, but it could be permanent," she laughed, throwing him a quick glance.

Frankie stood up and shook hands. "Pleased to meet you Mal. Uh, where are you from – the United States?" Mal smiled wryly, shaking his head. "Shame on you, Frankie, Mal's from Canada," Hetty scolded.

Mal turned, beckoning the other man forward. "This big guy is Leroy – he's from Jamaica. He's a great guy to have around if there's any trouble." Leroy proffered his huge hand to Frankie.

With the preliminaries over, Mal rubbed his hands together briskly. "Do you mind if we join you, or would you two lovebirds rather be on your own?"

Frankie shook his head. "No, no – we don't mind Mal. As a matter of fact, there's something you may be able to help me with so pull up a chair." As they settled. Mal sat back waiting. "OK, shoot. What's on your mind?" Frankie leaned forward. "I understand from Hetty you and Leroy have a business stake in a club. Well, I'm looking to buy into that kind of setup when I move up here."

Leroy chuckled softly, the sound coming from somewhere near his boots. "Yeah man, we got a tight operation – real tight, but I don't see us wanting to cut anybody else in. No offence Frankie, but we don't know shit about you, right Mal?"

The Canadian nodded in agreement. "Leroy's right as far as we're concerned, but we're not really looking for another partner right now. But I have a close pal who owns a great club in the West End and I happen to know he's looking to take in a partner for the right amount of dough. Do you wanna meet this guy Frankie?"

Hetty took a blood-red lipstick out of her handbag and renewed the colour on her lips. "This might be the sort of deal you were look-ing for," she murmured as she studied the results of her handiwork in a small mirror. Frankie downed the remainder of his brandy. "OK Mal. Can I leave it to you to set up a meeting as soon as pos-sible with your pal?"

Mal nodded. "Sure. Will tomorrow be early enough for you – yeah? Right!" Hetty excused herself and made her way to the Ladies, while Mal studied Frankie, sizing up his new acquaint-ance. "Would I be right if I said you've done time in the pokey – you know, an ex-con?"

"What the fuck has that got to do with him," thought Frankie as he studied the man across the table. "I didn't know it was that obvious Mal," he said evenly." Why the interest?"

Mal drew his chair up closer to the table. "I'll leave it to Leroy to explain it to you. After all, it's his baby."

Leroy grinned, this time revealing a gold tooth Frankie hadn't noticed before. "It's like dis, man. We want to set up a new team because there's plenty of money out there just asking to be picked up. We bin looking for someone reliable – someone we can trust." He looked at Mal who motioned him to carry on. "Your woman Hetty knows what kinda game we got going, so you could be our man." Frankie was about to reply when Hetty returned.

"There's not only me." he told them. "My two brothers will be here too and we always operate as a team, so perhaps we could work something out."

Mal finished his drink and stood up. "Something this important should be discussed somewhere more private. Whaddya say to chewing this over at Hetty's place, say around nine o'clock. There's something I have to take care of first." With that agreed, Mal and Leroy left the pub.

Hetty snuggled up close to Frankie. "Go on. Tell me what you think about those two," she prompted. Frankie rubbed his chin reflectively before replying. "In the short time I've known them they seem OK. But as for joining up with them as a team, I'll let you know how I feel about them after our meeting tonight.

———————

"So what is it you have in mind Mal," asked Frankie as they settled down. The Canadian and Leroy lounged in a squashy settee on one side of the large, oblong glass-topped table. Its twin settee on the other side of the table was occupied by Frankie and Hetty.

"OK Frankie, let me explain a few things first to put you in the picture." Mal pulled a cushion on which his back rested into a more comfortable position. "During the war I was stationed with my Army division in England, near Epsom. I was trained as an explosives expert." He let the words sink in. "After that, I bummed around a bit, eventually settling down here in London. That's when I met Leroy." He glanced at his companion who took up the story.

"If you haven't already guessed, I'm a Jamaican and made it to Britain with my family who have now moved on. I stayed here and eventually teamed up with Mal."

Frankie gestured with his hand, halting Leroy's explanation. "OK, I get the drift. You mentioned explosives Mal. Are we talking about blowing safes, bank deposit boxes or anything similar?"

Mal nodded approvingly. "Jeez Frankie, you hit it right on the nose. Don't tell me you're in that line of work too?" Frankie looked at Hetty before replying. "I take it we can all trust each other here, right?" He looked across at Leroy who hadn't said too much. "Right Leroy?"

The Jamaican's face split into a huge grin – all white dazzling teeth! "Right Frankie, right!" he replied.

Being more talkative than his companion, Mal filled in the blanks. "I generally supply the brains, Leroy supplies the muscle. Sometimes, but not often, it's the other way around," he admitted, gesturing in Leroy's direction. "He's a martial arts black belt, Third Dan. If you know what that means, then you know he's a hard cookie." That big grin flashed again as Mal paused trying to gauge the effect by Frankie's face. "He's also got a lot of Yardie friends – so there's a big spin-off in the drugs racket too if you're interested."

At this point, Hetty excused herself, heading for the kitchen and a cup of tea. Mal meanwhile continued. "There's a job that's just crying out to be pulled and no explosives either, but we do need some fresh faces. Get the picture?"

Frankie calmly turned Mal's remarks over in his mind. "This job of yours," he said finally. "What kind of job is it that's crying out to be done?"

Mal punched a fist in the air. "Attaboy Frankie, now you're cooking!" he enthused. "This is how it goes down. There's this guy who's a regular at our club and the more he drinks, the more he blabs. Can you guess what he does for a living?" Mal didn't wait for Frankie's answer. "The guy drives a frigging security van picking up payrolls from banks and delivering them to big factories or offices. Can you believe that?" he roared.

Frankie leaned forward. "So how do you see our next move?" he asked. "You and Leroy can't hold up the van – you'd both be recognised – especially him," he said, indicating Leroy.

"You're darned right we can't," Mal conceded, while Leroy just grinned. "But this guy doesn't know you and your team, am I right? This is how I see it." At this point, Hetty reappeared from the kitchen but all three politely refused her offer of "something to drink." As she again retired to the kitchen, Mal continued outlining his plan. "I know the companies, the routes and the times he delivers the money. I also know where his wife and three small kids live." He sat back. "Over to you Leroy – this is your scene."

Leroy gave one of his deep chuckles. "This is where I act the real bad guy Frankie. Me and one of your team call at the driver's house wearing some kind of disguise – like you know, a stocking over the head or something – not original but effective. Then hold the family hostage. Mal brought a Polaroid camera back from the States the last time he was there. These cameras are great as they can produce instant pictures. So we take a few Polaroid pictures of them looking frightened and your man hands over the pictures to you at a pre-arranged coffee stop on the driver's route." He took a folded piece of paper from his pocket and opened it.

On it were printed the words:

DON'T SPEAK. WALK OUTSIDE WITH US.
DO AS YOU'RE TOLD. NO ONE WILL GET HURT'

He handed it to Frankie. "All you do is to walk over to the driver's table and show him the note and the photographs for him to read and see. I tell you man, when he sees his family and your note, he'll co-operate big time and get the guard in the van to open it up. You bet your arse he will!"

Frankie nodded his approval. "We can't clear the van out though in full view of everyone one in the coffee shop, so what then?" he queried.

Mal patted his hand. "No sweat man. We just drive the van to somewhere quiet, tie the two security guys up and take the money. Easy!

Frankie stood up, stretching his aching back. "I like the idea," he said, "and I think it could really work, but we're all taking a hell of a lot of things on trust, seeing how we've only just met each other."

He stood there, trying to gauge the effect his words of caution had on his two companions, both of whom looked as though they hadn't expected a brake to be applied on their hopes of joining forces with Frankie and his brothers. It was left to him to break the silence.

"Either way, I expect we could all do with a drink," he said. "I'll get Hetty to rustle them up."

As he crossed the lounge heading for the kitchen Mal exchanged glances with Leroy. "My gut feeling tells me we can do business with Frankie and his boys but whaddya think big guy?"

Leroy sat there, just rocking back and forth as he considered the options. "Well the man got form – and he's got style too. We sure need extra faces if we're going to pull off some of the jobs we've sussed out." He stopped his rocking. "I say we go with the flow man – and do the deal."

Hetty reappeared carrying a tray of drinks with Frankie not far behind her. As she placed the tray on the table, Mal stood up and held out his hand to Frankie. "I say we go for it Frankie. So if you feel that you can trust us, as much as we're prepared to trust you and your brothers, let's drink to the success of our new business."

A few handshakes all round and several stiff drinks later, Frankie made an important decision. "Things have changed a hell of a lot over the last twenty four hours, fellers. This means I'll need to move my operation to London right away – starting now!" He pointed at Mal. "You'll need to confirm the time the meeting is set for tomorrow with your pal in the West End – OK Mal?" The Canadian nodded. "Yeah, that's right." Frankie turned to Hetty. "And you, beautiful, you'll have to be nice to your new lodger and his brothers. It will be just like one big happy family!"

Chapter 18

The waitress had just placed Ian James' cup of coffee in front of him when Jeff Brown walked in to join his boss for the regular morning boost of Colombian coffee at the Kardomah Cafe, situated opposite their place of work in Lloyds Bank, Queen Street.

"Morning Ian," said Jeff, sitting down, meanwhile attracting the attention of the attractive blonde waitress. "How did your weekend go?" he enquired absently. He really didn't give a shit. He was much more interested in the blonde, who had given him the eye on several occasions recently. "It's all harmless fun," he mused. "After all, I'm happily married but I wouldn't mind giving her one if it was offered."

His colleague stared at his untouched coffee before answering. "I couldn't stop worrying about the damage to the vault. I also had the security chief from London head office chewing my ear off on the phone on Sunday." He sighed. "Then my wife kept nagging me all weekend, saying I was damaging my prospects of promotion. Yes, you could say that I had a really rotten break. And you Jeff?" The truth was, he couldn't care less either how Jeff's weekend went. He took a slow sip of his coffee as the waitress swayed over to their table to deliver a second cup, making sure Jeff was taking note of her curvaceous presence. He flashed her a lingering look, signalling 'message received'.

Jeff added two lumps of sugar to the steaming brew then dragged himself back to the small talk at the table. "I went to see a rugby match on Saturday and my wife had several friends over for dinner yesterday. We enjoyed ourselves so much, I forgot all about the problems at the bank."

"Lucky swine," thought his boss. Still it was one of the crosses to bear as the bank's senior officer. He finished his coffee and stood up. "Ready Jeff? It's time to be going." As they departed, settling their bill on the way out, Jeff used the opportunity to flirt again with the waitress, resplendent in her tan and white uniform. "I like the Kardomah," he thought as they crossed Queen Street to the bank – "especially the girls that work there."

The bank's electric alarm bell situated high above the ornate front entrance clanged just once as Ian James unlocked the heavy, carved wooden door. He entered, deftly switching off the system located in the front porch. His colleague unlocked the inner door and both men made their way to their respective offices. Several minutes elapsed before they emerged and headed for the main vault. A number of ledgers and substantial cash would be required by the cashiers once the bank opened for business.

Both men were required to use their individual keys to release the massive locks. They swung the heavy door open.

The manager switched on the interior lights, blinking in the sudden glare that flooded every inch of the vault. Reality dawned on them both as they stood there, transfixed. Ian James felt as if a giant hand had reached into his chest and tried to rip his heart out. He let out a low moan, followed by another, louder moan, then screamed out in anguish. "My God, oh my God, what's happened here Jeff? What's happened?" His eyes darted about rapidly, trying to make sense of the carnage that confronted him – the doors of each safe now gaping open, having given up their secrets to strangers. His colleague sagged back limply against the cool, steel-lined wall of the vault. "I don't believe it, I just don't," he gasped. As if by command, their eyes were drawn simultaneously to the ceiling, now clearly showing the damage sustained during the raid.

A hasty examination of the safes revealed the scale of the disaster. Jeff turned to his boss. "It looks as though they've cleaned them out, but if it's any consolation, they didn't bother with the safety deposit boxes." Ian James' face was ashen. Trembling with shock, he knelt, absently collecting some of the papers and cardboard wallets scattered on the vault floor. "I worried all weekend that something might go wrong," he mumbled, almost to himself.

Meanwhile Jeff, who had been examining the safes and deposit boxes, spoke over his shoulder to his distressed boss. "There's no damage to the safes so it looks as though they must have used keys to open them. Where the hell would they have got them from?" he queried. By now, Ian James was on his knees, incapable of intelligent thought or action, totally consumed by the disaster for which he knew he was ultimately responsible. Receiving no reply from his boss, Jeff spun around. "Hey Ian, for goodness sake. Snap out of it," he urged. Helping his still-shocked colleague to his feet, he steered him to the doorway. "Let's get to your office, Ian. We'll have to notify the police and Head Office. The sooner we do that, the better." Once there, the manager sat down, thankful for the support his chair offered.

His deputy looked at his boss carefully. "Do you feel you can cope with speaking to Head Office just yet, Ian?" he enquired. "If not, I'll do it after I've informed the police."

Ian James raised his head from between his hands, "Thanks Jeff, but I'm feeling a bit better now. I'll do it," he added, his face still ashen. As his deputy disappeared to his own office, the weekend warning of his wife that his promising career within the banking group might be jeopardised by the vault damage, returned like a bad dream. It undermined his attempts to compose himself enough to make the telephone call he was dreading.

Jeff reappeared in the open doorway. "The police are on their way," he said. "They told us not to touch anything in the vault, in case we disturb any evidence but it's a bit late for that, I suppose."

Ian James nodded his acknowledgement and reached for the telephone. He was about to make the worst phone call of this life. The shit really was about to hit the fan.

Detective Sergeant Dave Parker jumped up from his desk in Cardiff's police headquarters, walked briskly across the floor of the open-plan office to the enclosed room opposite, its glass panelled door and gold lettering proclaiming the name and rank of its occupant. He gave two short raps on the door and entered without waiting for any response.

"It looks as though we've got a bank job on our hands this morning George," he declared to the big man seated at the desk studying some papers from an open file. "Lloyds Bank in Queen Street has been turned over and the bank people say that whoever did it has cleaned out the safes in the main security vault. They sound as though they're in a proper state," he added calmly.

Even when sitting down, it was clear that Chief Superintendent George Davies was big – huge in fact, even by Cardiff copper's standards. At six feet four inches, weighing in at seventeen stone and possessing huge, hairy hands that should have been fitted to a bulldozer, his appearance alone was enough to scare the shit out of the local criminal community.

Yet despite his size and fearsome reputation, he was a talented pianist with a feather-like touch despite his pork sausage-like fingers and much in demand at the police social club.

He placed his hands on the desk, pushed his chair back and slowly elevated himself to his full height. His craggy features, topped by greying, wiry hair and massive bulk had long intimidated criminals of every colour in Cardiff's multi-racial society. Behind his back, but never to his face, his fellow officers of all ranks claimed that he could have starred in any Boris Karloff movie without the need for an audition.

"I take it you've alerted the scene of crime team, yeah? In that case let's go," he rumbled, his voice seemingly being delivered from somewhere near his boots.

They descended to the basement of the large, white Portland stone building that made up part of Cardiff's widely-admired parkland civic centre. They were soon on their way, dispensing with the strident bell that normally heralded the rapid progress of a police vehicle en-route to a job. "It might wake up some of the residents," observed Davies drily.

As their vehicle pulled up with a scream of tyres right outside the front of the bank, the two detectives alighted quickly and stepped into the bank to be greeted by Jeff Brown, who glanced briefly at their warrant cards. A young police constable doing duty on his regular beat in Queen Street was standing just inside the doorway.

The constable saluted as Davies and Parker approached.

"I want you to stay here and prevent anyone other than our team and bank employees from entering the premises," growled Davies as he acknowledged the constable's salute. "Meanwhile, let your watch sergeant know where you are and what you're doing."

Following brief introductions to Jeff Brown, the trio strode past several bemused early arrival bank staff, all of whom were excitedly comparing their views on what might have occurred over the weekend. Ian James met the newcomers at the door of his office – again brief introductions passed between them, before he led them to the now discredited security vault – its shame emphasised by the gaping doors of the individual safes.

The manager briefed the two police officers as fully as he could on the events as he knew them. He confirmed that he'd notified his head office who had instructed him to close the bank for at least twenty-four hours. Davies growled his agreement. "Good, that's just what we need. Our team is on its way," he added, breaking off to take a closer look at the safes, the ceiling and the general mess on the floor of the vault.

It was several hours before the two officers returned to Davies' office. As they sat opposite each other across the desk, he glanced up at his younger colleague. "Whoever pulled this job, they were a smart bunch of bastards. It had to be a team, otherwise the money would have been too heavy to move."

Parker consulted the copious notes he had taken during their questioning session at the bank then cleared his throat. "I contacted the officer in charge of road patrols just in case they are still out and about on the road, but I doubt it." He sat down at his senior officer's bidding.

He again glanced at his notes. "We can't be certain what time the job was pulled, especially as the night-watchman was given a 'mickey finn', so they could be well clear of the city by now. By the way George, I've checked with the Infirmary and they say he's none the worse for wear, other than a rotten headache."

Davies looked up at his colleague. "We won't rule him out of the equation just yet. This has all the hallmarks of an inside job and he was in as good a position as anybody to help the vermin that pulled this score."

The big man sat back in his chair, arms folded. "We can bottle this city up as tight as a drum – and if the money's still here, we stand a bloody good chance of lifting them," he said reflectively. Parker leaned forward to make his point. "Yeah, but that's it. If the money's still here! On the other hand, they could be a team from outside the city. Maybe London, Bristol or Manchester."

He paused, then accepted his bosses silence as permission to continue. "But if it is a local team there's only one lot that really fits the bill and that's the Gallaghers! None of the rest are smart enough to pull a stroke like this," Parker added, standing up to leave.

Davies delicately extracted a slim cigar from its case, lit it and blew a thin stream of smoke from his nostrils. "I want you and your boys to question all the usual garbage, but I want you to leave Frankie Gallagher and that cow of a mother of his to me. You could also have a quiet word with your pals in the Met to see if any of the teams in the Smoke fancied doing a bit of gardening on somebody else's patch." With that, he dismissed his younger colleague with a nod of his grizzled head towards the door.

Dave Parker closed the door, made his way to his desk and sat down. The list of possible suspects grew as names and faces flashed through his mind. He glanced at the list, headed by the Gallaghers. "It looks like it's going to be a busy week," he thought as he reached for the telephone.

He searched for and found the number of a local scrap metal dealer. He consulted his list as he waited for a response to his call. "If anything has moved above or below ground over the weekend, Jerry Walsh would know about it," reflected Parker, tapping his pencil impatiently on the desk. He heard a cautious 'hello' in the earpiece. "Hey, Jerry, it's Dave Parker. I need some information, right?" He received a grunt in reply.

"I take it you've heard about the job at Lloyds Bank at the weekend?" At first there was nothing but silence, then another grunt. It could have meant either yes, no or neither. "Did you get that, Jerry?" he asked. "Remember, you've already got one foot in the shit. You might as well put the other one in."

There was another pause, then came the quiet reply. "I'll be in touch soon, Mr Parker." With that, the line went dead. For Parker, that was enough from his number one snout for now. He consulted his list again confident he'd started the ball rolling. It wouldn't be long before some of the skittles started falling.

The news that a very big reward was up for grabs for any information leading to the arrest of the Lloyds Bank robbers caused every low-life informant in the city to go into overdrive. It wasn't only the local press and radio that went to town on the story – the Nationals also grabbed their share, giving extensive coverage to the biggest-ever raid staged in Wales.

George Davies and his team had spent a fruitless week following up spurious leads from snouts who had crawled out of the woodwork in a bid to cash in on the substantial reward. Despite the local feeding frenzy, Davies used his experience to sniff out the best leads from his more reliable underworld contacts while also banging a few heads, but still drew a blank. He called yet another meeting of his more experienced officers.

"Gentlemen, we have before us, a crime designed to exercise the more enlightened minds among us. Naturally, I include myself," he added, his craggy face devoid of any expression. He settled his bulk in his favourite chair and continued. "The precision with which the robbery was carried out would suggest the involvement of a team certainly from outside our manor – and from outside of Wales for that matter."

Many heads nodded in agreement, digesting his words.

"But equally so," the big man continued, "we could be looking for a local team that were lucky enough to take advantage of a series of circumstances that fell at the right time – for them, that is."

Just as many heads again nodded agreement at his alternative suggestion. Davies then stood up and glowered at the gathering. "But I don't give a flying fuck where they came from as long as we nail the bastards – and the quicker the better!"

He held his massive hands up, silencing the babble that followed. His jabbed a pork sausage finger at Dave Parker.

"I want you and two of your people to really put the pressure on the Gallaghers – and I mean pressure, whatever you have to do."

He paused to fish a handkerchief from his pocket, blew his nose noisily and returned the crumpled piece of cloth to his pocket. Parker took the opportunity to speak. "We've been giving those alibis a real going over. Yet despite the fact we suspect their alibis are pure fantasy, we haven't been able to prove otherwise, yet." Davies stared at his colleague and leaned forward.

"Just keep at them. Have another go at Nell. Scare the shit out of them, but come back and tell me that we've got something to go on. Got that?" he barked.

Another pork sausage prodded the air, this time in the direction of Detective Sergeant Jackson. "If it's a local team, somebody will find the money burning a hole in their pockets. Find out who needs a new pair of trousers." Davies stood up, his anger clearly evident.

"We're being paid to uphold the law in this city, so get out there and earn your bloody money!" Upon which, Davies turned on his heel and left.

Dave Parker waited for his boss to disappear then rose from his seat. The silence that prevailed when George Davies was speaking was replaced by a babble of voices as ideas and opinions were aired on the progress of the investigation.

"Let's have some hush here," ordered Parker. "You've all heard what the guv'nor had to say, so the teams of officers on the case will get separate briefings this morning at twelve o'clock."

He eased his buttocks onto the desk, grateful for its solid support. "This is an important investigation, very important, especially for the chief super. Everybody who's got an axe to grind will be on our backs to sort it out." He paused to clear his throat. "I refer to the bank people, our own people and the top brass in the Met who regard us as a bunch of amateurs from the sticks."

He rose, with one final point to make. "Don't let the boss down – or yourselves." He picked up his briefcase, left the room and headed for the toilets. "I've earned this one," he thought as he undid his fly buttons.

As the result of his efforts disappeared anti-clockwise down the china basin plug hole, he re-fastened his flies and reflected on their findings to date. "Not much," he thought as he returned to his office.

Reluctant as he was to admit the possibility, given his desire to nail the Gallaghers for the job, it really looked to be the work of an out-of-town outfit. Whoever they were, they were well organised and there was a lot of work ahead to put them behind bars. Unless that is, we get a real break.

He looked at his watch. "Time for a quick bite." He left his office and headed for the canteen, his stomach rumbling. "Come to think of it, I do feel peckish."

Chapter 19

The Gallaghers were expecting a lot of heat from the police – and they got it! George Davies and Dave Parker probed relentlessly in their efforts to find cracks in the family's alibis, but so far had drawn only blanks.

Davies drummed his thick fingers on the edge of his desk for what seemed like ages while Parker looked on impassively. Finally, the drumming stopped and the big man spoke.

"I've just gone over the statements of that bunch of misfits who claim they played cards from early Saturday afternoon until well into Sunday morning at Nellie Gallagher's house. Christ! They've seen too many Hollywood gangster films that lot!" He snorted in derision. "She even claims that not a single penny changed hands in all that time, the lying cow!"

Parker checked through the sheaf of notes he was holding. "It seems as if most, if not all the Gallagher boys were there and the other card players have confirmed their statements. It looks like they took it in shifts to play, which makes it even more likely they're giving us the run-round." He shook his head doubtfully. "It's just like pissing into a gale force wind and having it all blowing back in your face!"

He looked quizzically at his boss. "Why should anyone want to play cards for the best part of twelve hours? It could only be that they wanted to establish some kind of alibi. It just has to be that!" he exclaimed.

Davies slammed his fist on the desk. "You're damned right it has to be that, the bastards!" he stormed. "It's up to us to keep pressurising them until somebody coughs!"

He returned to drumming his pork sausage fingers on the desk – then stopped abruptly. "That Frankie Gallagher. It's no coincidence that he happened to be out of Cardiff when the bank was turned over. This job has got his stamp all over it!"

He stood up. "I want you to get one of your men down to the railway station again and see if they can find a ticket clerk that remembers Gallagher buying a ticket to London."

He walked around the desk. "Make sure he's got up-to-date photos of him, right? It might be a long shot seeing that the robbery took place more than a week ago, but we need to go over every angle again and again Dave if need be, so see what you can come up with."

Parker replaced his notes in a folder and stood up. "There's something that clearly stinks about these alibis George and I've got a good idea where that smell is coming from!"

The place Parker referred to was remarkably quiet by Gallagher standards. The iron discipline imposed by Nell, and faithfully observed by her family, paid dividends as officers investigating the bank robbery failed to detect any unusual spending patterns among the suspects topping their list. It was almost an anti-climax later that week when a cousin of the family was arrested.

He had been caught red-handed heaving a small safe out of a first-floor office window onto a mattress, placed on the pavement below to deaden the noise of the safe's impact.

Parker thought they had a break when they found the clerk that had sold Frankie his ticket to London the day before the robbery.

"Yes. He remembered the man in the photograph, alright! A flashily dressed cocky sod he was too! He had the nerve to complain about the high cost of the return fare to Paddington! Said it was only half that price to get there by bus. So I reminded him that it would take three times as long to get there. That shut him up!"

The ticket clerk's remarks seemed to rule out Frankie but doubts still gnawed away in Parker's mind. The fact he bought a ticket didn't mean he used it. The other Gallaghers didn't have the balls or the brains to pull a job like this one without Frankie.

Nor had he returned from his trip to London, that's supposing he'd gone to London – a holiday, Nell claimed. If he hadn't, where the hell was he hiding out now?

The bloody thing stinks! fumed Parker. So, had a mob from out of town been involved? It was just possible he reasoned. Right now, that was one big unanswered question.

Nell meanwhile telephoned her son in London, to brief him on the police activity in Cardiff. Hetty answered the phone.

"It's for you," she called out. "It's your mother." He emerged from the bathroom, towelling his damp hair. She handed him the receiver. "Hello Mam. Is everything quiet on the Western Front," he asked jauntily.

"Quiet? Quiet you say," she rasped. "That pair of bastards Davies and Parker have been crawling all over the place giving us a hard time – and they've come up with nothing. Absolutely nothing!" Frankie chuckled, as much with relief as with cockiness. "That's great news Mam. We want to keep it that way for…"

The words died on his lips as she cut him short.

"Joe and Danny are leaving here the day after tomorrow to meet up with you. I'm going to miss them Frankie – just like I miss you."

He could almost see the tears brimming in her eyes as her voice betrayed her feelings. "There, there now Mam," he soothed. "It's not as though we've gone away for ever – it's just for a while that's all. And don't forget, we've got that money for you to enjoy Mam. You really deserve it for what you've done for us – for all the kids."

Nell slowly wiped her tears away. Even the money was less of a consolation at the thought of losing her sons to the attractions of London. But her thoughts inevitably returned to the job in hand, her voice a little steadier now. "I've told the two boys to travel to Bristol by bus, then catch a train to Paddington from there. The rozzers have been watching the comings and goings at Cardiff Station for days, so it's best we don't use it. They should be in London by five o'clock, tea-time tomorrow. Are you going to meet them?"

Frankie cupped his hand briefly over the mouthpiece as he turned to face Hetty. "My brothers will be here on Tuesday around five o'clock," he told her before returning to the call.

"That's great news Mam, I'm dying to see them. Yeah, I'll be at the station and Hetty has arranged a smashing flat for them in the house. It's on the ground floor just below us."

He continued to sound cheerful and confident for her benefit. "Don't worry Mam. They'll be well looked after." He said his 'good-byes' and turned to Hetty.

"That's another piece of the jigsaw in place and I hope to finish it after tomorrow's meeting with Mal's night-club friend." He took her in his arms, softly kissing her neck and ears. "Things are definitely looking up," he reasoned as they cuddled. "Let's hope they stay that way." They certainly were! Frankie didn't know it then but the most gorgeous, sensuous woman he had ever seen was about to walk into his life!

Chapter 20

The moment that Frankie first set eyes on Sabra, she literally took his breath away as she swept past his seat at the bar, his tumbler of brandy forgotten. He had been informed that the drinking club located in a boutique-filled lane just off Oxford Street attracted its fair share of beauties – it was the main reason for its clients being there. But this woman truly was an exceptional beauty, exuding an animal-like sensuousness often present in women of Mediterranean or Middle Eastern origin, but less evident in their northern European sisters.

His eyes, along with just about every other man in range, followed her progress down the length of the bar. Her sensuous body contours moved rhythmically under her short, shimmering blue dress, clearly unhindered by even the wispiest of underwear. She selected a table next to the club's office door and sat, giving her an unrestricted view of the club and its occupants. Depending where the men were sitting, one or two had an unrestricted view of the space between the top of her thighs. Her legs were slightly parted, but infuriatingly, not parted wide enough.

The barman jiggled a couple of bottles, added ice cubes to a glass and delivered the clinking, pale orange-coloured drink to her table, for which he was rewarded with a 'thank you' touch of his hand and a flash of strong white teeth framed by a flawless olive-skinned complexion.

Ignoring the other men in the room, she glanced across at Frankie, beckoning to him with a red-tipped, slender index finger while patting the chair alongside her with the other hand.

He didn't need any second bidding. Without wondering "why me." he slipped off his bar side stool aware he was the most envied man in the club as he strolled over to join her. That was the first surprise. The second was when she spoke.

"Hello Frankie. My name is Sabra. Please sit down – here," she emphasised, again patting the seat of the chair alongside. "Christ, she's even more gorgeous close up," he thought as he complied. The fragrance of her perfume so tantalising just minutes before as she drifted by at the bar, subtly conquered any lingering uncertainty that here was a woman of undeniable elegance.

He offered her a cigarette which she refused with a slight shake of her lustrous hair. He returned the slim case to his pocket, studied her face briefly and then spoke. "How do you know my name? I've never been here before nor have I ever met you. I would have remembered you if I had, believe me."

She laughed softly, placing a manicured hand on his as she spoke. "The club owner, Maurice Green, told me he had arranged to meet you here to discuss some business. You were pointed out to me earlier when I came in." Her thick, black luxuriant hair cascading over her shoulders, gleamed with healthy radiance in the soft lighting.

"Even her skin seems to glow," thought Frankie, "especially the deep, tempting cleavage revealed by her off-the-shoulder dress barely held up by its thin straps.

She smiled, enjoying his appraisal of her. "Do you like what you see?" Her question was unexpected, surprising him. He smiled back. "Yes, on both counts. I do like what I see – and I expect it's not the first time you've been told that. And I am here to discuss business with Maurice, who I've never met either. A mutual friend told Maurice I've been looking to buy a stake in a club and I understand, he's considering taking on a partner, so here I am. It seems it's a nice, classy place." Again, that soft captivating laugh as she shook that mane of hair. "If you and Maurice do team up, that means I'll be working for you – along with twenty or so other girls, or didn't you already know that Frankie?"

The questions on the tip of his tongue were cut short as the door next to their table opened and two men emerged.

Maurice Green opened his arms in welcome, then proffered his hand, his face showing surprise at the power of Frankie's handshake. "That's some grip you have their Frankie. I see you've met Sabra and of course you and Mal are already acquainted." The second man also shook hands, clasping Frankie around the shoulders in welcome. Maurice stood in the doorway. "Come on in, both of you. You too, Sabra. There's a lot to talk about."

Maurice, below average height, slightly portly and Jewish, with dark slicked-back hair, sat behind a large, polished wooden desk, while Frankie and Mal opted for a big, comfortable leather settee. Sabra had little choice other than to sit on a chair the other side of the desk. From there, she crossed her long, slim suntanned legs, seemingly twice as long as her body, their length emphasised by a pair of strappy high heels.

Maurice prepared and lit a Cuban cigar, then took several appreciative puffs. "Nice club, eh Frankie? Of course you haven't met the girls, yet." Taking Frankie's nod as an affirmative, he carried on. "I hear good reports about you and your brothers from Mal and now you're living here in London, you'll be needing to get some business, right?" Another couple of puffs was followed by a thick plume of smoke aimed at the ceiling. Mal patted Frankie several times on his shoulder. "I told Maurice you're an OK guy and looking to score in London. This will be a real good opening if you two get it together, right Maurice?" Just then, Sabra uncrossed her legs and then crossed them again – slowly. "Was that for my benefit?" thought Frankie. "If it was, she's doing a great job!" For two hours, the talk flowed back and forth as the deal on the table was hammered out, subject to the books being cleared by Frankie's accountant.

The member's drinking club and its trio of musicians was a front for a high-class call girl operation, overseen by Sabra. At one time she had been Maurice's girl friend and from the start, had been instrumental in recruiting the girls.

At the moment though, she was unattached. "That's perfect timing," thought Frankie. All the girls were strictly vetted by Sabra and those that passed her scrutiny were given the once over by Maurice, who wasn't averse to testing the 'goods' first hand. All 'business' with their clients was conducted in one of half a dozen up-market flats owned by the company, who also provided dinner and drinks for the clients. The 'take' is split with the girls, who certainly prefer being introduced to the quality of client frequenting Maurice' club. As a bonus, they often gave the girls expensive presents in appreciation of the level of service provided. It certainly beat walking the streets punting for customers!

Sabra rose from her chair and with an 'it's been nice to meet you', wave to Frankie, swayed out of the office, her body contours working overtime. There was time for a celebratory brandy with his proposed new partner and "I'll see you soon Mal," from Frankie, who hurried from the office while trying to appear casual. Sabra was nowhere to be seen and a few words with the barman confirmed she had just left the club.

As he hailed a cab to head back to Ladbroke Grove and Hetty, he mulled over the events of the last few hours. If the books were OK, he now owned half share of a classy, well-organised London club. Not bad for a kid from the sticks! But as for missing out on seeing Sabra home and having that sensuous, tanned body of hers next to his in bed, doubts clouded his mind. "Christ, I must be losing my touch," he uttered louder than he intended. "What was that you said, Guv?" enquired the cabby, the question breaking through his private thoughts as he settled back into the leather seat. "Er, nothing, driver. Nothing at all," meanwhile reminding himself, "there would be a next time soon and I just can't wait to slip between those legs!"

True to form, Frankie didn't have long to wait. Having obtained Sabra's telephone number and address from Maurice, a telephone call was all that was needed to set up a date with Sabra at her flat. It was a meeting that would change the rest of his life.

———◦×◦———

Frankie paid the taxi driver off, turned and checked out the number of the building. Satisfied he had the right one, he walked up the wide stone steps to the large, shiny black-painted door, paused and studied the index fastened to the wall, before selecting a button and pushing it. Nothing happened for thirty seconds so he pushed it again. He was rewarded when a woman's voice issued from the small speaker above the row of names. "Yes?" He moved nearer the speaker at the base of the index.

"Hi, it's Frankie." There was a slight pause followed by aloud click of the front door lock. He pushed the door open, which closed behind him, walked across the hallway to the lift and pressed the shiny button. The lift doors opened and he thumbed 'number 8' for the penthouse suite. The lift rose smoothly and rapidly before easing off and stopping. The doors slid open and he crossed the hall to the penthouse front door which was slightly ajar so he went straight in.

The rooms were palatial, and tastefully decorated with Italianate plaster-work ceiling coving and a matching central ceiling-rose from which an expensive chandelier hung. The quality of the furniture matched the decor. Frankie gave a low whistle of appreciation as he absorbed his surroundings. "Jesus, this place must cost a bomb. I wonder who pays for it?"

A voice called out from one of the corridors leading off the main lounge. "Pour yourself a drink Frankie. I'll be with you in just a moment." He glanced around the room, his eyes alighting on a tray of drinks sitting on the carved wooden sideboard. He helped himself to a generous measure of Brandy. As he sampled his drink, still fascinated by the display of money on show, he became aware of a movement behind him.

She stood there on the thick pile carpet, her mane of dark hair tousled and damp, looking even more ravishing than he recalled, a huge pink bath-towel wrapped loosely around her steamy damp body. Her perfectly-shaped generous lips parted in a sultry smile. "Hello Frankie," her voice was low and sensual. His intention of playing it cool vanished as his eyes devoured her.

He put his drink down and pulled her toward him, tugging at her towel until it fell to the floor. The sight of her fully-exposed body without even the flimsiest of underwear to defend her against his lust sent his feelings of desire into overdrive. Embracing her roughly, he explored her lips and tongue with his, while his eager trembling hands caressed, felt and squeezed her beautifully poised, firm-tipped breasts, before switching his exploration to the warm, moist valley between her thighs.

She slipped her hand down inside his trousers, revelling in the sensation as she gripped his hard swollen flesh. She fumbled with her other hand, unfastened his belt and eased his trousers and underpants down to his ankles. "Do it! Do it!" he said forcefully as she gripped his pulsating penis with both hands.

She licked the bulbous, shiny dome, sending waves of sexual ecstasy coursing through his loins, before thrusting it deeply into her mouth. She moved her head rhythmically, bringing him closer to a bursting climax with every stroke.

The sudden, unexpected sound of the front door being unlocked startled them into activity. They pulled away from each other as Sabra strode into the lounge, several shopping bags in hand.

Her look of surprise changed to one of amusement as she threw back her head with a peal of laughter.

"Hello Frankie. My goodness, I see you've already met my twin sister Eva. She's staying with me for the weekend." She threw the shopping bags on the settee and walked over to her sister, as Frankie hastily covered his embarrassment with his trousers. "So what do you think of Frankie, sis?" she asked as she kissed her softly on one cheek. Eva stooped and retrieved her towel, holding it in front of her nude body in a fun show of modesty. "Well, he's very cute – and he's got a really great way of introducing himself!"

In the moments that elapsed since Sabra's unexpected appearance, Frankie recovered some of his composure. "Christ that Eva's some woman – all woman! Now, unbelievably, there are two of them, or to be more precise, she's Sabra's identical twin sister!" Eva turned to Frankie, pulling her towel tighter. "Would you excuse me while I put something on?" Without waiting, she left the room, her rear end swinging. "Now where have I seen that before," he thought. His attention soon returned to Sabra, still highly amused at their antics.

"That was some stunt to pull on me wasn't it?" he chided her gently. He held her hands, drawing her closer. "I got your telephone number from Maurice and you told me that you'd be in when I called."

She again kissed him softly. "I'm sorry Frankie, but I was held up in town. Still, you seemed to be occupied when I arrived."

He laughed at the memory. "That's the strangest thing that's ever happened to me, but I must say that I did enjoy it."

She looked at him sideways. "I gathered that by the look on your face – and the size of your dick! I'm quite impressed."

He shrugged apologetically. "Identical twins, for Christ sake! How is anybody supposed to tell you apart?" Sabra kissed him full on the lips, slow and lingering, before breaking off and looking into his eyes. "Eva has a birthmark at the top of her right thigh – right next to her fanny. If I'd arrived ten minutes later, you would have found that out for yourself!"

She took his hand, led him across the lounge, down the corridor and into one of the three bedrooms. She turned to Frankie. "You told me when we first met that you liked what you saw. I think it's time you saw the rest of me." She slipped out of her dress and removed her underwear. Allowing several seconds for him to again marvel at the perfect contours of her nude body, her probing hands encouraged him to remove his own clothes. A voice from the corridor caused them to turn, revealing Eva, framed in the doorway. She too was totally naked. "Don't start without me," she breathed coquettishly as she joined them, allowing Frankie to gather them both in his arms. The effect on him was only too evident as his rock-hard erection strained to discover their havens of eroticism.

Never since his baptism into the adult joys of sex as a teenager had he ever seen such curvaceous, magnificently-proportioned breasts, crested with large brown nipples, now responding to gentle persuasion from his mouth and his sensitive fingers. Sabra grasped the stem of his penis while Eva gently massaged the soft fleshy dome until his fluid dampened her fingers. It was time for them to move onto the king-size bed that dominated the room.

Frankie lay on his back while Eva eased herself slowly onto his chest, straddling her thighs either side of his upturned face. She used her fingers to expose more of her vagina, into which Frankie inserted his writhing tongue as far as he could. Sabra meanwhile sat straddled across his thighs. She lowered herself onto his body and guided his erection between her thighs, coaxing him to penetrate her, then probing ever deeper. She moved up and down as he gradually timed his thrusts to match hers. As the tempo of all their movements quickened to near frenzy, the twins cried out as one, gasping in exultation as both climaxed within seconds of each other, their overheated bodies glistening with perspiration. Sabra shifted her position, easing herself away from his body before rolling sideways onto the wide bed, her lust sated – for now.

Eva dismounted from her pleasurer and kissed him on the mouth. "Now I want to finish what we started earlier, when we were interrupted," she whispered softly in his ear. Switching her attention to his lower body she grasped his penis, still remarkably swollen and horny and slowly thrust it deeply into her mouth while simultaneously masturbating him firmly. Unable to contain himself any further, his sperm erupted into her mouth, oozing from her lips as he cried out in pain and pleasure.

Frankie's introduction to the twins and their sexual proclivities was over for the time being, but the future promised many more such explorations of their lustful cravings to come.

Chapter 21

The arrival of his two brothers in London and the Gallagher's association with Mal and Leroy, plus his new partnership with Maurice Green, moved Frankie's life along at a rapid pace.

His relationship with Sabra intensified as his commitments at the club demanded more of his time. Meanwhile, Hetty remained blissfully unaware of her boyfriend's unfaithful behaviour. The occasions when she questions why he carries traces of other women's perfumes on his clothes are explained away by his unavoidable contact with the girls at the club. As for Sabra's expensive taste in perfume, he solved that simply by buying Hetty the very same brand. Her use of it easily masked his regular liaisons with Sabra.

But with Eva waiting in the wings, his infidelities didn't end there. They just carried on where he and Eva had left off from their first 'mistaken identity' encounter. Eva never gave a second thought to either her twin sister Sabra's feelings for Frankie, or for her husband, given his incurable weakness for other women.

Frankie knew her husband Larry – a diamond merchant in Hatton Garden, who was also a member of Maurice's place, The Kings Club. Eva told him Larry was screwing his way through the entire line-up of girls in alphabetical order! So far, he had reached 'M', the bastard!

But Frankie needed to turn his attention to the business of 'business!' The first security van hold-up went so smoothly, it sent the wrong signals to the newest Gallagher arrivals.

Joe and Danny were cock-a-hoop at their success, comparing their money haul with the 'London's streets are paved with gold' fallacy.

It took Mal's words of caution to bring them back to earth. "We wuz lucky to get a break like that," warned the Canadian. "That driver guy being such a big blabbermouth – it made our job a lot easier," he said with a shake of his head.

"Believe me, the next ones are gonna be a lot tougher."

Mal's wisdom was well-founded. Three more security van hold-ups and several small bank robberies later, they counted the cost of a change in tactics. A total of seven security men had been injured – some seriously, during the raids, either defending the payrolls or protecting the banks.

The gang had initially used pickaxe handles to terrify or subdue any opposition. These had now given way to sawn-off shotguns carried by Leroy and Joe. A blast from a shotgun into the ceiling of the bank commanded instant obedience from the customers or staff. Only the security men had ever attempted to prevent the robberies – and paid for their courage with a savage beating.

Frankie had always expressed his concerns to Mal over the use of firearms on the jobs they pulled and the prospects of anything going wrong with guns being involved worried him.

"One of these days something might go wrong and we could end up on a murder charge," he said, his concern clearly evident.

Leroy, sensing criticism of his methods, joined in.

"Hey Frankie, you're taking the whole thing too serious, man. We just show them the guns to frighten 'em. That's all."

In a surprising shift of loyalty, Joe backed Leroy's words. "It sounds to me like you're going a bit soft, Frankie. Like Leroy says, the guns are just to put the frighteners on people – I think we should keep them."

From Joe's forceful tone it sounded like the first real signs of dissent between the Gallagher brothers. It later prompted Frankie to check out Danny's views on Joe's apparent shift of support, when he and Danny discussed the matter in private over a drink.

Danny had some difficulty looking his brother in the eyes. "You won't like this," he began hesitantly, "but Joe and Leroy have been quietly branching out trying to get a piece of the action on the drugs scene." Frankie's sharp intake of breath made Danny look up. "Perhaps you've been too busy to notice, what with other things at the club," he said pointedly.

Frankie's face flushed with irritation. "Perhaps you've been too busy spending money to let me know there's been a problem with Joe!" he snapped. "Anyway, what the hell has it got to do with anybody what I do at the club as long as it doesn't get in the way of business," he snarled, jumping up from his seat.

"As for Joe and Leroy getting cosy with each other, that could be serious. Does Mal know about this – does he?" He paced the room. "We don't want to go pissing in somebody else's pool. That could bring us real trouble!" He turned round on Danny. "Where the fuck is he now, anyway?" he demanded.

Danny shrugged his shoulders. "He went out about half an hour ago – with Leroy, who said they had someone to see."

Frankie resumed his pacing of the room. "I'll bet they did, the idiots!" He stopped abruptly in mid-stride." I don't want Joe or anybody else from the family getting mixed up with drugs! There's all kind of filth out there pushing that crap onto the streets – and those that will knife you just to get their daily fix," he fumed. "I'm not going to let that happen to us! I'm buggered if I will!"

It was a vow that came too late. Even as the two brothers were discussing the thorny issue, Leroy and Joe had already fallen foul of a notorious Chinese Triad gang. When they tried unsuccess-fully, to hijack a consignment of heroin belonging to the Wo Shing Wo – one of the four main Triad gangs operating in Britain – their days were numbered. They escaped unhurt on this occasion, but their cards were now marked. The Chinese 'chop squads' would be looking for them and they would have to watch their backs. Constantly!

Badly shaken by Danny's disclosures, Frankie called in at Mal's club intent on clearing the air. He found the Canadian sitting in his office looking over some figures in a ledger.

"Hey there Frankie," Mal greeted him, in some surprise. "What's up, man?"

Frankie didn't beat about the bush. "What the fuck's going on behind my back Mal, between Leroy and Joe – and maybe you too for all I know!" he stormed, glaring at the seated Canadian.

Though completely taken aback by Frankie's outburst, Mal remained composed. Outwardly, at least." Take a seat Frankie, slow down and tell me what's bugging you."

Frankie repeated the main points of his conversation with Danny and the near-miss experienced by the pair with the Chinese Triads. "For Christ's sake, Mal. Getting on the wrong side of them through fucking around with drugs could mean us all ending up dead!"

Mal rose out of his seat, walked around his desk and stood facing Frankie. "When we first agreed to join forces, I told you there was some action on the drugs scene if you wanted it. You didn't. So there I am thinking that Frankie's not interested. OK!" He poured himself a drink, putting the stopper back into the bottle when Frankie refused.

Mal retreated to the chair behind his desk. "There are plenty of customers in my club who like to do drugs. Mostly, they try to bring their own into the club." He took a swig from his glass. "My bouncers keep them out if they're carrying, so the only way they can enjoy themselves is to buy their shit from me – or Leroy. Get the picture Frankie?"

Although his anger had subsided somewhat, Frankie was still upset that he had been sidelined by the others, including his own brother! "OK, I can see it from your point," he conceded. "But why is Joe involved without me knowing about it?"

By now, Mal was relaxed, no longer put on the defensive by Frankie's outburst. "I guess Joe was looking for a bit of action and Leroy asked him to help out. Joe just didn't want to upset you. That's all there is to it."

But that wasn't all there was to it. Three weeks later, Triad 'chop squad' members caught up with Joe in Queensway and dished out their particular type of retribution.

Using very large, razor-sharp melon knives, they hacked through Joe's bicep and calf muscles, rendering him crippled and in excruciating pain, writhing helplessly on the pavement as passers-by of Chinese origin walked by, frightened to go to his aid. They could have been the next victims if they had.

Police and an ambulance eventually arrived, but everybody questioned by the police had seen absolutely nothing – or anyone involved.

Joe had failed to give the Triads sufficient 'face' or respect when he tried to hijack their heroin. Now, repayment of his debt to them would be his legacy for the rest of his life.

The news of Joe's run-in with the Triads and his punishment soon reached a distraught Nell. She immediately travelled to London where she was met at Paddington Station by Frankie and Danny. She spotted her sons well before she reached the ticket collector. It was an emotional reunion.

As they made their way to the hospital by taxi, Frankie tried to allay his mother's fears. "Joe's not going to die Mam," he said gently "He took a severe beating and he's got some really nasty injuries, but the hospital people say he's going to pull through OK."

Despite Frankie's assurances, Nell sobbed fitfully, fearful she was about to lose yet another son. As it was, he would be a cripple for the rest of his life.

"I knew nothing good would come of any of you moving to London, Frankie," she said tearfully, her shoulders sagging under the stress of it all.

At the hospital, Nell met the surgeon who operated on Joe. He urged her to have faith in her son's will to recover. "He's a very strong young man, Mrs Gallagher and if anyone can cope with his injuries, it's your son."

As they walked out of the ward, the specialist stopped and turned to Nell. "Do you believe in God Mrs Gallagher?" he asked. "For if you do, then pray for your son. He'll never be the same active person, but he will be alert, alive and able to enjoy the company of his family and friends." The surgeon took Nell's hands in his. "After what he's been through, that's a reward worth achieving."

Several days later, having put his mother safely on the train at Paddington en-route to Cardiff, Frankie and Danny discussed the events of the last few days over a beer at the Lord Nelson pub. "I dunno about you Danny but I've been really pissed off over Joe getting involved in the drugs scene with Leroy – and now look what's happened! Our kid gets himself chopped by some Chinese bastards and now he's going to be a bleeding cripple for the rest of his life!"

Danny stared into the glass of beer he held, unable to look Frankie in the eye. It didn't go unnoticed by his elder brother. "What I can't understand Danny is that you knew Joe was fucking around with drugs and yet you didn't tell me," he said bitterly, his accusation ringing in his brother's ears. "If you had, this whole business with Joe and the Chinks would never have happened!"

Danny's face reddened, the truth hurting. "Joe said not to mention anything to you," he said lamely, "And I suppose you were getting a backhander from him for keeping quiet," snorted Frankie, brushing aside his brother's excuse. "I've had it up to here working with you and Joe," he spat out angrily. "I've always tried to play it straight with you two and all you can do is to kick me in the teeth."

He banged his glass of brandy onto the table and stood up. "I've got some unfinished business to discuss with Sabra – I'll see you later." With that, he stormed out of the pub without glancing back.

Danny sat there, stunned by Frankie's angry outburst. "I suppose he's right. I've been a daft bastard just for the sake of a few hundred quid," he brooded. His shoulders sagged. "I only hope that this business about Joe doesn't cause us to split up. If it does, it's my fault – and Mam will never, ever forgive me."

Chapter 22

The accountant sitting opposite finished jotting down some figures on the pad in front of him, looked up and pushed the pad across the desk towards Frankie.

"That's what you're worth in readies, give or take a thousand quid. I can give you the exact figure if you can give me a little more time."

Frankie pulled the pad closer, noting the scribbled figures. "So you reckon it's about three hundred and fifty thousand quid as things stand." He shook his head slowly. "It's not as much as I thought. Does that include whatever I get for cashing in my share of the club?"

The accountant smiled, looking at Frankie over the top of his spectacles. "No, no, no. Erm no! You could add on another fifty grand if Maurice pays you back what you put in – and I'm sure he will." He sat back in his chair studying Frankie. "It's a lot of money to have lying around loose. Are you going to invest it?"

Frankie pulled several folded sheets of paper from the inside pocket of his jacket and tossed them onto the desk. "These are details on a number of properties in Spain – on the Costa del Sol and the Costa Blanca." He leaned forward, his arms on the desk. "I've been thinking about moving abroad lately. I need to get out of London, or Britain even and Spain seems a good place to start looking."

The accountant picked up the papers and studied them for a while. "Interesting, yes. They seem interesting. Certainly worth a visit to check things over." He again smiled. "You know, there's a lot of, how shall I describe them, gentlemen who have taken off for Spain because things have become too hot for them here in Britain. But of course, you're not in that situation are you Frankie? And it's a big step to take, you know, a new country, a new language?"

Frankie grinned at his suggestion. "No way. Sure, everything will be new, but I'll cope most times and when I can't, I've got the money to help me along."

The following afternoon, Sabra lay on the bed contented as Frankie busied himself fixing them a couple of drinks. "Where on earth do you get your stamina from, Frankie Gallagher?" she called out drowsily. Their lovemaking had been exceptionally passionate, leaving her stomach and thigh muscles totally drained of energy.

Frankie returned with the drinks, placing them on the bedside table. "Why worry, as long as I can keep going at it," he responded. He settled down beside Sabra, conscious of the sensuous fragrances that exuded from the pores of her moist body. It was a distinct, personal aura that he could detect even with his eyes closed.

They lay there for several minutes in silent contemplation before Frankie spoke. "How do you fancy the idea of living in Spain?" His question was as puzzling as it was unexpected. Sabra stiffened, turning her head on the pillow to face him.

"Did you say how would I like to live in Spain," she queried. "I don't know. I've never given it a thought. Why do you ask?"

Frankie sat up, stretching across her for his drink. "It's something that appeals to me and I'd like to find out if it's as good as it sounds – endless months of sunshine, a slower pace of life. It's something I could easily get used to," he said wistfully.

Sabra reached out, her hand on his arm. "What's brought this on Frankie? I know that business with Joe has upset you and you may be feeling a bit down, but it's a big step to take, isn't it," she murmured, pulling him toward her.

He replaced his glass, then took her in his arms. "I've been to see my accountant and he says I'm pretty well placed for cash so that's not a problem. Anyway," he added, "if it wasn't for you, I would have probably given London the elbow by now." He kissed her gently. "If I do decide to go, say you'll come with me, say you will," he urged.

Sabra looked into his eyes, searching for signs of his love and fidelity for her. "Well, I don't have much in the way of family here in London except for my sister Eva. Then there's the club and my job of course, but surely it will be a much bigger wrench for you to leave Britain, wouldn't it?"

He nodded. "You mean my mother of course and she would be really upset, but I have my own life to live. I'm sure she would eventually understand," he said impassively. He jumped up from the bed. "I'm gonna have a shower. I've got some business to talk over with Maurice and you might as well come along, especially as it involves you."

His meeting with Maurice went smoother than expected. After all, he was a worldly guy and understood why younger men got itchy feet. He indicated their partnership could be dissolved and a satisfactory deal on the cash agreed. Maurice would also be losing his 'lieutenant' in charge of the girls, but he could always promote another, what the hell! "Mind you," he reminded Frankie, "that's always supposing that you and Sabra do leave town. It hasn't happened yet."

Mal and Leroy were a different proposition. Leroy and Frankie's relationship had soured ever since Joe's run-in with the Triads, so Leroy assumed Frankie was pulling out on his account. Mal meanwhile, felt he was being left in the lurch as far as the 'gangs' business was concerned. He was going to be left short-handed, even assuming Danny was going to stay in London if Frankie left for Spain. It was a question of 'wait and see."

With the idea of Spain now occupying, Frankie's mind, he and Sabra were soon on their way to Valencia on their fact-finding mission, having decided that the Costa del Sol was too full of crooks spending their ill gotten gains, as Frankie jokingly put it. The first step had been taken.

Arriving at Valencia airport around midday they cleared Customs, collected a rental car, took a look at their road map and were on their way. The early Spring sunshine beat down from a cloudless sky, making Frankie grateful he had chosen to wear a lightweight suit.

Even so, his jacket soon came off, despite the gentle breeze that carried the pleasant but unknown aromas of a fruit and flower-laden Mediterranean country.

Being a well-travelled person, Sabra had dressed for the occasion, her light cotton top and cotton skirt being ideally suited for the conditions. They negotiated their way through the outskirts of Valencia, a sizeable city and capital of the Valencian province, and despite a few missed junctions found themselves on the coast road, heading south-west to their destination.

Frankie concentrated on the uncertainties of driving on the 'wrong side' of the road while Sabra excitedly pointed out the glimpses of sandy stretches and rocky coastline washed by the blue-green waters of the 'Med'. It was a glorious day.

Twenty minutes later, they stopped at a roadside cafeteria for a break providing them with an opportunity to check their road map and more important, their Spanish currency. Their belief that 'everybody in Spain speaks English' was shattered when they found themselves confronted by Spaniards who, unbelievably, only spoke Spanish! Eventually, by pointing at faded photographs of the cafe's offerings and plenty of dazzling smiles from Sabra who was the focus of attention of the men at the bar, they got what they wanted – a very large brandy and two cups of strong coffee. Then it was back on the road again.

"How far do you reckon it is to Calpe from here?" asked Frankie, his eyes glued to the road as other drivers overtook him on hairpin bends going like bats out of hell!

As Sabra scanned the map, a signpost loomed up stating 'Cullera 3 km'. "Try working out the distance from here then," he urged as they bounced along the uneven road surface.

"You'll have to bear with me Frankie," she replied as she struggled to keep the map steady enough to read. "The printing is quite small so it's not too easy to make out, but for a start we don't go left down to Cullera. That's right on the coast. We need to stay on this main road for Calpe as I think it's about another 80 km or so from here," she said, adding somewhat hopefully, "I think that's about 50 miles."

Having digested that piece of information, Frankie lapsed into silence as he concentrated on his driving, while Sabra inwardly marvelled at the diverse agricultural landscape with its quaint farm buildings – so vastly different from the hustle and bustle of the grimy city she had recently left behind.

Little more than an hour later, having put Gata de Gorgos behind them, they saw the road signpost that lifted their spirits which read Benissa – Calpe.

It was then, as they swept downwards from the village of Benissa towards Calpe, that they were confronted by the sight of the massive Peñon de Ifach – a huge rocky headland jutting out to sea shaped like the Rock of Gibraltar to which it is often compared. It stood guard over the small fishing port of Calpe as it had done for many centuries.

"We can't be very far away now from our hotel – it's on this stretch of road somewhere." Minutes later, as they rounded a curve, the hotel stood less than a hundred yards further on.

A low, farmhouse style building with red-tiled roof and several shady arches typical of the area and featuring several mature palm trees, it was a welcome sight as they pulled off the road and parked on the tarmac near the large, double doors. Collecting their bags and locking the car, they walked into the cool, shady reception area, its intricate mosaic-tiled floor a masterpiece of statement to the devotion of its designer. Palm fronds were everywhere in their large terracotta pots.

A smiling, middle-aged woman appeared seemingly from nowhere.

"Buenos días, Señores," she greeted them. "Er, do you speak English?" asked Frankie uncertainly. The lady, her dark hair tied back, smartly attired in black with a crisp white apron, again smiled. "Yes sir, I speak a little English. Have you a reservation?"

Frankie took Sabra's bag and along with his own, placed them on the floor. "Yes, our travel agent made them in the name of Gallagher."

She studied the register. "Ah yes, Gallagher. I have it here. Pablo!" she called out, following which a young Spaniard in his teens appeared and picked up their bags.

"¿Que numero, Mama?" he enquired.

"Numero doce," she replied.

"You are in room 12, Señor Gallagher. If you let me have your passports and sign the register, Pablo will show you to your room."

Pointing out the lounge and dining room first, the youngster led them up the wide, tiled staircase to the first floor. He opened the door and took their bags in, placing them on a stand at the foot of the double bed.

"Here are your keys," he said in English. "I learnt to speak the language in school," he offered in anticipation of their next question. "My name is Pablo. If you need anything, just press the button over there," he said pointing to its position on the wall. "If you need to phone, pick up the receiver and give the number to Mama It will take a few minutes to put you through."

"So far, so good," thought Frankie. "Here Pablo, that's your name, yeah?" He pressed a small denomination note into the youngster's palm. Pablo thanked him profusely, handed him the keys and left, closing the door behind him.

Sabra sat on the bed, bouncing up and down. "It's nice and soft," was her verdict. "And the linen is lovely and clean – it smells of fresh air," she added. Frankie cupped her face in his hands and kissed her. "Why don't you have a shower while I phone the estate agent I've arranged to meet at the hotel?"

Sabra stood up and went over to the open window, breathing in deeply as she did so.

"Just smell that air and look at that view. It's wonderful, don't you think Frankie?" He moved up behind her and slapped her bottom. "Yeah, it's great. Now strip off and have that shower." He took his shirt off, the heat of the day sending trickles of perspiration running down his bare chest.

He watched her, fascinated as ever by the perfect contours of her naked, olive-skinned body. "I just can't wait to have our first session in Spain, but it'll have to wait for a while," he told her. "But keep it on ice for me."

He turned, looking for the telephone. Ten minutes later, Sabra emerged from the shower, still wet, her body glistening. She embraced him, kissing him softly, repeatedly. He stopped her, putting his hand over her lips. "Let me tell you this first. I got hold of the agent. OK? He's English, so no problems there. He said he'll meet us at the hotel around eight o'clock and take us out to dinner."

Sabra explored his lower body with her probing, restless fingers. He continued with some difficulty. "He said he'll also pick us up in his car tomorrow morning at ten o'clock and show us around half a dozen properties in the area. How does that seem to you?" Sabra undid his belt, easing his trousers down.

"And how does this seem to you? she asked huskily as she sank to her knees.

Chapter 23

"Well Mr Gallagher, do any of the properties we've looked at so far match up to what you're looking for?" The British estate agent looked expectantly at the couple seated opposite, praying there was a sale in the offing. It was after all, an expensive property and the commission would help to pay off his new Mercedes.

Frankie glanced at Sabra who was still busy looking through literature and photos of the numerous villas they had visited during the last few days. Now they sat in small cafe, enjoying a cooling drink and relaxing, while considering their options.

"I think that's the best one we've seen," said Sabra pointing at one located in the San Jaime estate near the former fishing village of Moraira.

Frankie nodded his head in agreement. "Yeah that's the one alright. In fact, I think we'd already taken a fancy to it," he assured the agent, whose slightly worried 'business' look was replaced by a beaming smile – all teeth on display. "I think you've both made a splendid choice, probably the best villa we have on our books. "It really is a magnificent place in a superb location overlooking the sea."

He quenched his thirst with a mouthful of carbonated water – "I never drink alcohol while I'm working' – and started collecting his sales literature. "You'll need to come down to my office in Calpe to sign some papers and place a deposit on the property you've chosen. Shall we go when you've finished your drinks?"

he suggested. "Now's a good a time as any," agreed Frankie "and while we're there I'd like to discuss one or two additions such as a security fence and a new wall by the swimming pool."

As the pair later relaxed on the shady terrace of a restaurant overlooking a nearby beach, the setting sun cast vivid orange highlights slanting across the horizon. Sabra embraced Frankie, pulling him closer. "This is a beautiful area," she murmured "and although I was reluctant at first to consider leaving Britain, I'm certain we'll be very happy here – and I've fallen in love with the villa." They kissed tenderly at first, then with increasing passion only to be interrupted by the sound of a polite cough. "Excuse me senor, but you table is ready – this way please." They linked arms, following the waiter to their table "Saved by the bell," grinned Frankie. "Another two minutes and I would have been inside your knickers!"

The following day, the estate agent confirmed it would be a further six weeks before all the relevant paperwork was prepared for their visit to the Notario and completion of the purchase of their new home. Their flight from Valencia to London later that day ended a hectic five day spell during which Frankie's determination to leave Britain was about to be realised.

There was much to do as preparations for their departure gathered pace. Yet the real reason for his five day absence was still completely unknown to Hetty. The expression 'thick as thieves' certainly took precedence as Danny, Mal and Leroy kept the truth of his visit to Spain – and more important – his close relationship with Sabra from his 'girlfriend'. As correspondence arrived at Hetty's house post-marked Spain, Frankie was forced to break the news to Hetty of his impending departure from Britain.

She was stunned by his revelation and further shattered when he told her he would not be taking her with him. "Why, oh why?" was the anguished question for which she repeatedly demanded an answer. Her tear-stained face and hollow-eyed look were testimony to a woman in torment as she searched for an explanation. "I know you were very bitter and upset when Joe was attacked but why should that affect us now," she cried. "Even if you have fallen out with Mal and Leroy, it's no reason to run away – especially from me," she pleaded. "We love each other Frankie – we do, don't we –

and I'm prepared to go wherever you want to take me. I want us to be together – always Frankie," she sobbed, her eyes red-rimmed with sadness.

Hardened though he was by his upbringing and lifestyle, his resolve nearly crumbled in the face of Hetty's appeals. "Sure, it was going to be a painful parting – for them both." But his mind was made up! It certainly was a painful parting for Hetty who, knowing Frankie's weakness for other women, became convinced there must be another woman in the picture somewhere. It was only much later that she learned it was Sabra.

An appointment with his accountant was the next stop on his agenda. When he was in Spain, he had opened an account with a leading Spanish bank, chosen for the difficulty it presented to would-be bank robbers! That seemed a very good reason to trust them with his money! Now that his deal with Maurice had been completed, the accountant arranged for this money and most of the other funds he held in Britain to be invested, less one hundred thousand pounds sterling to be kept handy for future emergencies.

Frankie's farewell to Mal and Leroy was less than cordial – more a question of 'keeping the door open' should any future liaison between them be desirable. The last and possibly the most difficult hurdle to be faced was a trip to Cardiff to deliver the news to his family that he was leaving Britain. It promised to be another tearful parting.

His arrival at his mother's home revived many memories of his earlier years spent there and the antics he and his brothers got up to. But nostalgia soon gave way to reality – that his visit home was a prelude to him leaving the country.

"It's not the end of the world Mam," he explained to an apprehensive Nell. "You can travel to Valencia from London in less than four hours – you really can."

But his assurances failed to move her as she was still struggling to come to terms with Joe's plight. "Look at the way our Joe is suffering since you decided to live in London and take him with you – you and your big ideas!" She bit her lip in distress now. "At least we can look after him better now he's been transferred to the Cardiff Royal Infirmary near his family – where he belongs!" she said bitterly. He looked at his mother pleadingly, noticing how much older and lined her face now appeared. "Aw, come on now Mam," he cried. "Joe wanted to go his own way against my wishes and tried to rip-off the wrong people – there wasn't much I could do to stop it happening. You know how headstrong Joe can be when he wants to," he said earnestly.

It seemed to Nell that her family was suddenly disintegrating around her. She looked up at Frankie. "I'm not getting any younger" – she sighed deeply. "Your father's no bloody help either just when I want some support – someone to lean on." Frankie put his arms around her, drawing her closer. "Look at it this way Mam. You can come and visit me from time to time. Just let me know when and I'll arrange your flight tickets." He searched for the right words. "Just think about it. It'll be great getting away from the damp weather here, especially in the winter. And I'll be nipping over to Cardiff now and again. It's no difference from me being in London, is it? he said hopefully.

Nell stared at her son, still unconvinced. "I suppose you're taking Hetty with you, are you Frankie?" He gave an uncomfortable laugh. "No Mam, I'm not. She's staying on in London" – he hesitated. "Danny says he would like to move in with her but I don't think she's ready for that – at least, not yet." Nell nodded her head shrewdly. "I suppose that means you've got another piece of skirt lined up to go with you." She didn't wait for his reply. "You haven't changed a bit Frankie Gallagher – not one little bit."

He spent the next three hours being brought up to date on the activities of his old adversaries, Davies and Parker. Nell confirmed that she nor any of the family had given them any reasons for further questioning on the so-far unsolved bank robbery. She patted his hand. "You needn't worry about them. We've been as quiet as mice since you left Cardiff," she told him, a hoarse, racking cough causing her shoulders to heave. "I've had a bit of a bad chest lately," she wheezed by way of explanation. It's nothing to concern yourself about."

He stood up. "I'll be staying here tonight if that's OK with you Mam and I'll be away to the 'Smoke' tomorrow. We leave for Spain in three days time." He leant over and kissed her plump cheeks.

"What do you say about a bit of a knees-up and a good drink in town with some of the family," He smoothed away a tear that threatened to become a trickle. "I'm not your baby any more Mam. You'll have to let go someday – you really will."

Chapter 24

Despite Frankie Gallagher's move to London, Dave Parker had never relinquished his interest in his old adversary's activities. He was still convinced the Gallagher's were implicated in some way or even responsible for that big Cardiff bank robbery, although he had never been able to prove their involvement.

During an inter-regional police conference held in London, Parker renewed his acquaintance with an old pal from the Met. Detective Inspector Matthews and he had shared accommodation while on their training course held at Hendon at the beginning of their careers.

Ignoring traditional police prejudices about sharing information, DI Matthews was only too happy to put Parker in the picture over a glass of beer, regarding Frankie's activities in London.

Matthews took a swig from his pint, then eased his belt off a few notches. "I've put on a few inches around the belly since we last saw each other, Dave," he explained. "Now, about this fellow Gallagher you were asking about." Parker interrupted his companion briefly. "I'd like to take a few notes as we go along." Matthews waved his hand. "You're welcome – anything that helps."

He then described Frankie's appearance at Maurice Green's club, apparently in a role that suggested he was more than just another punter. "One of my undercover officers who wangled a membership of the club later verified that your man had in fact bought a share in it." He leaned forward to emphasise his point. "Although we already had a pretty good idea about the place, my officer confirmed that the club is nothing more than a front for a high-class call girl operation." He settled back into his seat.

Parker looked up from his notes. "You reckon Gallagher has bought a share in the club. Do you know how much his share cost him and how he paid – in cash, for example?"

Matthews shook his head. "My man couldn't get close to that kind of information without setting off some alarm bells. But there's another connection between Gallagher and other criminal activities." He paused as he searched his memory for names. "Your bloke has been keeping company with another nightclub owner and his minder – I think his name is Leroy, a Jamaican – but both of them have been on the fringes of some bank and security van robberies. But so far, we've nothing concrete enough to bring a case against them." He took another swallow from his glass. "I don't know their surnames, but they are real shady characters and that Leroy is a real brute. He likes using force – especially on women, so I hear."

Parker nodded his satisfaction at the information he'd obtained. It wasn't as specific as he'd hoped, but he'd gained some new information. "Presumably these two you referred to have got some form. Do you think you could let me have a sheet on both of them?" he asked hopefully.

This time he was in luck. Matthews nodded. "Leave it to me Dave. Let me have your station's numbers and I'll arrange to have the information sent on, OK?"

Later that evening, Parker turned over the new information in his mind as the 18:15 train rattled its way back from Paddington to Cardiff. Was this the break he had long waited for?

It appeared Gallagher was splashing some money about in London, but where had it come from? As he settled back in his seat, Parker smiled to himself. One thing was certain. Gallagher hadn't won the football pools. Perhaps the first cracks were about to appear in the alibis that his family had clung onto for so long.

Five days later, as Matthews had promised, several sheets of information detailing the criminal records of Mal and Leroy were handed to Parker by the telex machine operator. There was also a separate sheet. Parker stared at its contents, his eyes widening in surprise. It stated that Frankie Gallagher and a woman friend had recently travelled from Heathrow Airport headed for Valencia in Spain. But it was the final sentence that really caught his eye. The words jumped out at him from the page "We have it on good authority that the two persons concerned are intending to settle in Spain. An expensive property has already been purchased to this effect."

———⧯———

That same evening, Charlie Gallagher sat in his favourite seat in his favourite pub. At least two hours had elapsed since his arrival and he was well on the way to being drunk. His watery eyes watched the comings and goings of the bar's customers. Some nodded a greeting, others said a 'cheerio' to the squat fellow in the corner, as they departed.

Charlie had decided it was time to declare his presence among them, regardless of respecting their privacy. He rose from his seat, swaying unsteadily as he made his way to the bar.

Glowering at those already standing there, he removed his greasy cap from his head and tossed it nonchalantly onto the sawdust-covered floor.

"I'll fight any man in the house," he bawled out aggressively, his head swaying from side to side. "Any takers then? No? I thought so, you gutless lot!" he muttered, stooping to retain his cap before returning to his seat. He sat there, muttering to himself, looking belligerently at everyone – seeing nobody.

He certainly wasn't aware of the shifty glances cast in his direction by the two scruffy men drinking at the bar, or their whispered conversation. Nor was he aware after leaving the pub that they followed his unsteady progress through the darkened streets.

As he reached the wide bridge that spanned the River Taff no more than two hundred yards from his home in Tudor Street, he was suddenly grabbed forcibly from behind – his unseen assailant wrapping his arms around Charlie's chest.

As he struggled to shake himself free, a second man stepped in front of the old boy and delivered several heavy punches to Charlie's stomach and chest, forcing him to sink to his knees As he went down, one of his trapped arms became free and he instinctively lashed out powerfully at the dark figure, catching him a very painful blow in the groin. The man gasped, then hauled Charlie to his feet before head-butting him twice while the person behind delivered a series of heavy punches to the old man's kidneys.

Charlie collapsed to the pavement groaning, his nose smashed and broken from the head-butting, his body searing with pain from his brutal beating. One of the attackers looked around, checking for any passers-by. There were none. The other man knelt down, rifled through Charlie's pockets, removing his wallet, spare cash and tearing his fob-watch away from his waistcoat. He picked up the old man's spectacles and tossed them over the bridge.

Together they then heaved Charlie up off his feet, grunting with the exertion and flung him over the bridge parapet, screaming with fear, to splash into the black swirling waters of the River Taff, some fifty feet below.

Scarcely conscious, he was taken by the swift-flowing tide along the black muddy river bank until he came to an uneasy, bobbing rest – his life ebbing away. He lay there, partly submerged face down, floating at the mouth of the vast brewery outlet pipes discharging their foaming waste into the black restless waters. Ashes to ashes, beer to beer and engulfed in foam, he drowned.

His body was discovered two days later. A verdict of accidental death was recorded. To some in authority, it might have seemed a lot simpler than setting up a time-consuming enquiry into the demise of an alcoholic.

To Nell and the family it was yet another shattering blow, bringing with it further grief to a closely-knit family that had already sacrificed three sons in the greater cause of their country.

Despite Charlie's aggressive approach to life and the inevitable aggravation his behaviour often created, his funeral attracted considerable attention. Family, friends, and even some people less sympathetic to his charms turned out in large numbers to give the old sod a send-off he would have surely enjoyed, if he could have. And who's to say he didn't?

Chapter 25

"I must say Sabra, I'm very envious of your place. It's absolutely gorgeous," gushed the tanned, slim, bra-less blonde dressed in a short, tight-fitting white dress. Sabra accepted the compliment from her guest with a dazzling smile before excusing herself to welcome two more guests at the front door of the villa.

Since their decision to live on the Costa Blanca, Frankie and Sabra had integrated well into a lively social scene comprising mostly members of either the Jalon Valley wine tasting club or the International Dining Club.

Its members met at various restaurants sampling the local cuisine or at a hotel conference room where general meetings were held. Comprising a pleasing mix of various European nationals, the language of choice on social occasions was usually English, Spanish – or both.

The evening was proving quite a success as the drinks flowed and the extensive refreshments consumed with gusto by the twenty or so guests. Sabra continued to circulate while Frankie chatted with a group of men no doubt comparing the assets of the various females present.

While she was mentally congratulating herself on how well it was progressing, she felt a touch on her arm. As she turned, the person flashed a friendly smile.

"We haven't been introduced yet but my name is Gail – I understand you are Sabra. That's my husband James over there," she said pointing to a tanned, good looking man with a full head of greying hair and matching moustache. His lifestyle had added too many extra pounds around his middle, like many others present. "Oh and thank you for the invitation," she exclaimed in a low, pleasant voice.

"It's a pleasure Gail," responded Sabra with a radiant smile, followed by the lightest brush of her lips on the newcomers' cheek. "My fellow is over there with your husband and the others. His name is Frankie and he's the one in the light tan trousers and white T-shirt.

Gail looked across the arched terrace. "Mmmm, yes, I know. He's already been pointed out to me. He's a very handsome chap," she added quietly, almost to herself.

"You make a very attractive couple," she smiled, returning her attention to Sabra.

"James and I knew the couple that owned your place before you. They returned to Germany – some personal problems within their family I understand." Gail paused, offering Sabra a cigarette, that was politely refused. "Mind if I do?" she enquired, then lit up at Sabra's slight nod of consent and blew out a blue plume of smoke. "Do you employ that quaint little Spanish gardener that the other couple used? It's quite extensive, isn't it?" she observed, looking around the stepped terracing with its mature palm trees and the large kidney-shaped swimming pool framed by several small lawns of dark green Bermuda grass – a not too common sight in sun drenched Southern Spain.

"Yes it is – and we still do have him come in twice a week. Why do you ask, Gail?" replied Sabra, slightly puzzled. "Have you ever employed him?" she enquired uncertainly.

Gail laughed softly, her eyes twinkling. "I'm sure you've noticed some of the young Spaniards working around the area – I have three that do various jobs around the villa."

She drew on her cigarette again. "One – my favourite, cleans the pool, another looks after the garden, while the third one cleans the windows."

Sabra smiled at her guest. "It sounds as though you are well catered for," she acknowledged. "Do they do anything else for you," she asked mockingly.

Gail turned away briefly to stub out her cigarette and sipped from her glass. "They certainly do," she replied mischievously. "One day James was out sailing – he sails nearly every other day – and I was sunbathing nude by the pool, when the pool cleaner turned up. I knew he was due sometime that day but not quite sure when. I just wasn't expecting him."

She clearly had Sabra's attention now. "This young chap sauntered over to my sunbed," she continued, "looked down at me and said "buenos días Señora," with a real cheeky smile on his face."

"He stood there just looking at me for a while then slowly pulled his shorts down to display the biggest penis I've ever seen! It was just like a horse's!" she giggled.

Glancing around to make sure nobody else was within earshot, Gail lowered her voice. "Then he started masturbating – very, very slowly, all the time smiling at me, looking me right in the eyes' Again Gail laughed. "What could I do? So I thought, here goes and said to him, I don't think we ought to waste that erection on yourself do you darling?"

"So I reached up, grabbed it with both hands and pulled him down on top of me. My god, he had some stamina that lad!" She blushed at the recollection. "He really screwed the arse off me!" Gail looked at Sabra, waiting for her response, but her hostess was still looking slightly bemused. "We still have a session every fortnight or so. It's been a real education for me." Gail shrugged her shoulders. "Now, I have it off with the other two as well on a sort of rota basis. It's very satisfying, giving me everything that James can't!"

They were interrupted by Frankie who had walked over unnoticed. "Hey, what are you two up to?" he asked, slipping his arm around Sabra's bare midriff. "You seem to be enjoying yourselves. Like to let me in on the joke?" he asked, while casting an approving eye over Gail.

As he had noticed earlier, she was a very attractive full-breasted woman with sun-streaked highlights in her fair hair and an absolutely gorgeous, inviting mouth. Sabra looped an arm around his waist, drawing him closer. "No way Frankie," she smiled, reading his mind while also answering his question. "This is strictly women's talk – and this is Gail, but I suspect you already know that. You were just speaking to her husband James," He completed Sabra's introduction with a brief light kiss on both of her cheeks as their eyes exchanged unspoken messages.

'Her eyes are really blue' he noticed. He was also very aware of her perfume as he drew back. Just one thought flicked through his mind without any prompting. 'She may well be one for the future.'

Gail was very aware of his broad shouldered, athletic body, his eyes taking her in, less than an arm's length away. Her mind too toyed with just a single thought. "I wouldn't mind giving him a test drive, one day" she mused as she checked out his flat stomach and muscular arms.

"Would you excuse me a moment Gail," he asked, resting his hand on her tanned, bare shoulder. The brief contact sent a shiver shimmering briefly through her body. "I have to make a phone call." He turned to Sabra, kissing her lightly on the lips. "I'll see you later."

As he disappeared through one of the archways, Gail switched her attention back to Sabra. "On the subject of gardening or whatever, if you're interested, I could send over one of my boys. I don't think you'll be disappointed with any of them," she said pointedly.

Sabra smiled, her head inclined to one side. "I don't think so just now Gail, but if I do become dissatisfied with my present arrangements, I can always let you know, can't I." She glanced across the swimming pool, which formed the perfect central feature with its terraced arches on three sides. Most of the other guests seemed to have collected there. "I think perhaps we should join the others Gail, before they think they've been abandoned."

As they skirted the edge of the pool, Gail had another attempt at gauging Sabra's fidelity to Frankie. "Most of this crowd are into wife swapping," she murmured as they strolled around the edge of the pool. "My husband James apparently, is screwing that blond over there in the short white dress. She told me so herself," Gail added without any trace of resentment.

Several hours later, the last of the guests gone, Frankie and Sabra relaxed on a four-seater, soft leather settee with big squashy cushions. "Well, that seems to have gone off successfully," she sighed dreamily. "I see we've been invited by that German chap and his girl friend to have lunch on board his boat tomorrow down at that small marina – you know the one near Calpe."

"That's for Wednesday isn't it," he affirmed. "Karl – that's the German bloke's name. He said it should be a great day out." Frankie stretched his arms above his head, yawning deeply. "Karl teaches water sports down there apparently. And now my tired little temptress, I'm knackered and I'm ready to hit the sack. Are you ready?"

Before Sabra could answer, one final thought passed Frankie's mind. "Jesus, I almost forgot! We have to collect our motor first from Global Cars in Moraira tomorrow morning. They said it would be ready at 10 o'clock."

Sabra slowly flexed her lithe body then slowly eased herself across the sofa towards Frankie. "Yes, I'm ready lover-boy – but don't get any ideas. I need my beauty sleep even if you don't."

Chapter 26

Frankie turned off the coastal road, two kilometres short of Calpe, before driving down the steep twisting lane that led to the small Marina. As they reached the bottom they could hear music coming from the small bar located underneath the restaurant that was situated at the waters edge, overlooking the quiet, sheltered bay.

They parked on the hard standing, selecting a shady space underneath several tall palm trees that fringed the boat moorings and strolled past a line of boats gently rocking in the calm, crystal-clear water. As they approached the small group of swimsuit-clad people sitting drinking under the canopy, sunbathing or swaying slowly to a Latin rhythm, Karl emerged from the bar, his arms linked around two attractive, deeply tanned young women – one blonde, the other a redhead, both wearing only the bottom half of their bikinis. Frankie noted with some interest how their firm, ample breasts bounced as they walked, Sabra noted Frankie's interest with an indulgent smile.

"Hey Frankie, you made it then," Karl called out, hugging him around the shoulders, then kissing Sabra on both cheeks. "I'd like you to meet these two gorgeous girls Katrina and Suzi. They're both from Germany and are staying with me for the summer," he yelled out above the noise of the music coming from the cassette player balanced on the window ledge of the bar. Following several 'mwah, mwah' kisses in greeting, Karl ushered them to a table near the water's edge. "Do either of you mind if we sit in the sun?" he enquired of the new arrivals. Frankie certainly didn't mind. He had two gorgeous 'twenty-somethings' with stunning breasts and big, firm nipples sitting next to him, while Sabra, with her dark complexion, positively relished the sun. She had to admit though, that the two girls were magnets for the men sitting around sunning themselves – including her own man!

As the foursome engaged in small talk, Sabra complimented the two fraüleins on the excellence of their English. "In school, it is taught as a second language," Suzi explained as Karl went to the window of the bar, to reappear shortly with a tray of drinks. "This is what you were drinking at your place the other night," he explained as he served them. "Is that alright?" He eased himself into the chair. "I've turned the music down a little so that we can talk." Their chat was interrupted by the roar of a large motor bike that skidded down the last few yards of the slope and slewed to a stop.

As the bare-chested rider dismounted and kicked the bike's resting bar into place, Karl stood up and beckoned the newcomer over to their table. "This is Maxie, the fellow I was telling you about. He teaches wind-surfing down here – he's a great guy!" he stated as Max and he hugged each other vigorously.

With the introductions completed, Max pulled up a seat while casting appreciative glances at Sabra. It didn't take much to figure out what was going on in his mind. She smiled at him, acutely aware of his presence. "I think I know what's going through your mind," he said unexpectedly. She started slightly. "What was he going to say?" "You think Karl and me look like brothers, maybe even twins. Right?" He laughed, throwing his head back.

"You'd be wrong. We're not even related." He downed Karl's beer in one swallow. "I was thirsty," he explained. "I'll get us some refills." As he stood up and went to the bar Frankie took Sabra's words out of her mouth. "You are alike Karl – very much alike." They were indeed. Above average height with a muscular build, they were both deeply tanned with longish shocks of sun-bleached hair and the type of moustaches favoured by many German men. "Maxie also teaches wind-surfing. You should have a few lessons with him – or me," he added with a slight shrug of his shoulders.

The conversation meandered along as they relaxed in the sunshine, the slightest of breezes from across the bay taking the edge off the heat of the sun. Suzi turned to Sabra and pointed to the warm sea lapping the stone jetty. "Katrina and I are going for a swim. Would you like to join us?" Noting her slight hesitation, Katrina touched Sabra's arm. "If you haven't brought a costume, swim in your panties – or nothing at all," she smiled. "That's how we like to do it," she pouted, as Suzi slipped off her own bikini bottom, then followed suit.

Their prominent pubic hairs were evidence that neither used depilatory creams or a razor, both used occasionally by Sabra. As she slipped off her shorts and cotton sleeveless top to reveal the panties she was wearing, she leant over Frankie and kissed him briefly. "You boys probably have plenty to discuss. We'll see you later," she said happily as Karl and Max noted every curve and contour of her superb body. The three descended the several stone steps into the water before striking out strongly for the middle of the bay. The men watched their progress as the two German girls sped to the front.

"I must compliment you on your girlfriend, Frankie," Maxie said admiringly. "She's one of the most beautiful women I have ever seen – and I've seen plenty in my time." He drank slowly from his glass, still watching the progress of the swimmers. Frankie raised his eyebrows in delight. "Yeah Maxie – she's some woman isn't she," he agreed, a smile playing around his lips at Maxie's assessment of the female form.

"He used to manage a brothel in Hamburg," Karl observed "and there were some terrific lookers there at the time. That makes him a bit of an expert I reckon – uuh, no offence meant Frankie," he ended lamely. Frankie chuckled at his discomfort. "None taken Karl. Tell me, what brought you two fellers to Spain?"

They looked at each other quizzically as he refreshed himself from his glass. "Well, it was some years ago when I worked at the brothel," said Maxie twirling his glass in his hand. "There were plenty of drugs around – the whole place was full of them." He shrugged. "That's where I ran into Karl. He used to deal in the stuff, so we came to an arrangement." He lapsed into silence, looking out across the bay. The pause was broken by Frankie. "So what happened?" he queried. Karl took up the story. "We did a lot of business – had a really good thing going for us. Then we got busted – big-time!" He scratched his tousled thatch at the memory. "Both us went to gaol for five years. I did the full time, no remission. Karl got nine months off-for good behaviour! Can you believe that? Him behaving!" he roared. The pair collapsed into noisy laughter, slapping each other on the thigh.

Frankie studied them as their laughing gradually subsided. "I take it you two might be interested if something came up – where you could make some money, real money. Am I right?" They glanced at each other. "Depends on what that 'something' was," replied Maxie evenly. "If it was the right kind of 'something' we could be very interested." He looked Frankie right in the eyes. "What do you have in mind?" he asked quietly.

"No point in being cautious now," thought Frankie. "Me and a couple of my brothers had a business back in Britain that was not entirely legal." They nodded, waiting patiently for the rest. "We ran into trouble with the law and ended up doing time, so I guess we're all members of the same club, yeah?" Now they understood. "So now you're looking around for some action," queried Karl. "I thought when I met you at your villa the other night you were a bit too young to be retired."

Frankie rubbed his nose. "Yeah, you could say that, so maybe we can work together. Can we drink to that?" Maxie thumped the table with his hand. "I'll drink to that," he cried, raising his glass as Karl acknowledged a shout from the water some fifty yards away as the three women swam towards the steps. "So will I," affirmed Karl. "So will I." He stood, stretching his arms. "Now the girls are back," he yawned, "I think it's time we pushed off and had lunch on my boat."

Chapter 27

There was one issue – and a serious one at that – that had long troubled Dave Parker's conscience. In all the years that had passed since Peggy had given birth to her daughter and then died following the accident, he had never attempted to discover what had become of the youngster. He only knew that her guardians – her grandparents in fact – had moved to live in Winchester, taking their grand-daughter with them. His curiosity to discover what type of person she had become finally persuaded him to trace her. She would be in her early twenties by now.

Parker had some initial difficulty in tracing her, even allowing for the considerable police resources at his disposal. The difficulty stemmed from the fact that he started by assuming the girl's surname would be Steele – the same as her mother and also that of her grandparents.

In fact, she was using the name of Lisa Jones in her career as a professional journalist and used this name as her by-line on all of the articles she wrote for the national magazine on which she worked.

When he did succeed in tracing her, he was delighted to discover a mature, self-assured attractive blonde young woman and was immediately struck by her appearance and bearing, both of which brought back vivid memories of her mother. He never made himself known to her – why should he? He rested content in the knowledge that she had been brought up by caring persons, enjoying the love and affection of the only family she had ever known.

The passing years had also seen Spain become the attraction for numerous British subjects with money to splash around. Many colourful characters, some with dubious backgrounds, were either living permanently on the Costas or used their foreign properties as a bolt-hole to stay out of the way of nosey newspaper reporters.

It was only a matter of time before rumours of Frankie's past eventually surfaced which soon attracted women whether single, married or divorced, eager to have a secret fling and sleep with a 'real' criminal without the risk of endangering their own well-ordered lives. It gave these high-maintenance ladies of leisure a real buzz that was absent from their day-to-day round of poolside parties, eating in expensive restaurants and shopping in the company of portly, out of condition husbands who drank far too much booze for their own good.

While fending off the numerous advances of females on heat, Frankie still enjoyed the company of several in particular who satisfied his needs. Sabra meanwhile remained on the sidelines, clinging to an increasingly fragile relationship, while enduring the embarrassment and humiliation that his liaisons brought in their wake.

His presence on the Costa Blanca was noted with particular interest in an entirely different quarter – that of the local Guardia Civil, based in Moraira. The Guardia are a military-style police force which once formed the personal bodyguard of Spain's deceased dictator General Franco. They now perform the duties of a frontline, heavily-armed force at the top of law enforcement in Spain, who have borne the brunt of the thirty years and more of the battle against the violent Basque Country separatists.

It comes as no surprise that they are very conscious of the presence of foreign villains settling on their patch in Spain. Keeping themselves informed of prominent foreigners' whereabouts and with whom they socialised in monied circles, was a distinct advantage whether they were criminals or not.

One officer in particular from the local Guardia Civil station stood out. Lieutenant Juan Luis Garcia is a dedicated, articulate policeman. His fluency in English and an ease with several other European languages, provided him easy access to the Costa Blanca's affluent foreign population eager to curry favour with the police.

It was at a fund-raising party for a Spanish charity held at Frankie's villa that Juan Luis and he first came face to face. It was Sabra who did the introductions, having just welcomed the police officer at the front door. "Good afternoon Señor Gallagher. It's a pleasure to meet you," he said, returning Frankie's firm handshake with an equally strong response.

"Lieutenant Garcia," said Frankie easily while sizing up the man facing him.

"Please call me Juan Luis," the Spaniard replied. "It's much less formal," he smiled, returning Frankie's unblinking scrutiny of him. In his immaculately-pressed olive green uniform, polished shoes, belt and an automatic pistol strapped to his waist, he presented an impressive image. Slightly shorter than Frankie, he was equally wide-shouldered and well built. With his thick, black curly hair, trimmed moustache, olive skin and perfect white teeth, he could have easily been cast as a Mexican general chasing the bad guys in a Hollywood Western.

"I trust you are enjoying our beautiful country Señor Gallagher. You have retired here?" he enquired amiably.

Frankie smiled back. "Call me Frankie – please. It's less formal and yeah, I have come here to live but I think it's a little early to think of retirement."

Garcia looked around, nodding in appreciation. "This is a very fine home you have here Frank. Originally, you know, it was a finca – you call them farmhouses in Britain. The builder who was employed to renovate it to its present fine state did an excellent job – it must be one of the best examples of its kind in the area," he stated admiringly.

"You seem to know a lot about my place," said Frankie evenly. The officer smiled." I make it my business to know a lot about many things Frank. It's my job." He looked around as Sabra approached, looping her arm around Frankie's waist.

"How are you getting on with the Lieutenant," she enquired, brushing her man's cheek affectionately with her lips.

Frankie looked straight into Garcia's eyes. "I think we're getting along just fine," he murmured.

Garcia gestured with his hands. "That's right Señora, but please call me Juan Luis," he appealed. "After all, I expect we shall be seeing much more of each other. By the way Frank, what kind of business did you have in Britain," he enquired blithely.

Frank studied Garcia's face. "This is a copper asking me questions about my past," he thought. "My family were in the removal business. Some still are," he replied coolly as visions of the money stolen by them flashed through his mind. "Now Sabra and I are here to relax and quietly enjoy the best your beautiful country can offer."

Garcia raised his glass in salute. "As you say in Britain, I'll drink to that," he said without the slightest trace of mockery in his voice.

Chapter 28

The front doorbell rang as Sabra applied a final touch of lipstick. "That'll be for me Frankie," she called out. "Gail is picking me up – we're having lunch in the village. See you later." Frankie waved a hand in farewell as the front door slammed shut behind the departing Sabra. He checked the time on his watch. He would be leaving shortly for a meeting with Karl and Maxie at La Bodega restaurant overlooking the Las Palmeras marina.

He tossed his English newspaper aside. It was nearly a week old, but that's all you could buy here on the Costa Blanca. "One day perhaps, they would be available on the day they were printed, he thought," not too hopefully. He stood up, walked around the pool, checking that the doors and windows of the rooms over-looking the pool area were locked. Satisfied, he walked through the large, cool lounge, stripping off his T-shirt as he headed for the shower.

Maria, the young Spanish woman that came in to clean around the villa twice a week, glanced up from her polishing as he went by. "Now there's a man I would like to take me to bed" she fanta-sised as he went on through to the shower and turned the water on. She silently crossed the lounge and looked furtively through the partly-opened door of the bathroom.

Frankie stood there naked, applying shaving cream to his face. She blushed and quietly backed away from the door, feeling ashamed by her boldness. "I'm sure he would make a wonderful lover" she enthused, but dismissed the idea almost immediately. "On the other hand, Francisco the pool cleaner is pretty good." she conceded. "He fucks like a rabbit."

Karl and Maxie were already seated at the bar when he strolled into La Bodega. "Hiya fellers," he greeted them. "Make mine a Magno," he said as he shook hands and perched on a bar stool. Maxie nodded to the barman who poured out a generous measure of Magno, a good quality brandy. "That's another thing I like about Spain," he enthused as he took a taster from his glass. "They never skimp on measures here, do they?"

"I've ordered a table for two o'clock," stated Karl, "so that gives us plenty of time to talk." He glanced around briefly. "I think it would be more private at our table," he suggested, indicating the near-presence of the attentive barman. They collected their drinks as Maxie pointed out a table in a secluded corner of the restaurant.

Frankie put his glass down on a beer mat. "I've got an account at the Banco Trujillo on the outskirts of our village – you know the one, next to the big supermarket, what's it called? yeah, Centro, that's the one." They nodded their recognition. They knew the one.

"What, with opening my account and the number of times I've been in there since settling up buying the villa, I've had plenty of chances for a good look around the place." They waited patiently, wondering what he was going to come up with. He didn't disappoint them. "I think," he said slowly, "it would be an ideal place to rob." He took another swallow from his glass and replaced it on the beer mat.

Karl was first to react. "That's some thought Frankie! I take it you have first hand experience in these matters – it could also cost a lot of money to set up. What do you think Maxie?" His fellow countryman nodded vigorously. "It's bound to cost a real bundle of marks, make no mistake." Frankie shook his head.

"The money's not the problem. It's finding the gear we need to crack the bank's security systems – that's the problem. For a start, this bank is perfectly situated for knocking over. It's well away from the village which means there won't be many people about."

He paused as he mentally recalled his visits. "There are never that many Guardia Civil around on a normal day so you can bet there will be less while the fiesta is on. I tell you," he reasoned, "it's the ideal place – and the ideal time to go for it!"

He was so convincing, it momentarily silenced his companions as they mulled over his idea. Then Karl spoke up. "I think we know the guy you should talk to Frankie. He's one of yours – you know, British, but he's based in Portugal and" – he paused, somewhat uncertain. "I don't know if he's away just now but he's worth a call. He's a registered arms dealer. If anybody's got the stuff you need, he's your man." Frankie, suddenly seeing his idea becoming a reality, slapped the table with his hand.

"Now you're talking! How do I get in touch with this bloke – have you got a phone number or an address?"

Karl stood up. "I've got his business card in my wallet. It's in my car. He says he's a porcelain importer. I'll go and get it," he said edging past them to leave.

"Do you always leave your wallet in your car," Frankie asked. "Isn't that a bit risky. What if somebody broke in and stole it. You'd lose everything."

The German shook his head, smiling. "I don't think so Frankie. I've got Bruno keeping an eye on my stuff," he said as strolled from the restaurant.

"Who's Bruno, for Christ's sake," asked Frankie, getting no answer from Maxie.

Karl unlocked the driver's seat door of his Mercedes saloon car. As it swung open, a large white Staffordshire bull terrier bounded out of the car, tail wagging, greeting his master. Karl grabbed the excited dog by the ears, wrestling affectionately with him for a while before breaking off to reach for a large leather wallet under the driver's seat. He took the card from it and replaced the wallet under the seat. "Bruno!" The sharp command from Karl brought the dog bounding back from the nearby palm tree. It leapt onto the front seat and settled down as his owner re-locked the car. Karl returned to his companions and handed Frankie the card. "That's the man you want," he said as he sat down.

Frankie studied the details on the card. "OK. I'll give him a call and set up a meeting." He took another swallow of brandy and replaced his glass. "By the way Karl, Maxie filled me in about Bruno. I like it, I really do," he said with a laugh.

"Fancy having that bastard clamped around your balls for the next six months. They never let go, do they? Painful!"

An hour or so later, as he drew up outside his villa, he saw a car he didn't recognise parked under the outer carport. He unlocked the front door and walked through to the lounge. Gail was seated on one of the leather settees, her deeply tanned legs crossed.

"Hello Frankie," she greeted him. "Sabra said you wouldn't be back yet. She's in the shower." He crossed over to her, giving her a light kiss on her cheek and sat down next to her on the wide arm of the settee. "Had a good time shopping or whatever you ladies do?" he asked light-heartedly."

"What we ladies do best is not shopping Frankie," she said resting her hand on his thigh.

He looked over his shoulder in the direction of the bathroom. The shower was still hissing away loudly. He leant over and kissed her fully on her lips. As their mouths explored each other, she unzipped his trousers and felt for his penis. The way she expertly freed it from his underpants said much for her familiarity with men's underwear – while they were wearing it! She stroked it gently to encourage it to full size then placed her lips over the bulbous end.

Frankie glanced quickly over his shoulder to the bathroom. The shower was still going full blast. He put his hand on Gail's head, forcing his swollen member deeper into her mouth. "Suck me, suck me harder, faster!" he gasped. As she obeyed, the sound of the shower stopped. Gail pulled away from him, but it was too late. His semen spurted in bursts over her cotton top as he jumped up from the settee. There was no way to disguise the identity of the wetness that soaked her.

She leapt up from the settee. "Quick! Outside, now!" she urged crossing to the terrace door. Frankie followed, not knowing what to expect. The hose used for cleaning down the poolside tiles lay coiled nearby. Gail seized the hose. "Where's the tap to switch this on?" she called out hoarsely.

Frankie at last cottoned on. He hurried to the wash house at the end of the pool and switched on the water. Almost immediately, water gushed out the hose which Gail turned on herself. He joined her and taking the hose, sprayed her until she was soaked right through, with Gail squealing loudly in mock surprise. The noise brought Sabra hurrying from the lounge wrapped in a large bath towel, concern written all over her face. "What on earth is going on – what the hell do you think you're doing Frankie?"

He turned to face Sabra as Gail's shrieks changed to laughter. "It's all right Sabra," she gasped, her dress soaked and dripping with water. "It's that Frankie of yours. He caught me admiring some of your flowers and turned the garden hose on me without warning – the swine!" Sabra embraced her while casting reproachful looks at Frankie. "It's about time you grew up. You're just like a big overgrown child!"

She led Gail into the lounge, waving away Gail's protests at the wet trail left on the tiled floor. "You'll need something dry to put on Gail. Come into the bedroom and pick something out." Frankie went into the outhouse and turned off the water.

As he replaced the hose on its hook, he heaved a sigh of relief. "That was close," he breathed. "If I'm going to lay Gail, it'll have to be somewhere a bloody sight more private!"

Three weeks later, Frankie stood waiting outside the local Town Hall in Altea – an attractive fishing village located mid-way between Calpe and Benidorm. He looked again at his watch. Five to eleven. He'd arranged to meet 'Mr Smith' at eleven o'clock. He scanned the people strolling past in the warm sunshine. Nobody that looked like an arms dealer. What did an arms dealer look like, he wondered. Would he be carrying samples of weapons on him? Would he look like a spy? It was all very relaxed here in the square. Except for him. He was itching to meet this Mr Smith and felt somewhat impatient.

At five minutes past eleven a man rose from one of the aluminium tables set outside the cafe opposite and walked slowly to where Frankie stood waiting. "Mr Gallagher?" he murmured discreetly. Frankie turned to look at the man who had spoken to him. The short, thin grey-haired man with a droopy moustache and rimless spectacles, wore a suit and carried a briefcase. That set him apart from all the other people in the square in their T-shirts and shorts.

"Mr Smith?" Frankie replied, somewhat surprised. "Your first name wouldn't be John by any chance would it?" he asked, tongue in cheek. "It would indeed," replied the thin man. "How perceptive of you Mr Gallagher." He looked about him. "I have a client here in Altea who has kindly allowed me use of his office for our meeting," he said thinly. "Shall we go there now?" Frankie readily agreed, but couldn't help noting that the man's suggestion was more of an order.

Shortly after Mr Smith's earlier exchanges with a person in the office, they were ushered into a small room that was one of a number housed in an up-market property developers business. As they sat opposite each other across the boardroom-style table, Mr Smith placed his clasped hands on top and spoke. "How do you think I can help you Mr Gallagher?" he murmured, his face totally expressionless.

Frankie drummed his fingers on the table briefly before replying. "I won't waste time beating around the bush," he said drawing a deep breath before continuing. "I need some equipment that will knock out security systems – of a bank. A big bank that will have all the best gear installed to prevent break-ins." He paused, waiting for a reaction from Mr Smith. There wasn't one, so he carried on. "I'll also need something that will take care of any security people nosing around at the time."

The thin man studied him. "Anything else, Mr Gallagher?"

Frankie flipped through the mental shopping list he carried. "Yeah – there is something else. Can you fix me up with something that will video record the comings and goings of people over, say, a four or five hour period?"

Mr Smith nodded his head and smiled wanly.

"What I'm looking for is a gizmo that will be very difficult to detect," Frankie continued.

Mr Smith smiled indulgently, then opened his briefcase taking out a number of colour leaflets. "From what you tell me Mr Gallagher, I think you will find what you require among these examples." He spread them out on the table. "For outdoor surveillance without danger of detection, I would recommend the AE60 Antenn-Eye system." He looked up at Frankie. "Let me explain. This system can be placed in a car with its antenna fitted to the car body as you would with a normal telescopic car aerial. The difference is that the AE60 allows totally discreet undercover photography and video taping through its tiny wide-angled lens aperture in the stem of the aerial." He glanced over the top of his spectacles and was rewarded by Frankie's rapt attention.

"Use of this camera," he continued, "can give you detailed recorded information regarding bank activities, security arrangements, movement of officials, money deliveries by security vans and so on." He again checked Frankie's attention.

"While the camera's field of vision varies from ten to sixty degrees, it can rotate a full 360 degrees if required. You will of course need somebody with the ability to fit the camera, aerial and tape recorder into your car – a competent car mechanic familiar with installing car radios and that type of thing, I would suggest. That deals with surveillance, would you agree, Mr Gallagher?"

Frankie nodded enthusiastically. "I've got just the man to put that stuff in. That's a great start Mr Smith, but how about the inside of the bank itself?" The thin man sniffed. "All in due course Mr Gallagher. "The next step I would suggest is to render the bank's security systems and local telephone connections unusable. To do this, we need the Wiretap Torch." He turned the leaflet around to give Frankie a better view. "The Wiretap Torch was originally developed for use by the Central Intelligence Agency in the United States, but now its sale is totally banned in that country. Some of the details are on the leaflet but there are more," he advised, turning it over to reveal several illustrations.

"It was originally used as a 24-hour 'search-and-destroy' laser against bugs and telephone taps. As you can see, it's about the size of a box of Cuban cigars – and easily carried in one's pocket." Frankie studied the leaflet, then looked at Mr Smith.

"How would that get me into the bank vault – it doesn't look much," he pointed out. "Patience Mr Gallagher, patience," the thin man replied.

"First, any device or mechanism that is electrically or mechanically controlled can be burnt out in a selected target area and rendered useless. That takes care of the alarm and telephone system. Next, there is the bank vault door. Here, the same principles can be applied."

He paused, sketching out a brief diagram to illustrate his point. "Two small holes are drilled in the bank door, into which two fine wires, like needles, are inserted. Once the wires are in place, they are connected to one of the bank's telephone extensions." He looked at Frankie. "I take it you are still following me, Mr Gallagher," he enquired primly.

"Of course, Mr Smith, of course," Frankie assured him.

He returned to his sketch. "The telephone is then placed near the vault door and a second phone is used to dial the extension. Within seconds of the connection being made the metallic innards of the locking system will be rendered useless by a process of 'total burnout'. It's a very satisfying result Mr Gallagher," he concluded, clasping his hands together.

He tapped his pen on the table cutting into Frankie's concentration on the leaflets. "Have you any idea when you may require this equipment? I normally rent it out for up to four weeks at a time and there are other businessmen who require it."

Frankie looked at the man opposite, his brow furrowed.

"Why can't I buy the stuff straight away – then it doesn't matter when I need it, does it?" he asked curtly.

Mr Smith pursed his lips. "Well as each item costs about twenty thousand American dollars, it can be quite expensive. It's far cheaper to rent it, don't you think?" he murmured calmly. "But I can let you have the car aerial camera today."

Frankie blew out his cheeks in exasperation. "Yeah – I suppose you're right," he agreed reluctantly. "We'll need the rest of the gear in two weeks, but what about the stun guns – how much do they cost?" Mr Smith jotted some figures down on a pad.

"Two weeks you say. Oh, as for the stun guns, you'll have to buy those outright. I get them from a different source from the other equipment. They'll cost you about three hundred American dollars apiece." He put the leaflets back into his briefcase and snapped the catches shut. "Are we in business then Mr Gallagher?" he intoned as he rose to his feet.

Frankie got up and extended his hand. "Yes, we certainly are Mr Smith. I'll send you a list of my exact requirements and you can confirm the total price, including the camera. I'll pay in cash on delivery, or to any account you nominate by a bank transfer." As they departed from the building and went their separate ways, Frankie felt a rush of adrenaline coursing through his body. "It's good to be back in business," he thought as he strolled back to his car. "Yeah, it feels really good."

Chapter 29

T he battered green SEAT 1400 car parked opposite the Banco Trujillo was just one of a dozen cars whose occupants went about their daily business of shopping or banking. Occasionally, a man would open the SEAT's front door and sit inside reading a newspaper or listening to the radio. It was the sort of activity that went unnoticed among the crowds of people visiting the popular supermarket. What also went unobserved was that its occupant removed a video cassette from the recorder underneath the dashboard and replaced it with another.

Several days later, the three men lounged in comfortable chairs or the settee in Frankie's villa intently studying the television set on which video films recorded earlier that week were replayed.

"There's a security van pulling up outside now, fellers. Can we check the time of its arrival by the video clock?" Frankie enquired, a little anxiously. "Yeah, there it is," he cried, writing down the time shown on the film. "How many security guards are there," queried Maxie. "There's two going into the bank, but there's another one still in the van," said Karl.

"That trolley they're wheeling. Where did that come from?" he asked. "It was brought out by one of the guards," confirmed Maxie. He looked across at Frankie. "This film is a great help. It gives us a very good idea on which days the big cash is being delivered. It shows who's doing what – and when," he enthused.

Frankie injected a note of caution as he changed one of the tapes for another. "This is only the start. I agree it's a big help, but the hardest bit is getting into and out of the bank – with the money." He paused to press the 'play' switch on the recorder. "Then, we have to stay out of gaol afterwards! I hear these Spanish gaols are really rough!" His words brought his colleagues back to reality.

"When do you think we'll be ready Frankie?" asked Maxie as he returned from the drinks trolley with some more refreshments.

Frankie spread his hands out wide. "That I don't know until I hear from our Mr Smith. Once we get our hands on the rest of the stuff, it'll be a couple of days after that."

The two Germans quietly digested the information they had gained to date before Karl spoke. "Those stun guns Frankie. How do they work?"

Frankie smoothed out a folded leaflet given him by Mr Smith. "The stun guns are known as the Security Blanket," he explained, indicating the illustration on the leaflet. "They are disguised as ordinary flashlights or torches, but they generate a high-intensity black beam that temporarily incapacitates, or knocks out the person it's aimed at for up to two hours without them suffering permanent injury," he claimed. "The SAS and Special Forces use them. It's real cloak and dagger stuff, he hooted."

Mr Smith was as good as his word. Apart from the video camera already in Frankie's possession, the remainder of the equipment arrived by special delivery direct to Frankie's villa.

Allowing themselves several days to get used to handling the various items and make a few more trips to the bank to produce a fairly accurate layout of the premises, they were ready!

The fiestas held in celebration of the historic earlier battles between the Moors and Christians in a bygone century provided a perfect cover for the raid. With the local police forces and other security personnel relaxing their normal vigilance and enjoying the fireworks, processions and bands, Frankie and his men struck.

The raid went like clockwork. The premises were unguarded, the equipment worked and they got away with more than one hundred million pesetas, equivalent to £540,000, give or take a few pesetas!

The Guardia Civil, local police and bank officials were stunned by the audacity and expertise used to carry out the raid. Worse still from their point of view, the robbers had succeeded without leaving any traces likely to lead to their early arrest.

It later emerged that the investigation was being hampered by the criminal's use of highly sophisticated methods and equipment never previously encountered by the law enforcement officers. That certainly helped to explain their blanket of silence imposed on Press coverage of the robbery. They had been made to look like a bunch of amateurs – and they knew it!

The highest-ranking locally-based Guardia Civil officer was Lieutenant Garcia. He was also the most experienced in matters of bank robberies. His desk was littered with files containing photographs and records of Spanish criminals with a track record in robbing banks. He lit up a cigarillo and sat back in his chair. His sergeant, sitting at a second desk in the cramped office, was also pouring over several similar files.

"Eh – Felipe! We have a lot of work on our hands." Felipe looked around, his baggy eyes looking more tired than ever. "We can narrow it down to the scum we're looking for by taking out all the bank robbers we know are already in gaol," said Garcia.

Felipe nodded his head philosophically thinking, "that's why he's a Lieutenant and I am only a poor sergeant." Garcia continued to sift through the files. "That will get rid of... uh, let me see – he studied the list in his hand. "Twenty seven of them. But that still leaves..." He again consulted his list. "Twenty two others." He blew out a large cloud of blue smoke that tried to hang in the still warm air of the shady, two-tone green-painted office, only to be defeated by the slow turning fan that passed for air-conditioning. "That's always supposing it was some of our chicos that pulled it off. We could be looking for someone from outside," he said shrewdly.

His sergeant nodded, trying to convey he had already considered that possibility. He was an experienced member of the Guardia Civil with twenty two years service behind him. That's if you consider one year's service repeated twenty two times over as being experienced – then he was 'experienced'. These days his thoughts were concentrated more on his short, plump wife dressed all in black, his five children and his coming retirement and pension. "Yes lieutenant, it's possible," he agreed quickly, scratching the 'five o'clock shadow' that had appeared on his chin at least six hours earlier that day.

Several sharp knocks on the door announced the arrival of a subordinate Guardia Civil holding a sheet of paper. "There's a telex marked for your attention that's just arrived from Britain Lieutenant. Shall I wait for your reply?"

Garcia noted the name and location of the sender printed at the top of the sheet. "No – er, no. You can go." The man nodded briefly and left the room closing the door behind him.

Garcia studied the details on the telex. It was from a British police officer, a Detective Inspector David Parker, based in Cardiff. The message read: "Have heard of bank robbery that took place near Moraira, Alicante Province, two days ago. I understand the methods used were very sophisticated. Are you aware that a well-known British criminal by the name of Frank Gallagher, experienced in robbery, is resident in your area. His presence is a major coincidence. You may wish to follow up this line of enquiry. If there is any assistance or information I can pass on, please contact." Message ends.

Garcia read and re-read the message several times, meanwhile recalling meetings with Gallagher on several social occasions. The mention of Gallagher's name in the telex took Garcia completely off guard. He made a point of keeping tabs on newcomers in his area, especially foreigners. But to learn that Gallagher was a criminal with a track record for robbery – that came as a shock!

The apparent ease with which the robbery had been carried out rankled with Garcia and severely dented his pride. It was a bitter pill to swallow. Now there's this British policeman trying to tell him who might be responsible for the crime! Bastardo! Doesn't he know that we Spaniards place pride above most other things? Take that away and what is left?

Still, he reasoned – once his initial resentment had subsided – to be in possession of this new, possibly crucial piece of information without Gallagher being aware, gave him a distinct advantage over the Briton.

Since the robbery had taken place, Garcia and his fellow Guardia Civil compatriots had been forced to take their meals on the hoof due to the pressure, eating where and when they could. Today, he decided, he was going to a nice restaurant and have a civilised meal – with his girlfriend. His wife was not expecting him home, so why not?

He returned to his office in a better frame of mind, the good food and several glasses of his favourite wine succeeding in soothing his dented pride and his irritation at the British policeman's effrontery. But, he eventually conceded, it might be a line of enquiry worth pursuing. He pulled the nearest file to him and flicked it open. He studied the names and faces in front of him. Unless he got a break, it was beginning to look like a very long haul. He loosened his belt and returned to the files.

Chapter 30

The crowds of newly-arrived aircraft passengers from London thronged the arrivals concourse of Valencia Airport. Some were met by family or friends while most of the others made their way to the waiting tour coaches or proceeded through to the car parking area.

Lisa Jones collected her hire car from the car rental company and three hours later walked into the reception area of the local English language newspaper, the Weekly Bulletin, based in Calpe.

Shortly afterwards, she was ushered into the office of its editor, Jack Marshall. Two mugs of coffee arrived on his desk as if by magic as he greeted his visitor.

"One of the tricks of the trade," he explained, smiling at Lisa as they shook hands. "I'm Jack Marshall. Welcome to Calpe and our little empire. Please sit down, oh, and call me Jack." She smiled a 'thank you', pulled up a chair and sat down, crossing her long shapely legs.

"I'm Lisa Jones. Thank you for offering to help me while I'm here." She took a reporters pad and a pencil out of her handbag. "It's my pleasure," he said, taking a quick sip of coffee.

"We had a call from your magazine last week saying you were coming over to the Costa Blanca to research and write a special feature about the activities of some of our more interesting British ex-pats. Is that right?"

Lisa flashed him a dazzling smile. "Yes, that's right Mr Marshall. I thought..."

"Jack," he broke in."

"Yes, Jack. she smiled. "I thought you may be able to point me in the right direction." He handed her a list. "You'll find a few interesting characters in that lot. There's names, addresses, phone numbers. I think you'll get what you're looking for. She glanced briefly down the list, then took a business card out of her handbag and handed it to him. "You may wish to have this," she said.

"Mmmm – I see you're a photo-journalist so you'll be taking your own pictures then?" Marshall observed. She nodded and handed him a magazine she had taken from her briefcase.

"Perhaps you could turn to page 48," she suggested. "That's the start of an eight-page spread I did for last month's edition." His eyes widened as he flicked through the pages.

"I must compliment you Lisa. This is highly professional work." She murmured her thanks and returned the magazine to her brief-case. "This is lovely coffee, Jack. It's far better than the brown sludge we serve up in our office," she said, smiling at the memory.

He chuckled and removed his spectacles, cleaning them with a piece of soft cloth. "Believe me, it's not always this good. I laid it on especially for you," he joked. He moved around the desk as she rose, to shake hands.

"I'll have to leave you now Lisa. I know we are both busy people, but let me know if I can be of any further help."

Later, in her hotel room, she sat studying the list and a detailed map of the area. She reached for the phone book. "I've got some calls to make so I may as well get started." After an hour or so on the phone, she had several appointments lined up. Her first two were set for late afternoon with a several volunteers from two small charity groups and two animal sanctuaries.

The charity people she had chosen represented only a few of the many voluntary groups manned by British ex-pats who did a wonderful job on the Costa Blanca. Among other things, they raised funds for good causes, helping people needing assistance with hospital transport and medical aids such as wheelchairs and translation of Spanish paperwork. In all, they provided a series of services greatly appreciated by the foreign residents and all done on a voluntary basis.

It was eight o'clock that evening before she returned to her hotel room. After a full day that had started with an early flight from the UK, she felt she had earned a drink. A generous measure of gin with plenty of ice and a splash of tonic, followed by a hot shower would be the perfect answer.

As she headed for the shower, she passed a full-length mirror on the wall. Slipping out of her cotton top, shorts and panties, she checked her reflection in the mirror. Her closest friends – and quite a few men – often compared her to a young Marilyn Monroe. Well, she had the blonde hair and a beautifully curvaceous figure, emphasised by firm, round up-tilted breasts – so they might have a point, she conceded. After all, it wasn't a bad thing to be compared with one of Hollywood's love goddesses!

As she waited for the lift in the fourth floor corridor of the hotel, she felt nice and relaxed in a new short-sleeved red silk blouse and short white skirt, looking forward to a really splendid meal – on expenses of course!

Lisa ordered a taxi through the hotel reception desk and was surprised at the prompt response which was unusual for a small town. She settled comfortably in the back seat and gave the driver her destination. "The Don Santos restaurant por favor."

She strolled through the entrance, noting it was very well appointed and hoped the quality and service matched the tasteful decor. Having been shown to a table by an attentive waiter and ordered an aperitif, she checked the menu and ordered her meal.

As she sipped her drink, she noticed three good-looking, casually-smart dressed men standing chatting at the bar. It came as no surprise that all three men had noticed her, despite the many tables being full. After all, she did stand out from the crowd – any crowd!

From the similarity in their appearance, she guessed two of the men were probably brothers, both around forty years of age. The third person was somewhat older, early fifties or so, perhaps, she surmised, mildly surprised that she was spending time checking out the male talent at the bar! An hour or so later as the 'look-alikes' prepared to take their leave of the third man, he caught the attention of the barman and spoke to him briefly.

Shortly afterwards, her waiter, who by now had already served her coffee and liqueur, brought a bottle of champagne over to her table.

"Excuse me Señorita, but this champagne has been sent over to you by the señor at the bar. That one," he said pointing at Frankie. "Will you accept it?"

"I know the one you mean, she murmured to herself. He seems pretty smooth and very sure of himself." "Would you thank the gentleman and tell him I would be delighted to accept," she told the waiter, who then put the bottle into the ice bucket and departed. She flashed Frankie a dazzling smile then raised her liqueur glass to him in acknowledgement.

Her feelings of expectancy and arousal were cut short as her well-wisher finished his drink at the bar and rose to leave. He crossed to her table and was even more dishy up close, she noted, even though he must be twenty years older than her.

"I hope you didn't mind me sending the champagne over. Please enjoy it," he said.

As he turned to leave her table she put her table napkin down and caught his arm, looking up at him. "Am I supposed to drink this on my own – or was it your intention to join me?" He grasped the back of the chair opposite her, a trace of a smile on his lips.

"Yes – that was my intention," he said evenly. "But I just wanted to see how you would react if you thought I was leaving. After all, you've been giving me the eye ever since you came into the res-taurant!" he mocked her, a twinkle in his eye.

Such was his aplomb, she was momentarily lost for words." I must say Mr... er, what do I call you?"

He pulled up a chair and sat down. "Frankie will do. Frankie Gallagher. It's my name. And yours?"

"I'm glad the other two have left," she thought, her curiosity aroused. "It's Lisa. Lisa Jones." He took the bottle out of the bucket and felt it with the back of his hand. "It's not quite chilled enough yet," he observed, his attention now fully directed at the striking beauty before him. "Lisa Jones," he repeated, turning her name over in his mind. "Nice name."

She stared at Frankie, intrigued by his manner. But it was more than that. Although he was a total stranger, there was something about him that she found instantly attractive, even familiar. Why, for goodness sake! There were plenty of good-looking men around eager to pick her up. It wasn't his looks – he was handsome in a rugged sort of way – but something less definable. A warm, almost inevitable affinity. She roused herself as she realised he was speaking to her. "I didn't intend to spoil your meal. Had you finished?" he asked.

"Mmmm... yes. I'd like some of that champagne now," she murmured still studying his face. As she lifted her glass to drink, Frankie noticed a band of lighter coloured skin on the third finger of her left hand. He took her hand in his. "Does that mean," he said pointing at her finger, "that you've had a row with your boyfriend – and thrown his engagement ring away?" he asked with a cheeky grin.

She pulled her hand away. "No, not quite – but close. I've recently divorced my husband after two years of marriage – and nearly two years of his adultery! It was his ring. Naturally, I don't wear a ring now."

He nodded understandingly. "I think you did the right thing if you don't mind me saying so. You can never trust a man that's always trying to get into other women's knickers."

She smiled wryly, slightly surprised at his candour and sipped from her glass. "And how about you? There has to be a woman somewhere in the picture."

He looked at her provocatively. "Several women in fact. I like to keep my options open. I'm sure you are familiar with that."

Inwardly, Lisa contemplated the man facing her. 'He sounds like a real bastard, this one, but that's the only ones I seem to get involved with. He's just thrown out a real challenge' she thought. 'Is it one I want to take up? Mmmm... I suppose I could be persuaded – eventually. A one-night stand won't ruin my life and I'm a big girl now. I think I ought to find out if he's as good as he thinks he is.'

Frankie studied the astonishingly beautiful young woman opposite. 'I don't think it's going to be too difficult to get her into bed the way things are going,' he mused, his thoughts interrupted when she spoke.

"Do you live near here or are you on holiday?" she enquired. He took a couple of black olives from the glass dish on the table and put them in his mouth. "I do, but I've only lived here a short while – this year in fact." As he spoke, it seemed to her as if her senses became more acute. She couldn't explain it but she was clearly being drawn closer to this man.

It wasn't long before a second bottle of champagne replaced the first in the ice bucket. It was when they were half way through that one when Lisa decided to end her first night in the Costa Blanca in style. She would take this man to bed. "I can always put it down to research," she reasoned impishly.

She reached across the table and took his hand gently in hers. "We could have a nightcap back at my hotel. It would be much more comfortable. Do you have a car?"

He squeezed her hand, then released it – slowly – his eyes only for her. "Yes, I do, of course, but first, let me settle up your bill," he added hastily as she reached for her handbag.

"That's not necessary, Frankie, but thank you anyway." It was the first time she had called him by his first name. It sounded so natural.

At the hotel, Lisa unlocked the door of her room and stepped inside followed by Frankie. He closed the door firmly behind him. "Do you like music?" she asked, as she put her handbag on the dresser.

Frankie shrugged. "Yeah, I don't mind," he said crossing to the window to look out on the scene below. The town had become a blaze of lights since he and his two friends had popped in for a drink at the Don Santos restaurant.

Lisa tried the four station switches of the radio fitted in the console alongside the bed. She whooped as the final one responded with a slow, rhythmic Latin beat.

As he turned away from the window, Lisa was moving sensuously toward him in time to the music, her shoes discarded. He crossed to the bed and sat down watching her as she took the fine chiffon scarf from her neck and swayed toward him. Next, she slowly unbuttoned her blouse, removed it and dropped it on the floor.

Her skirt and panties followed, revealing the full perfection of her nude statuesque, curvaceous body. He remained seated on the bed, mesmerised by Lisa's sensuous movements as she took his hands and placed them on her breasts. Her calculated action caused his nerve ends to tingle with an electrifying sense of arousal as he rose to embrace her. The gentle contact of their lips gradually became more demanding, slowly stimulating them until it built to a frenzy of unbridled passion as they explored each other's body with a forcefulness that left them exhausted and drenched in perspiration.

It was sex in its most basic sense, but it was also much more than that. For two people, that just hours ago had been total strangers, their raw union had ignited passion of an intensity neither had rarely experienced. Unbeknown to them however, it was a passion that concealed the seeds of its own destruction.

Chapter 31

Lieutenant Garcia descended the flight of stone steps and made his way to the third room on the left of the corridor. The notice on the door read 'Departamento Fotográfico'. He opened the door and as he entered the room, he immediately became aware of the acrid smell of the chemicals used for developing and processing films. The room was empty but the red light glowing above the door of the photo laboratory indicated it was occupied and in use.

"Pedro," he called out as he knocked the door several times and waited. "I'll be with you in a minute," came the muffled response from inside as Garcia occupied himself looking at the dozens of photo prints festooning the walls, one of which was dominated by a large colour poster of a nude female on a beach advertising a film manufacturer's product. He was about to light up a cigarette then checked himself as he remembered the strictly observed 'no smoking' rule of the photo laboratory.

Several minutes later, the red light above the door went out and Pedro emerged clutching a handful of newly-printed photographs. "Hi, Juan Luis. That car crash near Benissa yesterday, he explained as he hung the prints on a line to dry, using small pegs.

"Nasty business, very nasty," observed Lieutenant Garcia as he looked at the carnage and death of all five people involved in a two-car head on crash.

"The way people drive with their minds on everything except

the roads," he exclaimed. "It's no wonder they end up in accidents like that.

Pedro pointed to a tray on his desk. "By the way, the pictures you're waiting for are in there, Juan Luis. Help yourself while I finish pegging out another lot out to dry."

There were a dozen or so 30 x 20 cm colour pictures, taken using a long range telephoto lens, showing three men and three women in various groupings on a small cruising boat and another six prints featuring just one couple.

From the pictures it was clear that some kind of party or celebration was taking place on board the boat, owned by one of the men pictured.

Garcia scrutinised the pictures carefully, using a magnifying glass. He mentally congratulated the Guardia Civil officer involved in the undercover surveillance operation ordered by himself. The pictures were sharp and clear making it easy to identify those under scrutiny.

Of the six people, three men and two women were known to him. Two of the men were Germans who ran a wind-surfing and water-skiing school at the Las Palmeras Marina, near where the pictures were taken. They were shown with their two girl friends. The Germans were suspected of bringing drugs ashore from a rendezvous with drugs runners anchored twenty kilometres or so offshore at a pre-arranged pick-up point.

The third man was Frankie Gallagher, seen with a blonde woman unknown to Garcia. To describe the activities of Gallagher and the blonde as 'partying' wasn't entirely true. In the six pictures in which they were shown naked together, it was obvious they were having full blown sex in the sunshine!

Garcia lingered over the pictures of the two, noting their various body positions with salacious interest. "These people look as though they're enjoying themselves, don't you think so Pedro?" he observed. The technician looked over his shoulder and grinned. "It just goes to show what people get up to on these fancy boats Juan Luis, but don't worry. We'll never be able to afford one on our pay," he sneered.

"You're damn right there," thought Garcia, "nor the kind of

women he gets to screw. That blonde! She's all woman from what I've just seen! The lucky bastardo!"

The lieutenant had been aware of Gallagher's association with the two Germans for several weeks now. The surveillance operation he had set up since receiving that telex from a previously unknown police source in Britain, might well bear fruit, he thought.

It resulted in all three men being added to his list of suspects in the Banco Trujillo robbery in which little progress was being made, much to his intense annoyance and dented pride.

Garcia wasn't the only person interested in keeping tabs on Frankie and the people he associated with. Sabra was only too aware that Frankie had a roving eye. Even Gail and some of her friends had made it clear they would like to slip between the sheets with Frankie! But lately, Sabra had detected signs that his obsession for her had perceptibly cooled.

When he received a call out of the blue from his sister Lydia telling him that their mother had suffered a severe heart attack and had been transferred to hospital, Frankie made immediate plans to fly back to Cardiff to be at her side. Nell may be battle-hardened but her heart attack had left her frail and vulnerable.

The bad news from Cardiff, provided Sabra with the opportunity to accompany Frankie, judging it to be the moment she could win back his love by showing her genuine compassion for his ailing mother. The first-ever meeting between the two women seemingly justified her optimism.

Having discovered in which ward Nell is, Frankie and Sabra enter the twelve-bed room anxiously scanning the faces of its occupants. Frankie spots his mother but is shocked by her appearance. She seems to have physically shrunk and her hair has turned grey, almost white in places. Her face, once so strong and resolute, is much thinner, pale and lined, revealing the changes her condition has cost her.

As he crossed to her bed, her eyes lit up in recognition as her Frankie gently embraced her, fearful of squeezing any remaining life out of her. "Oh Mam," he cried, kissing and hugging her while the tears rolled down her cheeks.

"I knew you would come Frankie. I knew my boy wouldn't let

me down," she whispered, as the distance between Spain and the hospital disappeared with their embrace.

As he gently wiped away her tears, Nell noticed Sabra standing silently at the foot of the bed. Frankie eased his mother back onto her pillows and beckoned Sabra forward.

"Mam, this is Sabra. She's travelled from Spain just to meet you." Sabra leant forward and gave Nell a brief kiss on each cheek. She smiled warmly at Nell. "I'm really delighted to meet you Mrs Gallagher. I'm only sorry it's in these circumstances," she said quietly, her concern for the older woman clearly evident. "Is there anything you need Mrs Gallagher – a drink or something else?"

Nell smiled at her. "No thank you my love. Why don't you sit down and then we can talk." She looked at her son, patting his hand. "She's a very beautiful girl Frankie. I hope you're looking after her." Sabra's eyes met his. Nell's words echoing exactly her own hopes and expectations.

By the time the visiting hour had expired, the two women had forged a bond that was inevitably centred on the person that both of them loved very deeply – Frankie Gallagher.

Dave Parker walked into his office, threw his jacket onto a chair and sat on the edge of his desk as he sifted through the messages that had accumulated in the last few hours of his absence from the office. The third message he read was the one that grabbed his attention.

It read: "Frankie Gallagher seen in Cardiff in company of woman, identity unknown. It is understood that he has been visiting his mother in C. R. Infirmary. Duration of visit to Cardiff not known. Ends."

Parker re-read the message, then flicked the key of the intercom on his desk. After a brief delay, the voice of his detective sergeant came through on the loudspeaker. "Yes Dave?" Parker rounded the desk and sat down.

"Jim. What time did you receive the message about Gallagher

being back in Cardiff?" There was a pause before the reply came back. "At ten o'clock this morning. Anything else?"

Parker pushed his chair back and stood up. "Yes. See if you can find out how long he'll be in town – oh! And the name of the woman he's with. That's all." He switched the intercom off.

During the next three days, Sabra and Frankie visited his mother in hospital for as long as the visiting hours permitted.

As they were driving away from the hospital, Frankie pointed to the large country-style pub some two hundred yards ahead. "Fancy a drink? My mouth's dry as hell after that place," he said glancing across briefly at her. "I don't mind," she agreed with a slight shrug of her shoulders. He checked the rear view mirror then signalled as he turned off the road into the car park.

They chose a quiet corner in which to sit as Frankie went to the bar to order. He returned with a double brandy and a gin and tonic. "Just look at that," he scoffed. "There's just about enough brandy in there to wet the bottom of the glass."

He shook his head, recalling the generous measures served in the bars in Spain.

"Your mother seemed slightly better today," Sabra observed, taking a sip from her glass.

"Yeah. I think you're right," he agreed. "It's just as well though, because I'll need to go to London for a day or so. I need to settle one or two bits of unfinished business.

He checked her reaction. She didn't seem upset, so he pressed on. "I'll be going tomorrow. Do you think you can keep an eye on Mam while I'm away?"

She looked at him doubtfully. "Yes, of course. How long do you think you'll be away? Two days you said?"

He nodded. "About that." She sipped her drink slowly, looking at him closely.

"Give my love to my sister Eva – if you see her," she said slyly. "I will – if I see her," he replied somewhat tongue in cheek.

The next day, Parker unexpectedly received some photographs at Police HQ offices in Cardiff, wired to him from Spain. The contents of the pictures really startled him. They were accompanied by a message from Lieutenant Garcia. It read:

*Pictures obtained during surveillance of Gallagher and
known associates also under suspicion for drugs offences.
All are now suspects in recent Banco Trujillo robbery.
Regards, J. L. Garcia (Lt), Moraira, Alicante, España.*

Several of the photos pictured two men and two young women
unknown to him, taken aboard a boat. The other photos pictured
two people clearly having penetrative sex on board the same vessel. He stared hard at the photos – shocked in sheer disbelief as
he recognises the two persons involved. The man is undoubtedly
Frankie Gallagher. But he is stunned as he recognises the young
blonde woman in their passionate embrace as Lisa Jones – the
daughter of Peggy Steele – and Frankie Gallagher!

What incredible circumstances could possibly exist whereby a
father and his own daughter would be openly making love – especially in the presence of others, unless they were absolutely and
totally unaware of their true relationship? Parker is an experienced,
seasoned police officer, but even he is sickened by the shocking
disclosures of their intimacy together! "Gallagher and his own
daughter, for Christ sake! It's beyond belief!"

All his years of training and discipline in both the Armed
Services and the Police Force are strained to the limit as his
intense dislike and even hatred of Gallagher now bubbles to the
surface. His desire to seek revenge on Gallagher is tempered only
by his concern for protecting the young woman from the trauma
that would surely follow in the wake of disclosure of their shame-
ful relationship.

He flicked the switch on the intercom. "Jim!" he yelled. "Jim!"
Again that delay before he got a response. "Yes, hello Dave. What's
up?" Parker hesitated, uncertain how to play it.

"Have you got those details on that woman who travelled from
Spain with Gallagher?" There was another pause while his colleague searched through his notes.

"Mmmm… yeah, here they are Dave. Her name is Sabra Levy,
she's from London and you can contact her at this telephone number.
It's the Gallagher house." Parker jotted the number down, uttered
a hurried "thanks" and flicked the intercom switch off.

He dialled the number, his hand slightly shaky. A woman answered the phone. He asked to speak to Sabra Levy. "She's not here at the moment," came the reply. "She's at the hospital and will be back later – I don't know when. Can I ask who's calling?" He ignored her question. "Can you just ask Sabra to phone this number when she gets back?" The woman at the other end of the line wrote the number down and repeated it back to him. "That's right. Thanks." he said and rang off.

The number he had given her was the private line on his desk. Not everybody wanted to go through the Police HQ switchboard for reasons best known to themselves. It was more than an hour later that the call he had waited for impatiently came through.

The woman's voice said, "I've been asked to ring this number. Who am I speaking to?" Parker took a deep breath. At least his anger had subsided now. "This is Detective Inspector Dave Parker of the Cardiff City CID. Thank you for returning my call."

He heard a sharp intake of breath on the other end of the line. Fearful she would ring off, he quickly spoke to her.

"Miss Levy, there is a personal matter of some importance that has been brought to my attention and it is very much in your interests that we meet as soon as possible." There was a prolonged period of silence on the other end of the line.

"Miss Levy – are you still there?" he asked anxiously. "Miss Levy!"

She finally spoke. "I take it that this may involve Frankie, is that right? But why me? Why do you want us to meet?" she asked.

He could understand her puzzlement, but a meeting with her was vital. "Miss Levy, we've never met, but I really do have to see you," he pleaded. "Trust me. It's very important, believe me."

Sabra hesitated, uncertain of her position, especially in Frankie's absence. She was fearful of putting him in jeopardy. But the detective sounded sincere enough. She made a sudden decision, hoping to God she wouldn't regret it. "Where do you suggest we meet, Mr Parker?"

He heaved a sigh of relief. "I'll pick you up in an unmarked car at your address. Tell any member of the family that you've ordered a taxi to do some shopping. Agreed?"

Twenty minutes later as a car drew up outside, she let herself out of the house and got into the rear seat next to Parker.

After he quickly identified himself with his warrant card, she spoke to him. "I've been worried sick since we spoke on the phone Mr Parker. Can you explain what is so important that we have to meet like this? What's this all about?"

He gave a reassuring smile although he was about to detonate an explosion that could affect her life. He tapped the driver on the shoulder. "Take us somewhere quiet," he instructed him.

Twenty minutes later they pulled up at a spot overlooking the sea in the small seaside town of Penarth. The nearest houses were located some two hundred yards away overlooking a pitch and putt mini golf course.

Parker turned to face Sabra. "I take it you and Frankie Gallagher are very close – well, you are living together in Spain."

She nodded. "Yes, we are very close, you can be sure of that," she replied, still puzzled as to where this was leading.

He rubbed his chin doubtfully before continuing. "You'll know I'm not speaking out of turn if I say your boyfriend has a reputation for being a ladies man, so you won't be surprised to hear that he's been keeping company with another woman." He was having difficulty putting this across as he soon discovered.

"Is that all this is about – another woman?" she flared. "Don't you think I know he's had an occasional fling elsewhere in his time? My god! You've brought me out here to tell me that!" she stormed angrily.

Parker held up his hands in a gesture meant to calm her. "Believe me Miss Levy, it's not that simple." He took an envelope from his pocket and extracted the photos it contained. "This will undoubtedly hurt, but you must see these." He held out the pictures. "That woman he's with...' he hesitated, "that's his own daughter! Believe me. I know her and I know that she's his daughter!"

The effect on Sabra was instant and shattering. She stared transfixed at the pictures, unable to tear her eyes away from the carnal images displayed. She broke down sobbing quietly at first, then bitterly until she was sobbing uncontrollably as her body shook with pain and emotion.

"His daughter," she sobbed. "Why his own daughter? Where did you get these from? Who took them? Who gave them to you?"

Parker, appreciating the value of tears as a release in these circumstances, watched and waited for several minutes until the shaking of her shoulders and severe distress subsided.

"Although it won't be any consolation to you, I'm not even sure that he knows the woman he's with actually is his daughter. But why I should give him the benefit of the doubt, God only knows! Surely, even he can't stoop that low!"

Later, as he dropped her off near the Gallagher home, she felt incapable of facing any of them, especially as her tear-stained make-up betrayed obvious signs of distress. With the briefest of apologies, she collected her belongings and booked into a city-centre hotel.

Her efforts to contact Frankie at Maurice's club proved futile. He hadn't indicated where he was going once he had finished his business with the club. Did that mean he was on his way back to Cardiff? She desperately wanted to speak to him and clear up this dreadful, unbelievable nightmare now that news of his involvement with his daughter had become known. She was also fearful that should it reach Nell, it could have a serious, possibly even a fatal effect on the old lady, given her fragile state of health.

While devastated by Parker's revelations, Sabra realised there was something positive that could come out of this dreadful mess. Now she was thinking more clearly, she realised she may now have the means of destroying Lisa's passionate relationship with Frankie – once and for all! But who does she confront first with the truth?

Desperately seeking some advice she contacts Parker, explaining her dilemma. While not wishing to become entangled any further in the bizarre circumstances in which Sabra now found herself, as he was responsible for breaking the news to her in the first place, he gives her the name and telephone number of the magazine for whom Lisa works.

Having decided that Lisa needs to be made aware of her own and Frankie's extraordinary situation, Sabra's course of action becomes a simple matter. "Let's get rid of the opposition first – then I can tackle Frankie."

Chapter 32

"Hey, Lisa! You're wanted on the telephone." The copy boy who had answered the call in the editorial office put his hand over the mouthpiece.

"Who is it?" she called out from the other side of the office. "Can I call them back?" The young man took his hand away from the mouthpiece. "Can I ask who's calling?"

He listened briefly and replaced his hand over the mouthpiece. "It's someone called Gallagher – Frank, I think he said."

She dropped the pile of papers she had been reading onto the desk. "I'll take, I'll take it – don't let him go," she squealed, hurrying across the office to where the young lad stood, still patiently cradling the receiver.

"Some special kind of lover boy then, is he?" he quipped with a cheeky grin. She snatched the phone from him and shooed him away with her free hand. "It's private – go away," she smiled, repeating the gesture with her hand.

"Hello Frankie? Oh my goodness, it's wonderful to hear from you. Where are you calling from? From England! What, from here in London? Wow! Yes, yes of course we can meet up this evening. Do you know where my office is? You have the address? That's brilliant! I finish at six o'clock, so can we say – seven? It will give me time to freshen up for you. I'm dying to see you again Frankie. Bye, my love. See you later."

As she returned to her desk, the last thing she could concentrate on was work! Frankie's call had really brightened up her day.

But it was another unexpected call that ruined her plans for that evening.

Sabra dropped the first bombshell when she told Lisa that she and Frankie lived together in Spain and that Lisa's appearance on the scene had jeopardised their whole relationship. It didn't take Sabra long to establish her knowledge of Frankie or her claim on him! But it was the second salvo from Sabra that really blew Lisa's world of romance to smithereens!

Lisa was totally dumbstruck as Sabra stuck the knife in and gave it a cruel twist! "Did you know that you're not Frankie's girlfriend at all. How could you be – when you're his daughter!"

Lisa stood there swaying, her legs shaking as she felt faint. The waves of nausea rose from her stomach as she reached for the chair behind her and sat down.

Swallowing deeply, she managed to speak. "What kind of sick crank are you?" she hissed down the phone as workmates turned slyly to eavesdrop on the one-way conversation. "You must be stark staring mad to come up with such filthy, horrible lies just to try and take Frankie away from me," she snapped, her eyes now blazing. "That's the most disgusting, filthy lie I've ever..."

Sabra's interruption cut her protests short. "You may not believe me – despite the fact that it's true! But there's a senior police officer in Cardiff that can and will prove that you're Frankie Gallagher's daughter! I have his phone number. Just call him and ask him for yourself!"

Despite the silence from the other end of the line, Sabra persisted. "Write this down – and call him!" She gave the numbers, then repeated them to Lisa to make sure. "I'm just astonished you don't want to find out the real truth for yourself!" With that final condemnation, Sabra slammed the phone down.

Lisa replaced the receiver, slowly, still paralysed by the dreadful horror of that woman's allegation. Avoiding everyone's eyes, she collected her handbag from her desk draw and left the office – her eyes red and burning with her tears. She fled to the female toilet room, locked herself in a cubicle and collapsed on the seat, whimpering like a wounded animal.

Her grief welled up, consuming her entire body as she recalled the mental pictures, those disgusting, filthy pictures painted by Sabra's accusation. She must get hold of herself! She must think clearly! She would contact Frankie and tell him of Sabra's evil, malicious call. That's what she would do! What would he say? Would he deny it? Of course he would, wouldn't he?

This Sabra bitch! Who is she? Was she really Frankie's only true love? That woman! She would invent any poisonous story to keep me and Frankie apart, wouldn't she? Some women would kill to keep their man. Many have! But why did she say these filthy lies? They couldn't be true, could they?

Lisa took the screwed-up piece of paper on which she had scribbled the policeman's number from her blouse pocket and stared at it numbly. As she read the figures, she realised that this scrap of crumpled paper could release her from her torment and despair – or it could condemn her to a life of self-disgust, unable ever to forget her moments of unnatural passion with Frankie Gallagher. To phone – or not. It was a harrowing decision to make.

She unlocked the door, checked to see if the toilet room was empty and then emerged to study her reflection in the mirror. She saw a stranger, saddened by despair and fearful of what might prove to be true, her red-rimmed eyes swollen and puffy. She rinsed her face in water in an attempt to repair the ravages of her tears, brushed her hair and left.

Lisa made her way to the ground floor of the building by lift, walked out into the street and made her way to a group of telephone cubicles manned by a young man. "Number 5," he said, pressing the reset button to zero on the timer by which she would be charged for her call.

She checked the number and dialled it, half-hoping there would be no reply. There was.

"Hello, Dave Parker,"

She started at the response, hesitating, then spoke. "Mr Parker, my name is Lisa Jones. I believe you know of me, although we've never met." She stopped, unsure of what to say next.

"Yes – how can I help you?" he replied, now realising to whom he was speaking.

Lisa took a deep breath. "I was informed today by a woman I've never met or ever spoken to before, that I have a father whom I've also never met, that she claims is Frankie Gallagher." She paused. "Can you tell me if this is true and what proof there may be to substantiate it. Please, please help me if you can,"

He hesitated briefly then answered. "Yes Lisa. It's true. I'm very sorry you've had to find out..." He stopped as the woman on the line cried out – a cry of anguish!

There were many seconds of silence before Lisa composed herself enough to speak, albeit with a tremor in her voice. "If necessary, can you prove my family relationship with this person beyond any shadow of doubt, Mr Parker?" she pleaded, her voice choking with emotion.

He again hesitated. "Yes Lisa, I can. I knew your mother very well – we were good friends and I can assure you that this fellow Gallagher is indeed your father. Regrettably, I have undisputed evidence to that effect," he told her.

They spent the next minutes speaking of the background of the triangle that linked Lisa, her mother and Gallagher. Parker also discussed his friendship with her mother as teenagers. Lisa thanked him for his help in such distressing circumstances, with a hint that they might just meet one day.

She couldn't face returning to work. Instead she took a taxi to her flat, wrote a letter to her company claiming compassionate circumstances, a brief letter to Frankie Gallagher and headed for Winchester and her roots. There was plenty for her to think about. It was time for reflection – and more tears.

Chapter 33

Frankie Gallagher stood waiting outside the office block as its people spilled out from the large revolving doors onto the pavement. Some faces showed tiredness, others were smiling as they joked with their colleagues, a night of relaxation and a few drinks in prospect. He looked at his watch. Ten minutes past seven. He again scanned their faces hoping to see Lisa, but to no avail. He gave it another ten minutes then pushed his way through the door and walked over to the reception desk."

"Evening sir," said the security guard, acknowledging Frankie as he approached the desk. Frankie smiled a greeting.

"Hi – I've been waiting for a friend who works for the magazine company, but she's failed to show up. Can you ring them from here and see if a lady named Lisa Jones is still in the office? I'd appreciate it."

The guard nodded affably. "Certainly sir, I can do that for you." He dialled a number on his exchange console and spoke into his phone. "Hello, this is Security on the ground floor. I have a chap here enquiring if a Lisa Jones is still in the office." The guard listened, nodding occasionally, then replaced the phone. "Apparently sir she left the office earlier this afternoon and hasn't been back. She didn't leave a message I'm told."

Frankie stood there, momentarily nonplussed. "You're sure that's what they said?" he queried, still not satisfied.

The guard nodded. He'd already done this guy a favour, so what more did he want? "Yes sir," he re-affirmed. Frankie muttered his thanks, left the building and stood there as the homeward-bound traffic increased in density. He spotted a telephone kiosk some thirty yards away, hurried towards it fishing some coins from his pocket. He dialled Lisa's number at the flat. There was no reply. Frankie waited several minutes then dialled again. Still no reply.

He ran their earlier conversation through his mind. He was certain neither of them had said anything likely to cause any change in their plan. In fact, Lisa had seemed especially happy at the prospects of them spending some time together. So the question remained. Why had she failed to show up? He decided he needed a drink and made his way to the bar on the opposite side of the road.

He ordered a brandy, sat down and continued to consider the possible motives for Lisa's non-appearance. He made a decision. He'd finished his business with Maurice for the time being and there seemed little point in hanging around in London – especially as he'd been unable to contact Lisa.

He tried her number once more from the bar's pay-phone. No reply, so that clinched it. He finished his brandy, left the bar and flagged down a passing black taxi cab – destination Paddington Railway Station. An hour later, he was on the train back to South Wales.

Frankie phoned his mother's house on arrival in Cardiff only to be told that Sabra had left and booked a room at the Royal Hotel in the city centre. "Don't ask me why," said Frankie's youngest sister. "She just upped and left." He replaced the phone.

"Now why the hell did she do that," he pondered as he made his way out of the station's main entrance.

The Royal was located just across the road from the station. In fact, he could see it from where he stood, it taking him less than a few minutes. His enquiry at the reception desk revealed she was staying in Room 24. "Can you tell Miss Levy I'm on the way up? The name's Gallagher." With that, Frankie made his way to the lift and pushed the appropriate button.

Sabra was waiting at the open door, greeting him with a sensuous kiss and a warm embrace reserved for the special person in her life. Frankie grasped her by her shoulders. "Why did you leave the house. Sab? Is Mam still OK? Is anything wrong?" The questions tumbled from his lips, mirroring his concern. Sabra put one finger gently on his lips, stemming the flow of his questions.

"Your mother's doing just fine, Frankie. She looked very much better in hospital today. Naturally, she wanted to know where you were," she smiled, thinking meanwhile to herself, "that's something I'd like to have known as well," although she hadn't expected to see him for a day or so longer. "And why did I leave your Nell's house and book into the hotel? This is why," she said huskily.

Sabra took Frankie by the hand, placing it deep inside her inviting cleavage. Her breasts, inadequately protected by the flimsy material of her dress, failed to conceal the sensuality of her curvaceous, olive-skinned body.

As his fingers brushed across her rapidly hardening nipple, the contact sent pulses of lust surging through his loins. Frankie swept Sabra off her feet onto the nearby bed. The exotic fragrances exuding from her slightly moist body further heightened his senses which were already about to go into overdrive. She initially submitted to Frankie's carnal promptings without resistance, suggesting she was about to fully surrender.

Sabra's submission didn't last. Her own level of eroticism rapidly soared to pure whorism, enveloping the couple in a raw sexual frenzy that left them totally and utterly drained.

An hour or so later, an expert massage in the hotel set them up for a relaxed dinner in Frankie's favourite Bute Street restaurant – an area of Cardiff known by many in its popular guise as Tiger Bay. Despite their earlier, inflammatory lovemaking and the subtle romanticism of the restaurant, it was clear to Sabra that Frankie had something on his mind that was occupying his innermost thoughts – and they bothered him.

The feeling persisted into the following day during their visit to see Nell at the nearby Llandough Hospital. The couple's concerns for Nell's condition were eased by the encouraging opinion of the nursing staff who confirmed that Nell had indeed responded well to the treatment she was receiving. Such was their optimism, that Frankie and Sabra felt it was possible for them to return to Spain in a day or so. A further, somewhat emotional visit to see Nell the next day, a final evening's drinking with several close family members and a few friends and they were soon back on their way to Spain – and their home on the Costa Blanca.

Despite the generous welcome of their friends upon their return and the relaxed surroundings, Frankie's subdued manner persisted in spite of Sabra's efforts to bring back the sparkle that was his hallmark.

While he remained in the shadow of uncertainty having still not had any contact from Lisa, for her part Sabra could at least console herself with the salacious knowledge of Lisa and Frankie's family connection. It was knowledge that was certain to result in an end to the threat posed by Lisa as a love rival when Sabra had been feeling at her most vulnerable.

Frankie's mood of suppressed emotion couldn't last long – and it didn't. The resulting rows and flare-ups frequently left Sabra in tears, fearful that he was about to walk out for good. It was a situation she had long dreaded despite the humiliations she had suffered through his addictive attraction to other women.

Sabra spent literally a whole afternoon turning over the thorny problem that was etched indelibly into her mind as she sat alone watching television without seeing or absorbing anything of any significance on the screen. Frankie's poker playing date with a couple of pals provided the opportunity to give the subject of Lisa her undivided attention. Was this the moment to play her trump card and dispose of the Lisa problem once and for all? Sabra sighed deeply and decided it was. She'd confront Frankie with his latest sordid affair, but one that was likely to have the most painful and damaging of consequences. With that thought, she turned her attention once again to the television – and the only TV channel available in Spain – despite the fact that it was in Spanish!

The slamming of a car door at the top of the drive – the shouted 'cheerios' heralded Frankie's return. As he appeared in the archway that led into the lounge Sabra looked up, smiling a welcome. "Enjoy your card game Frank?" she enquired, patting the sofa.

Frankie slumped heavily onto the leather cushion next to Sabra. "Yeah, it was OK. I even managed to take five thousand pesetas apiece off those two tight bastards from the Estate Agency. Miss me babe?" he quizzed her, as he gave her a meaningful kiss on the lips while his right hand slid deftly under her brief top, encouraging the dark brown nipple to swell and rapidly firm up.

In response, Sabra squeezed his crutch, gently fondling his manhood while he stretched his arms above his head. She smiled, her white even teeth framed by a perfectly shaped generous mouth. "Don't settle down Frankie – we're not going to have a session. I've something important to tell you." She stood up. "Fancy a brandy?" Sabra didn't wait for his response, but poured his drink anyway – a generous measure of Magno.

She returned to the settee, placing his drink on the coffee table, before resuming her place alongside him. He sighed contentedly, totally unaware of what was to follow. "Right then Sab, what's so important, go on, spill it." He took an appreciative sip of his drink, relishing its fiery flavour.

Sabra touched his arm causing him to make eye contact. She wanted that – eye contact. She wanted to see Frankie's reaction – through his eyes – to what she was about to reveal.

"This woman Lisa, Frankie – yes Lisa! I know it surprises you that I know about you and her. Well, she's not so much a woman more of a girl I suppose. So, just how serious is it this time Frankie? Tell me," she urged.

The mention of Lisa's name jolted Frankie, causing him to sit bolt upright. I've got his attention now, thought Sabra watching Frankie intently. His face paled under his tan, his mouth tightening. "What do you mean for Christ's sake? What Lisa? Who the hell's she?" he rasped as Sabra continued.

She'd started and she wasn't going to back down now! "That's a good question Frankie – a damn good question coming from…"

"What the fuck are you driving at?" he interrupted. "Go on – tell me?" he shouted, his voice rising as his anger started to cut in.

Sabra leaned forward to emphasise her accusation. "This Lisa – she's not just your latest girl friend, is she Frankie – is she? How could she be?" Sabra paused, "The real truth is that she's your daughter Frankie – yes your daughter! Do you hear what I'm saying?" Lisa is Elizabeth – the daughter you thought had passed out of your life for good when your real girl friend died after that car crash all those years ago!"

Sabra stood over Frankie, her disgust disfiguring her striking features. "For God's sake Frankie – don't you realise what I'm saying? You've been fucking your own daughter!" Her eyes brimmed with tears. "What kind of monster does that make you," she sobbed.

She sank slowly to her knees in front of Frankie, saddened yet strangely flushed by the release of her pent-up feelings – the cause of the bombshell that had literally ripped Frankie's thoughts asunder just moments earlier.

His grasp on the glass in his hand loosened, the liquid spilling onto the marble floor. Frankie just sat there, shaking his head in disbelief, stunned into silence by her unspeakable claim. Finally he spoke. "That can't be true Sab – it just can't be true! Wherever you heard that, whoever you heard it from is just feeding you the most vicious lies to cause trouble between us."

He rose to his feet, avoiding Sabra's eyes as he crossed to the drinks trolley, fixed himself another brandy and took a sizeable mouthful.

Sabra, now regaining more of her composure yet with a bitterness welling inside her as the true depth of his treachery to her was about to be laid bare, added further evidence of her source of information. She grimaced. "It's no lie. It's the truth! That policeman in Cardiff – Dave Parker – he told me. He showed me proof. That girl Lisa, she's your daughter for sure, "she added with even greater emphasis.

"Parker! Parker!" Frankie raged. "Do you believe that lying bastard? He'd say and do anything – and I mean anything – to get at me," he yelled. He paced the floor, his mind a whirl. If what Parker had told Sabra was true, what grounds did he have for proof? How could it even be a remote possibility? The child had been taken away to live somewhere in England by Peggy's parents after her death and brought up as their own child.

And yet the nagging doubt, now given substance by Sabra's revelation, still caused a stab of fear through Frankie's insides. The vivid memory of Lisa failing to turn up for their London meeting flooded back to him. There just had to be an important reason for her failing to show. Was this why she disappeared without trace, with not even a word then – or since? The truth, if that what is was, felt like a burning hot dagger being driven deep into his guts! Frankie needed time to think – to seek refuge from Sabra's unrelenting scrutiny – and his own humiliation! Now wracked with feelings of shame and guilt, he turned to the one real friend he could depend on – brandy, in copious quantities.

It took an urgent telephone call from his eldest sister Lydia, in Cardiff, to jolt Frankie out of his two week, alcohol-inspired stupor. Nell's health had unexpectedly deteriorated to a degree that caused the hospital authorities to fear that her days were nearing an end. If nothing else, Nell had been a fighter all her life. Now she was doggedly hanging on, showing the same fierce determination from which her family had inherited its powerful sense of survival. The question on everyone's lips was, "Could Nell win her biggest battle against all the odds that seemed stacked against her? The next few days would provide the answer. Meanwhile the family watched – and waited.

Chapter 34

T he regular flight service between Valencia and Cardiff airports had proved a real bonus for Frankie and Sabra especially now in view of Nell's fluctuating and worsening health. The old girl had battled bravely against the odds, hoping fervently that Frankie, of all her family, would be at her bedside to comfort her through her latest crisis. But Nell's lapse into a deep coma and the unlikelihood of ever coming out of it made it clear she was near her end. Nell had been a hard taskmaster to her family during her emotionally eventful and often difficult life, but she was loved by her closely-knit family with an intensity borne out of devotion and a deep-set respect.

Her family's anxious wait and Nell's frail grasp on life came to a quiet end when she died peacefully without ever recovering or being aware of her family's stressful three day and three night hospital vigil.

Frankie Gallagher's departure from Spain, to be at his mother's bedside, had been unobtrusively observed by those persons who made it their business to keep an eye on the comings and goings of the Costa Blanca's criminal community. As a gesture partly of goodwill but mainly on a basis of "you help me and I'll help you," Lieutenant Juan Luis Garcia tipped off his opposite number in Cardiff, DI Dave Parker – more information that was again greatly appreciated by the South Wales Serious Crime Squad.

Parker had already intended to be present at Nell's funeral, in a bid to pick up useful information from the gathering of the Gallaghers. Frankie's presence was the icing on the cake.

Nell's laying to rest might have been blessed with a bright sunny day. Instead, it was a dull, overcast damp day that only served to emphasise the smell of the freshly-dug earth from her grave in the Culverhouse Cross cemetery and the over-long grass of the plot that had already been host to several earlier Gallagher family members.

The mourners shuffled around the open grave as they sought to obtain their positions – some seeking front-line prominence, others choosing a form of anonymity to provide the sombre grey/black background deemed so necessary on these occasions. Some faces gave evidence of their owner's unease at their closeness to a deeply personal religious ritual. Others, silent though tearful, with their private thoughts remaining private, at least for the time being.

Dave Parker's unmarked police car drew up a discreet distance away from the graveside gathering. He got out, gave his driver a brief instruction to park out of sight and slowly made his way towards the crowd gathered at the graveside. Parker had intended his arrival to be discreet but his appearance brought an immediate reaction from several men and women members of the family who uttered various oaths and uncomplimentary remarks, one or two making a move in his direction.

It was Frankie who stepped away from the graveside, urging them to remain calm, motioning them to stay where they were. With that, he strode to where Parker stood motionless, his eyes never moving from the policeman's face. Frankie stopped some ten yards or so from the man he had detested with an unbridled, burning passion since their early school-days.

"What the fuck are you doing here Parker," he said through gritted teeth. "This is not the time or the place for an arsehole of a copper – especially you, of all people!"

By now, the attention of the entire congregation was focused on the pair as they eyed each other with mutual loathing. Parker took a deep breath before replying. "I don't expect you to believe this Gallagher, but I've come to pay my respects to your mother. She was a proud lady and..."

Frankie took several quick paces forward, bringing him within touching distance of Parker, his sudden movement causing the policeman to stop short. The venom in Frankie's voice could have been cut with a knife. "You've what?" he spat out. "You've come to pay your respects to my mother! You've never had any respect for her or any member of my family at any time in your poxy life, you lying bastard!"

He moved even closer, thrusting his face within inches of Parker's. "We don't need you or your stinking respect now or any other time Parker," he snarled, "so fuck off out of here while you can, or I'll set that lot on your rotten carcase. You'll be lucky to get out of this place alive!"

Parker had never lacked for courage in his lifetime – and he didn't now, but common sense told him he couldn't reason with Frankie Gallagher in his present frame of mind. "I'll go Gallagher," he said evenly, "but I'm warning you now. You step out of line just once more on my patch and I'll put you inside for a long stretch." With that, he took a couple of paces to the rear, turned his back on Frankie and headed in the direction of his waiting police car without a backward glance.

Dave Parker pushed open the door of his office in the Cardiff City Police headquarters in Cathays Park, took off his raincoat and hung it on the coat stand in the corner of the room. He slumped down heavily in his chair, still inwardly seething at the treatment he'd had to put up with from Frankie Gallagher at the cemetery.

He picked up the several notes that had been left on the desk by Sergeant Jim Cooper and studied each one in turn, evaluating what action – if any – was required. It was the last one though that grabbed his attention. He flicked the switch and spoke into his intercom. "Jim! Jim!" he repeated, louder this time.

There was a further delay of several seconds, then the voice of Jim Cooper crackled through the speaker. "Yes Dave – sorry to keep you waiting. I had someone on the phone. How can I help?"

Parker again briefly checked the details on the note in his hand. "There's a message here from a Lisa Jones and a contact phone number. When did she telephone and did she say what she wanted?" he asked. Parker impatiently heard the rustling of papers, then Cooper spoke. "Yes, erm, she said she needed to speak to you about an important matter and asked if you would ring her when you got back to the office. Oh – and she rang about twenty minutes ago, so I suppose she might still be wherever she rang you from," he added helpfully.

Parker was already picking up the phone off its hook. "Thanks Jim," he replied. He checked the number on the note and dialled it. The phone at the other end rang six times.

Parker's expectation was lessening with each ring, when a voice responded. "Hello?" The voice was quiet almost defensive. "Hello? it said again. Parker grabbed a pen and pulled a notepad closer. "This is Dave Parker of the Cardiff City police. I have a message to ring this number. Is that Lisa Jones?" The silence from the other end only lasted four or five seconds but it seemed longer leading the policeman to believe the other person had rung off. Then – a reply.

"Yes it is, thank you for returning my call." A fleeting image of Lisa Jones' face flashed through Parker's mind as he heard her voice, visualising her speaking. "My mind has been in an absolute turmoil since I heard that this person Frank Gallagher is supposed to be my father." She hesitated... "I mean, I still can't believe it, despite what I've been told – it's just so bizarre and horrible. In fact, it's left me totally drained," she added, her voice betraying her pain. Her air of utter despair was all too evident to her caller despite the distance between them.

Parker cleared his throat. "I really am sorry that you find yourself in this situation Miss Jones and I know it came as a shock, but unfortunately, it's true. Frank Gallagher is your father." Despite all his years as a policeman, he felt himself clearly moved by the predicament in which she found herself. His thoughts were interrupted as she spoke, emphasising her words.

"My grandparents have been my parents in virtually every respect throughout my life. Whenever I've raised the question of my real parents, I now know that they protected me from the real truth, despite our closeness and the love we've shared."

There was a lengthy pause as she dabbed at her eyes with a handkerchief, Parker sensibly remaining silent until she resumed speaking.

"I knew my mother had been killed in a car accident but I'd

always been led to believe that my birth was the result of a very brief relationship – a one night stand in fact, with the identity of my father never known. It seemed so final, so utterly conclusive, that I just accepted it. I once visited my mother's grave in Cardiff, so there seemed no reason to question their version of events – until now, that is," she concluded, her voice dwindling to a whisper.

Parker stood up to relieve the ache in his back. "I knew your mother very well and we were close. Gallagher, your mother and I went to the same school – in fact, we were all in the same class. If you feel a meeting might help in any way... he stopped short as Lisa cut in.

"I would prefer that we didn't meet. This is a situation I really don't want to prolong any more than necessary. I'm sure you understand," she said. Given the circumstances, Parker could only agree. "Yes of course," he replied, "as you wish." Lisa paused – "There is something I would hope you can do for me if you could," she said. "Since the last time we spoke I've written a letter that I want to send to Frank Gallagher. I haven't been able to bring myself to face him directly, Would you be able to pass it on to him in some way?"

She lapsed into silence, prompting Parker to say, "Miss Jones, hello? Miss Jones?" There was a brief silence then, "I'm still here," she replied. "I just want this whole dreadful business to be a chapter in my life that I can put behind me – once and for all. If you could give me your address, I'll send it on to you. Will that be acceptable?" she enquired. Parker briefly considered her request before replying.

"Yes of course. I'll arrange that when I get your letter," he said as the intercom on his desk buzzed. "I'm on the phone," he barked, flipping the buzzer key back up. "It just leaves me to wish you well in the future, Miss Jones, but let me give you my address." With that and a quiet murmur of thanks, she rang off.

He put the telephone receiver back on its cradle and eased himself back into his comfortable chair, as he ran the details of their conversation through his mind. She was dreadfully upset, that was clear – but then, she had every reason to be. While Parker had at one time briefly considered that Gallagher might have known in advance that Lisa was his daughter, the policeman dismissed this from his mind, having finally admitted to himself that it was only his intense dislike of Gallagher that had led him to that unlikely conclusion. All it needed now to draw the whole unsavoury episode to an end, was to pass on Lisa Jones' letter, thereby ridding herself of Gallagher's presence once and for all.

Chapter 35

His mother's death, followed by the arrangements for her burial, the need to settle her affairs and the manner in which they affected the family, convinced Frankie that he and Sabra would be best suited staying on at the Royal Hotel – at least for a few more days. Being away from Nell's house spared them from the constant flow of well-wishers, welcome though they were and appreciated by the family as they expressed their condolences. The hotel by comparison was a retreat of relative calm – a situation Frankie needed as he continued to come to terms with the unwelcome revelation regarding his and Lisa's family link. The presence of a London jewellery company exhibiting their products in the hotel's conference room gave the place an extra air of activity providing a boost to Sabra following several sombre days before and after Nell's funeral.

Following breakfast at the hotel, Frankie was going to be absent for most of the day on 'company business' which gave Sabra the opportunity to check out Cardiff's renowned central shopping area. The city centre featured several major department stores and a host of covered arcades with their wealth of small specialist shops brimming with unusual gifts and was indeed a shoppers paradise. But several hours later and well into the lunch period, even a dedicated shopper like Sabra needed a break, so with a glance at her watch she decided she'd stop at one of the fashionable cafes for a coffee and a bite to eat.

As she strolled past the medieval landmark of St John's Church, someone called out to her from the doorway of the Old Arcade public house – part of the famous Brains Brewery chain – a pub noted for its Brains SA and Brains Dark beers and one that featured numerous memoirs of its boxing and rugby connections, past and present with framed photographs and team jerseys.

Danny Gallagher again called out as Sabra approached. "Sab – hey Sab! Let's give you a hand with that lot," pointing at her numerous shopping bags. "Christ, you've been busy haven't you," he exclaimed. "This must have cost you a few quid!"

Sabra stopped as several passers-by jostled their way down the historic old street with its fourteenth century church and imposing clock tower. "Hi Danny," she greeted him, glad even for a brief break from her shopping spree. "It's OK. I'm just popping into the cafe over there for a break then it's back to the hotel. By the way Danny," she enquired, "now that your mother's funeral matters are settled, when are you thinking of going back to London?"

He scratched his nose reflectively. "Sometime next week I expect – Monday maybe." He hesitated. "By the way Sab, could you do me a big favour? I need to get to the bookies before the next few races start at three o'clock and I've got a couple of nags that are dead certs running." He looked at her expectantly.

"Yes, If I can. What do you want me to do?" her curiosity clearly aroused. He reached into his jacket pocket and pulled out something solid wrapped in a yellow duster cloth. He glanced anxiously up and down the street. "I can't show you here in the middle of the street." His stage whisper gave her scant warning of what to expect next. "It's a gun – Frankie's gun. I borrowed it to scare the shit out of a shyster that owed us money – nearly £2,000! He's a two-timing pick-pocket whose missis is a very busy shoplifter – nice couple," he sniffed. "He soon coughed up when he saw the shooter! By the way, it's loaded, but the safety catch is on," he added as he handed her the weapon.

Danny's casual reference to a loaded weapon took her off guard. "What do you want me to do," she repeated cautiously, surprised by its unexpected weight. She took the cloth-wrapped parcel and gingerly placed it in her handbag, fearing it would go off at any moment. "Good god Danny, are they all as heavy as this," she exclaimed, testing the weight of the bag and its unwelcome passenger.

He nodded. "More or less, but in any case, this one has a full clip of ammunition in it – that's thirteen bullets in all." He blew his nose enthusiastically into his soiled handkerchief before replying. "I'd like you to give it to my brother. Oh – and tell him that I got the money. That'll please him."

It was clear he was in a hurry as he stood in front of her, changing his weight from one foot to the other as though he was ready to sprint away. "As I explained Sab, I've got a couple of really hot tips and I want to get the money on before the three o'clock race." With that, he patted her on the hand and with a hurried "Thanks Sab," he strode off in the direction of the church and the bookmakers premises situated in the adjoining street.

With the gun now in her handbag, all thoughts of a leisurely taken cup of coffee and a cake were dismissed from her mind. As the hotel was handily situated only some 200 yards or so away in nearby St Mary's Street, she adjusted the distribution of her shopping bags making them more comfortable to carry and set off.

The hotel doorman rapidly offered his help with the bags as she approached the main doors. "I would never have made it through these doors with this lot," she laughed, flashing a dazzling smile as they exchanged bags.

"My pleasure madam," he responded, his eyes drinking the sheer beauty of the vision that stood less than a yard from him – the fragrancy of her expensive perfume bridging the gap between them just enough to send his juices coursing. He carried her shopping over to the reception desk, awaiting her next request. Whatever he was expecting, he was disappointed.

"Can you have these sent up to my room and ask Mr Gallagher to join me in the cocktail lounge, please."

The reception clerk nodded to the doorman – a signal for him to return to his post at the front door. Sabra murmured her thanks as he dialled her room number. The clerk put the telephone down.

"There's no reply I'm afraid madam, but I now seem to recall that Mr Gallagher claimed your room key earlier this afternoon. If he's not in the cocktail lounge it's just possible he popped out for a while and took the key with him. Oh there is one thing. A gentleman called while you were out and left an envelope for Mr Gallagher. He didn't leave his name." Then with a disarming smile and – "Will you excuse me please" – he turned and consulted a stack of mail deposited on the table at the rear of his little domain.

Sabra looked at the envelope, her curiosity aroused. She held it to her nose and sniffed it several times. There was a clear hint of perfume but not one she could identify. Sabra hesitated briefly then turned away while she considered several questions that Frankie's absence posed. Why had he returned to the hotel so early after saying that he would be 'on business' most of the day – and well into the afternoon at that? Why had he collected the key and then left the hotel taking the key with him? Why didn't he leave a message with the desk clerk, or a note for me if he had intended leaving the hotel even for an hour or so?

Still turning these questions over in her mind, she made a call from the hotel call box to the Gallagher house. No, they hadn't seen Frankie. – "We thought he was with you." She decided not to ask the clerk to let her in to her room – after all, the shopping was out of the way. Might as well have a drink then look in at the jewellery exhibition.

Finding a quiet corner in the cocktail lounge, she ordered a drink before retrieving the envelope from her handbag. Still wondering about the identity of the sender, her suspicions soon won the battle against her principles, so she opened it.

Her senses quickened as she saw Lisa Jones' signature at the foot of the brief letter. Sabra read and re-read its contents several times, her sense of sheer relief mounting each time. The simple words jumped out at her from the page. It read...

Frank Gallagher,

I have given considerable thought to the stressful circumstances in which I find myself and it has proven to be an episode in my life in which I still have doubts over my ability to cope. It is an horrendous task of an immensely personal nature.

Nevertheless, I want to express the utter disgust I felt when I was given proof that the man I had fallen in love with, was in fact, my own father! The extraordinary circumstances that brought us together are truly beyond belief – but it happened and it is something I have to live with for the rest of my life. Now, I want to make it absolutely clear that I never ever want to see you again or have any future contact with you under any circumstances.

LISA JONES.

If ever Frankie needed convincing that Lisa wanted him out of her life completely – even in a father-daughter relationship, this letter killed off any future hopes that may still linger.

She replaced the letter in its envelope and returned it to her handbag. At least, she could savour the permanent removal of a serious love rival at a crucial time.

Somewhat refreshed by the Martini, she made her way down the corridor to the display hall and on arriving at the entrance, pressed the bell. After a pause of several seconds there was a buzz as the door-locking mechanism was released by a member of the security staff. The quality of the merchandise on display was eye-catching – so were the smartly dressed shapely female sales staff, complete with their flawless makeup. No doubt their glamorous presence enticed male customers to spend more than they had intended on their female companions.

She glanced at her watch. Four thirty. Time to try her room again – this time making straight for the lift, her mind fully preoccupied. She entered the lift and pressed the button for her floor. It was only when the lift doors opened, did she realise that she was on the wrong floor, indicated by the different decor and hall furniture.

Hesitating in the doorway while debating whether to go down one floor or use the stairs, she became aware of a door opening in one of the rooms some way down across the hall and a figure stepping out into the empty hall. She stared at the figure in shocked disbelief despite the fact he had his back to her. Pausing just long enough to embrace the near-naked blonde young woman in his arms and kiss her passionately, Frankie made his way quickly down the hallway to the stairs leading to the floor below.

Sabra stood there stunned, unable to move. Her body felt trapped, her muscles seemingly unable to function, so much so, that she lost her grip on her handbag. It fell with a thud on the carpeted floor.

Still brutally shocked by what she had just witnessed yet even now uncertain her dazed mind was playing some cruel trick, she finally stooped and retrieved her handbag. It felt heavier than ever. New questions queued up to be answered in her confused state. Had he been away from the hotel at all after leaving her this morning? What was the 'business' he was supposed to be seeing to? If he had been on 'business' and returned, why hadn't he attempted to contact her? The grim irony of that last question struck her. Because he had been shacked up all the time with some tart, that's why! No wonder the bastard hadn't answered her phone calls!

Still shaking with barely-suppressed anger, bitterness and pain, she made her way down to the ground floor and approached the reception desk clerk.

"Good afternoon Miss Levy. Have you seen Mr Gallagher yet?" he enquired politely.

"I've seen the swine alright," she thought, somehow forcing a flashing smile at the clerk. "Yes, everything's fine thank you, but you can perhaps help me."

He leaned forward eagerly, anxious to be of service.

"I was hoping to contact a friend of mine named Charles Cohen who said he was staying here – in room 30 – or perhaps 32 I believe."

He adjusted his gold-rimmed spectacles, flicking over the pages as he consulted the register." Mr Cohen you say – Cohen? Hmmm, no. We don't have a Mr Cohen booked in at present. And you said Room number 30 or 32, I believe? There followed a brief silence as his mind clicked into automatic gear. "As it happens Miss Levy, most of the rooms on the third floor are presently occupied by the people running the jewellery exhibition in our display hall – and there isn't a Mr Cohen among them I'm afraid. You might find the exhibition interesting," he added helpfully as he closed the register firmly.

Thanking him somewhat tersely, she made her way to the lift, her smouldering resentment burning fiercer with every step. Can you believe that, she fumed. Frankie found the exhibition interesting – especially one of the sales assistants, the lying bastard! His mother's just died and all he can think of is getting inside the knickers of some cheap tart!

The lift doors opened and as three people got out, she suddenly changed her mind, turned abruptly and made her way to the cocktail bar, ordering her favourite dry Martini.

As she sat, twisting the glass endlessly with her fingers, she was oblivious to her surroundings – seeing nothing, her mind in a turmoil. Anger continued to burn in her chest at his latest betrayal. The way he lies! He does it so easily, then thinks nothing of it! There just had to be a way of changing him but how many women have thought that about their men. It would take something pretty drastic – something totally unexpected – but what? when he was so easily distracted by the first piece of skirt that flashed her fanny at him. Numerous thoughts entered her mind, most of them too fanciful or just plain ridiculous. But there was one thought that stuck. It was drastic that was for sure, but she could try putting the frighteners on him with the gun.

She reached for her handbag and unzipped it. The bulk of the cloth-covered gun reminded her how afraid she was of its presence in her bag. She unwrapped the cloth and removed the gun being careful to conceal it below the level of the table. She stared at the weapon in her hand, turning it over and noting the safety catch. Was it on or not? She couldn't tell and couldn't remember what Danny had told her. She tried the catch, easing it over. It moved easily – too easily she thought.

The problem with Frankie and other women was so bad, perhaps she could frighten him by telling him she'd use the gun on him if he didn't change his ways. It was a desperate measure, but then she was getting desperate! But would he believe even for a minute that she meant what she said? He knew, and more importantly, she knew she would never harm the man she loved so intensely no matter how he behaved.

She replaced the gun in her handbag not bothering to wrap it again. Then, swallowing her Martini and mentally bracing herself for the showdown with Frankie, she left the bar and headed for the lift.

Sabra pressed the doorbell of her room. There was a delay of twenty seconds or so causing her to ring it again. As she did so, the door swung open. Frankie's face broke into a wide smile as she pushed past him and sat on the bed.

"Hey babe, have you missed me while I've been away? he greeted her. He sat alongside her on the bed but his intended embrace was brushed aside as Sabra stood up and walked several paces across the room, her back towards him.

Frankie laughed uncertainly. "What kind of game are you playing, babe. Can I join in?" It was his turn to be shocked when she swung around, the gun in her trembling hand. "What the hell do you think you're doing with that – and where the fuck did you get it?" he growled as he stood up, causing Sabra to step backwards, keeping the distance between them.

"Come on Sab," what game do you think you're playing at," he repeated. "This is a joke, right? Right Sab?" he spat out angrily as he stepped toward her.

"Stay there Frankie – I mean it," she said evenly, a semblance of some control returning despite her shattered feelings. She pointed the gun at his chest." You lied again to me today – like you've lied so many times before." She stifled his protest with her upraised free hand. "The only business you had today was to spend time fucking some tart from the jewellery people. I saw you with my own eyes as you left her room this afternoon."

As she took a deep breath to calm her jangling nerves he took his chance to speak, but again she cut him short. "There's no way you can deny it this time – I saw you both in her doorway this afternoon you rotten bastard!" her voice rising as she recalled the vivid, hurtful scene.

Frankie's display of angry surprise suddenly softened to one of guilty admission. He spread his arms wide, palms upward in a gesture of mock surrender. "OK Sab – you caught me out. You know it's not the first time. Anyway," he continued, "It's not the end of the world either, is it?" By now, his attitude was much more relaxed, his smile designed to calm her nerves. "You know she meant absolutely nothing to me – none of them ever do. "You're the only one Sab – the only woman that I really care for and love. You know that for sure, don't you Sab," he added, again moving toward her.

She shook her head. "No, you're not getting off that easy Frankie – not this time." The gun was becoming difficult to hold steady but she adjusted her grip and kept it aimed at his chest. Inwardly, her stomach churned as she wrestled with the problem of ending her charade of a show of strength – had she played it right to convince him that enough really was enough? – or should she keep him on tenterhooks about her intentions with the gun?

"I want you to promise me Frankie – and I mean not just now or the next few days but for all the time we're still together – that you'll stay away from other women and keep your trousers zipped up every time you fancy some tart or other." She hesitated, then added, "or I'll be tempted to use your own gun on you for real. Do we understand each other Frankie?"

He looked at her, still trying to decide if she was momentarily upset at catching him out, or if she really meant what she said. He decided to go along with her – at least for now. Anything to keep her happy.

"OK Sab," he replied. "If that's what you want, it's a deal. I'll be on my best behaviour from now on. Now – just give me the gun," he pleaded in a 'little boy lost' voice – still humouring her.

She looked down at the gun. "Did I put the safety catch back on," she wondered. "Which way does the catch go?" Her hesitancy and their 'truce' encouraged Frankie to close the gap between them, still smiling disarmingly. "Come on Sab – give me the gun – please! You might hurt yourself." His smile was fixed as he tried to take the gun out of her hand.

Startled by his sudden move, Sabra jerked the gun upwards, as he tried to wrest it from her trembling, white-knuckled hand. The thunderous explosion as the gun went off shattered the stillness of the room, forcing a full-throated, piercing scream from Sabra's throat, her body frozen with fear.

The bullet smashed through Frankie's cheekbone just below the left eye and blew a hole the size of an egg as it exited from the rear of his head. He fell backwards slowly as if in slow motion then slumped onto the floor.

Sabra's wide frenzied eyes reflected the sudden terror of the carnage before her. Her heart seemed gripped by a giant fist as she tried vainly to respond to the violent events of the previous few seconds. She wanted to scream – loudly – but she couldn't even utter a whimper. The gun slipped slowly from her trembling fingers, falling with a dull thud on the carpeted floor. Luckily, it didn't go off a second time. She knelt by his crumpled body, the blood from his shattered head slowly spreading into a pool, the mess staining her clothes. She cradled his head as best she could, trying to avoid causing him any further pain, oblivious of the soft, red pulp oozing slowly from his horrendous wounds.

Frankie's eyes flickered faintly, then opened seeing nothing but the red mist that swirled before him. "My god he's still alive!" she sobbed. "Where can I get help?" – her mind clouded with terrifying indecision. She leaned closer, trying to make sense of the low noises coming from his blood-flecked mouth.

A sudden loud knocking on the door followed by the bell ringing startled her. "Hello. Hello! Are you alright in there?" came the voice. "This is the manager. One of my staff thought she heard an explosion in this room. Can we come in and see if we can help?"

Hearing only Sabra's moaning, the manager used his pass key, opened the door and stood there, caught off guard by the scene revealed. "He's still alive, but only just," sobbed Sabra. "It was a dreadful accident. Can you get help straight away?"

The manager strode across the room carefully avoiding the couple and the blood-splattered carpet. Picking up the bedside phone, he dialled reception. "Johnson!" he snapped into the mouthpiece. "Call the police and the ambulance service. There's been a dreadful accident in Room 24. We need their help – and quick!" He replaced the receiver, a grim look on his face.

He went into the en-suite bathroom and emerged with some towels which he handed carefully to Sabra. "These might be of help," he suggested. She smiled weakly and placed a towel carefully under

Frankie's savagely-lacerated head. He continued to lay there motion-less – his very life steadily ebbing away by the second.

Sounds of a number of people hurrying in the corridor proved to be two ambulance medics who immediately busied themselves tending to the injured man once they tactfully asked Sabra to give them the space they needed.

Shortly afterwards, a couple of plain-clothes men and a uni-formed police officer entered the room. DI Dave Parker took in the chaotic scene with a practised eye and addressed the man stand-ing near the doorway.

He and Sergeant Jim Cooper flashed their warrant cards at him. "I believe you're the manager sir," – more of a statement than a question – to which the manager nodded his confirmation.

"Yes, the injured man and his companion booked in here recently, in the name of Mr Gallagher and Miss Levy." Parker shot a glance at Sergeant Cooper. "This is a turn up for the book Jim. Look at the state of him. Frank Gallagher, eh? – this said without any hint of pity. He turned to the constable standing in the doorway. "Make sure you keep everybody else out of the room and arrange to tape off the corridor for ten yards in each direction to prevent people from trampling all over the scene, until we've had a closer look. Got that?"

Followed by Cooper, he strode into the room, noting the gun on the carpet. Parker pointed to the gun. "We'll need that."

Sergeant Cooper pushed a pencil into the barrel of the weapon, lifted it and gave it a brief visual examination "It looks like one of ours Dave – it's a Browning Hi-Power 9 mm self-loading version. Takes a handy thirteen rounds of ammunition." He then put the safety catch on. "Its been fired recently Dave," he observed as he slipped the gun into a small plastic bag he fished from his pocket. Parker nodded. "It only takes one," he remarked drily.

Despite the mess her tear-stained face had made of most of her make-up, Sabra's extraordinary beauty still shone through. He held out his hand to her. "Miss Levy, I'm sorry we have to meet again in these dreadful circumstances. Perhaps you would like to sit down and tell me briefly what happened? He turned to Cooper. "Get Miss Levy a glass of water will you Jim?"

As Cooper disappeared into the bathroom and returned with a tumbler of water, Sabra tried to compose herself enough to recall the events that led to the shooting. While she was speaking, one of the medics caught Parker's attention as they prepared to lift Frankie onto the wheeled trolley with extreme care.

The medic shook his head several times signalling what little chance their patient had of surviving, had all but gone. By now, Sabra had finished her faltering account of the accident and Parker stood up.

"You'll need to come down to Police headquarters with us Miss Levy to give us a full statement and we'll take it from there." At that point, the medics prepared to leave but Sabra stepped to the side of the trolley and avoiding the drip tubes, gently cradled Frankie's heavily-bandaged head in her arms, whispering inaudible words of love and comfort.

Frankie's eyes again flickered as he tried to respond. She leant closer trying to catch his words. He finally spoke.

"That's nice Mam. You haven't cuddled me like that since I was a little kid."

As the medics pushed him slowly past the detective, one of them turned and said, "I think he mentioned his Mam. Do you know her?"

Parker sighed deeply before replying. "Yes. You could say I knew her. She was a strong-willed woman named Nell and I even went to her funeral. But I'll tell you this," he added, pointing to the shattered figure on the stretcher, "as far as the police are concerned, there'll be no flowers for Frankie."

End

ISBN 1-905597-05-3

9 781905 597055

90000>

Global - Moraira - Head Office Centro Comercial Los Pinos C/Moraira - Benitachell Moraira 03724 Alicante, SPAIN Tel : (+34) 96 649 0356 / 0359 Fax : (+34) 96 649 0340	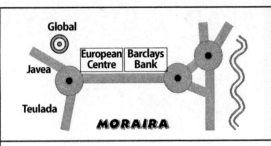
Global - Denia C/Valencia Km.3 Denia 03700 Alicante, SPAIN Tel : (+34) 96 578 6256 / 8976 Fax : (+34) 96 578 8976	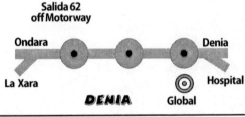
Global - Javea C/Cabo La Nao Km.1 Javea 03730 Alicante, SPAIN Tel : (+34) 96 579 5305 / 4327 Fax : (+34) 96 579 4327	
Global - Torrevieja N332 Cabo Roig Torrevieja 03180 Alicante, SPAIN Tel : (+34) 96 532 2169 / 1847 Fax : (+34) 96 532 1847	
Global - Onteniente Avenida Textil 51a Onteniente 46870 Alicante, SPAIN Tel : (+34) 96 291 1630 / 5441 Fax : (+34) 96 291 1651	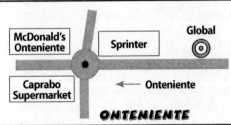
Global - Roquetas de Mar Alicante, SPAIN Tel : (+34) 95 032 9386 Mobile: (+34) 679 408 273